THE
LAST
GRAVE

Also by T. F. Muir

THE
LAST
GRAVE

T.F. MUIR

CONSTABLE

CONSTABLE

First published in Great Britain in 2025 by Constable

Copyright © T. F. Muir, 2025

1 3 5 7 9 10 8 6 4 2

A CIP catalogue record for this book
is available from the British Library.

ISBN: 978-1-40872-402-6 (hardback)

Typeset in Dante MT by Hewer Text UK Ltd, Edinburgh
Printed and bound in Great Britain by Clays Ltd, Elcograf S.p.A.

Papers used by Constable are from well-managed forests and
other responsible sources.

MIX
Paper | Supporting
responsible forestry
FSC® C104740

Constable
An imprint of
Little, Brown Book Group
Carmelite House
50 Victoria Embankment
London EC4Y 0DZ

The authorised representative
in the EEA is
Hachette Ireland
8 Castlecourt Centre, Dublin
15, D15 XTP3, Ireland
(email: info@hbgi.ie)

An Hachette UK Company
www.hachette.co.uk

www.littlebrown.co.uk

For Anna

AUTHOR'S NOTE

First and foremost, this book is a work of fiction. Those readers familiar with St Andrews and the East Neuk may notice that I have taken creative licence with respect to some local geography and history, and with the names of some Police Forces, which have now changed. Sadly, too, the North Street Police Station has been demolished and a block of flats constructed on the site, but its past proximity to the town centre with its many pubs and restaurants would have been too sorely missed by Gilchrist for me to abandon it. Any resemblance to real persons, living or dead, is unintentional and purely coincidental. Any and all mistakes are mine.

www.frankmuir.co.uk

CHAPTER 1

'According to the satnav,' Jessie said, 'we're nearly there.'

Detective Chief Inspector Andy Gilchrist slowed to a crawl. In the eerie gloom of a winter morning's fog, his car's headlights were as weak as candlelight. Homes either side offered glimmers of light and life through curtained windows. Ahead, at the foot of the hill, where the road opened up to the dark waters of the River Clyde, the world seemed to sink into deeper darkness. Mist swirled and shifted in the riverside winds, one moment lifting as if about to clear, the next thickening to a damp haar.

He'd taken the call from Dainty two and a half hours earlier – *I need you to see this, Andy. I'll explain when you get here* – after which he'd contacted Jessie; Detective Sergeant Jessica Harriet Janes, formerly of Strathclyde, now his trusted associate at Fife Constabulary, and back at work only a month earlier, after being hospitalised from a violent assault. At that time in the morning, traffic had been sparse on the drive down from St Andrews, until they hit backup on the M80 on the outskirts of Glasgow. From then on, it had been slow going. But once on the Clydeside Expressway the commuter plug speeded up as if puzzled by the earlier hold ups, only to revert to a stop–start drive between traffic lights. They'd followed the satnav through Dumbarton town centre, across the River Leven, then onto Clydeshore Road where the windscreen wipers now jumped to life, sweeping the glass clear on automatic.

'Don't tell me it's started raining,' Jessie said.

'It's the Clyde. Cold air over water, meets warm air over land.'

'You make it sound like a love story.'

'No love story, believe me.' He slowed down to negotiate a sharp left turn into a road appropriately named Clydeview, and parked behind a dark-red Volvo that he recognised as belonging to Strathclyde Police Detective Chief Inspector Peter Small, more affectionately known as Dainty.

Outside, he clicked his key fob and stepped onto a stretch of weed-riddled grass that lined the riverside road. He gripped the cold metal railing that ran the length of Clydeview, and stared across the black waters of the Clyde. On the opposite shore, lights from the village of Langbank danced like scattered stars. At his feet, it seemed, waves brushed the shoreline, nothing more than a narrow length of sand and gravel and grass that bordered the bottom of the seawall.

Jessie stood next to him. 'Not quite the French Riviera.'

'We're missing the sun.'

She chuckled at that. '*And* the glamour. *And* the seaside cafés. *And* everything else, come to think of it.' She clapped her hands, and shivered. 'Jeez, it's bloody freezing.'

'Cold.'

'What?'

'It's cold. It's freezing in the Arctic. Here, it's cold.'

'Oh excuse me Mr Attenborough. I stand corrected.' Her gaze drifted down the Clyde, as if following the path of abandoned flotsam. 'I tell you what,' she said. 'I could do with another coffee to heat me up.' She looked around her. 'Where're we supposed to be meeting Dainty, anyway?'

Gilchrist removed his mobile, tapped the screen, and got through on the second ring. 'That's us here,' he said, without introduction. 'We're at the end of Clydeshore Road. Where are you?'

'Follow the footpath down the river,' Dainty said. 'Half a mile or so. You can't miss us.'

Gilchrist returned his mobile to his jacket pocket, and pulled up his collar. 'This way.' As he strode off, Jessie by his side, he thought she might not have exaggerated the chill after all. His breath puffed in the frigid air like steam. It really was bloody freezing.

The asphalt footpath ran along the side of the Clyde, a great place to have an early morning jog, he thought. He shrugged off a cold shiver, or maybe it was a sense of guilt – he really had to get back to running along the West Sands. But with all that was going on in his personal life, jogging and exercise of any kind had to take a back seat for the time being.

As if reading his thoughts, Jessie said, 'How's Irene keeping?'

He grunted, and said, 'Putting a face on it, is about the best way to describe it. I don't know how she does it.'

Jessie grimaced, tightened her lips for a moment, then said, 'Still on medication?'

3

'Painkillers. Lots of them.' He didn't want to explain that despite his best attempts to persuade Irene to go into a hospice, she'd steadfastly refused. *Home is where I live, and home is where I'll die.* So, home it was, although the lounge now looked more like a hospital ward than a family living room. He'd organised nurses to visit four times a day – first thing in the morning, then midday, again in the early evening, then back for the final dose of pills and a tuck into bed. And throughout it all, Irene continued to smile. Christ, if he could only be half as upbeat—

'Jeez, Andy, I don't know what to say. It's so . . .' She shook her head. 'It's all so bloody sad.'

He grimaced in silent agreement. At times it felt so much worse than bloody sad. It felt so bloody unfair, as if the God he didn't believe in was playing a brutal joke on the world, punishing the good, instead of the bad.

'Looks like that's them,' Jessie said, nodding ahead.

Despite the footpath being blocked from vehicular access, a white transit van straddled the walkway. The SOCOs – Scenes of Crime Officers – must have driven in from the other end of the path, he thought. Crime-scene tape flapped like bunting from riverside gusts, guarded by two uniformed officers assigned to prevent the gathering of inquisitive dog-walkers and pretend joggers from interfering in what Dainty had already pronounced a murder investigation.

On the other side of the seawall, the Incitent was set up by the water's edge, looking oddly natural in that location, as if some holidaymakers had chosen to camp on the banks of the river. The sun had risen above the horizon – dawn, if you could call it that – and cast a weak light over the scene. Even from a hundred yards distant, Gilchrist could make out Dainty in a group of three, his

4

small stature giving the uninformed the impression of a boy among men. How wrong could they be?

As Gilchrist approached, Dainty had his back to him, and put his mobile to his ear as the other two parted; one strode off along the footpath, the other walked to the SOCO van and removed a mobile, at which point Gilchrist recognised DI Annie Melton. Several years ago, he'd heard rumours that Dainty and Annie were having an affair, which was dispelled by the quick transfer of two detectives to Northern Constabulary, about as far from Glasgow as the Scottish Police Force could finagle. You messed with Dainty at your own risk.

Dainty caught sight of Gilchrist as he and Jessie were signing in. Without a word, he slipped his mobile into his pocket, nodded to the forensic tent, then vaulted the metal railing and jumped down to the river's edge.

'Looks like Spider-Man's had his porridge this morning,' Jessie said.

A set of aluminium ladders had been set up by the SOCOs, which Gilchrist used to help Jessie over the wall and down onto the narrow stretch of sandy gravel. He followed, and met Dainty at the entrance to the tent.

Dainty nodded to each in turn. 'Andy. Jessie,' then said, 'Either of you heard of Mike Elgin?'

'Isn't he a reporter?' Jessie said. 'One of the broadsheets. Can't remember which.'

Dainty grimaced approval. '*Was* a reporter. Freelanced for the last two years as an investigative journalist. Does true crime podcasts. Turns out he's been missing for three days. Pulled out of the Clyde this morning.'

Jessie nodded to the tent. 'I take it he didn't drown.'

'Which is why I phoned you.' This to Gilchrist, as if she hadn't spoken.

Gilchrist held Dainty's hard gaze for a moment, before saying, '*Turns out*, you said. Turns out he's been missing. So no one called it in?'

Dainty grunted. 'Got it in one.'

'And this is where his body was pulled from the river?'

Dainty nodded. 'An early morning dog-walker called it in. Said a body was lying at the edge, looked like it had been washed ashore.'

Gilchrist let his gaze drift across the river. On the opposite bank, houses, trees, cars, seemed to stir alive as dawn pulled them out of the night's gloom. The Clyde had to be at least a kilometre wide where they stood. The power of all that water flowing seawards was incalculable. He turned back to Dainty. 'It doesn't make sense,' he said. 'Three days in the Clyde would have the body out to sea. Not turning up here. Unless it ended up in the Clyde yesterday.'

'Not according to Cooper,' Dainty said.

Something fluttered in Gilchrist's stomach. 'Cooper . . .?'

'The one and only. She's back. Used to work in Dundee,' he added, as if to make sure Gilchrist hadn't forgotten her. 'Took up her new post a couple of months back. Already been and gone this morning. According to her, the body's been submersed in water for three days at least. No doubts about it.'

Jessie said, 'Well if Queen Becky says three days, then three days it is.'

Dainty ignored Jessie's quip. 'The body could've snagged on an underwater piling or something. Currents can be fickle. With activity up and down the river. Another way to look at it is . . .' He shrugged. 'We got lucky. Really lucky.' He paused, as if giving

6

Gilchrist time to gather his thoughts. 'But that's not what's troubling me.'

'I'm listening.'

'Four weeks ago, Leila Hazazi was reported missing. Last seen leaving a pub in town, heading for the subway. She never made it. No one's heard from her since. No phone activity. No credit card, bank, or social media activity. Nothing. At first we thought she'd maybe just pissed off out of it. Worst case, taken her own life.' He shook his head. 'But we've now escalated it to a murder investigation.'

Gilchrist said, 'And Leila Hazazi is . . .?'

'Mike Elgin's partner. In life, and in work. Another investigative journalist.'

'So the two deaths are linked?'

'I don't think it's coincidence. Do you?'

Gilchrist grimaced. 'Anything to do with whatever story they were working on?'

'Don't know that yet. But yeah . . . it's more than a possibility.'

'Where did Hazazi and Elgin live?'

'Glasgow. West End.'

'So . . .' Gilchrist said, letting his thoughts come together. 'If they worked and lived in Glasgow, and were murdered or disappeared in Glasgow, what does this investigation have to do with us, or more specifically, Fife Constabulary?'

'Get kitted up, have a look at the body, then tell me what you think. His wallet and phone have been removed and taken to the Office. Phone's buggered from the water, of course. But our IT guys'll do what they can with it, although I'm not holding my breath.'

With that, Dainty walked off, mobile back to his ear.

CHAPTER 2

The first thing that struck Gilchrist was that Mike Elgin appeared much younger than he'd imagined – somewhere in his late twenties, early thirties. The second, that he was better dressed than expected. Somehow, the thought of a newspaper reporter eking out a living as a freelance investigative journalist conjured up an image of older-man beer bellies, scraggly beards, dog-eared wallets needing topped up, and an altogether scruffy appearance.

But the man who lay on his back at his feet was none of that.

A three-piece suit, with gold pocket watch and matching fob-chain, spoke of sartorial extravagance. Soft hands and manicured fingernails told him that Elgin had never worked a hard day's night in his life. Slim waist, broad shoulders, suggested he'd kept himself fit, or at least watched his weight. Trimmed beard and a neat back and sides added to the image of someone who took pride in his personal appearance.

'What is he?' Jessie said. 'A model for *Gentleman's Journal?*'

Gilchrist kneeled by the body. It struck him that Dainty hadn't mentioned cause of death. Jessie's comment about not having drowned had been left somewhat unanswered. This was a murder investigation, per Dainty. So how had Mike Elgin been killed? Of course, all he had to do was speak to the forensic pathologist, Doctor Rebecca Cooper, who would no doubt have her own opinion on cause of death. But he knew from past experience that she would be reluctant to speculate until she'd completed a full post-mortem examination, which required the body to be relocated to the mortuary.

No, Dainty had kept cause of death to himself because he wanted a second opinion. Which is why he'd phoned Gilchrist. But Cooper was the best forensic pathologist Gilchrist had ever worked with. So why would Dainty need a second opinion from him? He seemed to be finding too many questions, and not enough answers, although as he stared at the body it was becoming clearer that Dainty wasn't interested in a second opinion on cause of death, but of something more pertinent to the murder investigation.

But what?

He leaned forward, placed the palms of his hand on Elgin's chest, and applied some pressure. The chest sank, which caused a flutter of bubbles at the nostrils. He pressed firmer, and a whitish froth foamed at the man's lips.

'Shit,' Jessie said. 'He drowned?'

'Looks that way.'

'So why does Dainty think he was murdered? He could've tripped and fallen into the Clyde. An accident. Or taken his own life. Jumped from a bridge. What're we missing?'

'Clearly something.' Gilchrist let his gaze drift the length of the body. Shoes intact, brown leather, handmade, barely a scratch on their leather soles. Socks striped all the colours of the rainbow – a sartorial slip, or personal statement? Heavy woollen suit, dark blue checks, burgundy lining, matching trim at the pockets and buttons – clearly handmade. White button-down shirt – Egyptian cotton? Silk burgundy tie, half-Nelson knot. Silk handkerchief in the top pocket to match. Gold cufflinks in the shape of the letter B. Double cuffs with burgundy embroidery stitched in the letters MPE – Michael middle-name Elgin, he thought.

'What's the letter B stand for?' Jessie said, toying with the cufflinks.

Gilchrist frowned. He'd seen that shaped letter before. 'Could be Bentley,' he said.

'As in Bentley car? Jeez, is this guy loaded? Are we in the wrong job?'

'It's just a guess, Jessie. Settle down. We'll check it out.' He glanced at her. 'Here. Have a look at this.' He peeled back the sleeves on the right arm, as far as they would go, then the left. 'What do you see?'

Jessie frowned, shook her head.

'How about . . . what *don't* you see?'

'No watch?'

'He has a pocket watch.'

She shrugged. 'No bracelets? No rings?'

'No jewellery of any kind,' he agreed.

'Don't cufflinks count?'

'That's not it. There's something else. Might not be important.'

She leaned closer, frowned, then shook her head again.

'Tell-tale stubble?' he tried.

'What?' She leaned closer. 'He shaves his arms?'

He slid the sleeves back down. 'And no tattoos. At least, as far as we can tell.' He patted the suit from top to bottom – nothing

10

in the pockets – then slipped a hand into the inside jacket pocket. Empty. No wallet, no mobile, just as Dainty had said. He avoided the urge to scratch his head in comic puzzlement. If this was a murder victim, he was missing something. But what, he couldn't say at that moment.

'What's this?' Jessie said, her fingers brushing the man's beard at his jawline. 'Is it a birthmark? Or . . .?'

He pressed his hand to the man's face, rubbed his fingers through the beard. No raised skin, only what looked like a couple of red marks an inch or so apart, that were neither raised nor open. He peered closer, parting the facial hair as best he could. Was this what Dainty was wanting him to confirm? Could this be the reason Mike Elgin, investigative journalist, male model about town, had found himself in the Clyde and consequently drowned?

He pulled back, pushed to his feet, and faced Jessie.

She raised her eyebrows. 'Are you thinking what I'm thinking?'

He nodded. 'He's been tasered.'

'So . . . someone attacked him.'

Gilchrist tried to picture the scene in his mind's eye.

Had Elgin been meeting someone, perhaps by the River Clyde? On the landscaped walkway? Or on one of the bridges that spanned the river? If so, and it was a big if, would an experienced journalist like Elgin have agreed to meet out of range of CCTV cameras? If he'd had any suspicions or fears for his life, Elgin would surely have met where his meeting could be recorded on CCTV. On the other hand, the meeting might have been arranged by his killer-to-be, or killers-to-be – now why had he thought there might be more than one killer? – then it might have been set someplace beyond the reach of CCTV cameras. But Scotland, particularly within city limits, had to be one of the most CCTV-ed countries on the planet. All they had to do was examine recorded CCTV footage, and they would find who tasered Mike Elgin. Of course, trying to work out where the meeting could have been held in a city of over a million people – if there even had been a meeting – was an impossible task. But if you focused on footage by the River Clyde, surely that would improve the odds—

'Earth to Andy?'

He turned to see Jessie frowning at him. 'What's that?'

'I was saying, before we jump to any conclusions that might result in us looking kind of foolish, we should turn the body over. Check it out more thoroughly. Just in case.' She placed a hand under the body's shoulder. 'Help me. He's a dead weight, excuse the pun.'

He nodded, his thoughts not fully back to the present. But he assisted Jessie in rolling the body over onto its side, just enough to permit her to search for signs of obvious wounds. He said nothing while she ran her fingers over the back of the head, then leaned closer as if she'd noticed something.

'You see this?' she said, more to herself than Gilchrist. 'Looks like a cut. More graze than cut. It's not open. Could've happened before the attack, or after. Who knows. But it's not severe enough to knock him unconscious, I'd say.'

Gilchrist said, 'Tasered. But not accurate enough, so it doesn't immobilise him. He stumbles. Falls into river. Hits the back of his head on the way down. But only a graze.' He paused, letting his mind work the scene, then said, 'If he's still conscious, couldn't he swim?'

Jessie squinted up at him. 'Fully clothed. Shoes on. Even if he could, it might've been a struggle just to stay afloat. Or

12

maybe where he fell in he couldn't pull himself out for some reason.'

Just then, the side of the tent flapped, and Dainty said, 'Got a minute?'

Not a question.

Gilchrist eased the body onto its back again, leaving Jessie to finish up whatever she felt she had to do, then followed Dainty from the tent.

DI Annie Melton stood facing them,

'Tells us what you think,' Dainty asked.

'Could Elgin swim?'

'How the fuck would I know?' Dainty grumbled.

'We need to find that out. Could be important. Because he drowned. Which you knew, of course.'

Dainty raised his head and eyed him as if suspicious. Then he tightened his lips, and nodded. 'And . . .?'

'I'd say he's been attacked. Tasered. Then either fell into the Clyde, or was pushed.'

'So not suicide.' A statement, not a question.

'Not if he's been tasered.' A pause, then, 'It'd be man-hour intensive, but if we could approximate time and place we might find CCTV footage of the actual incident.'

Again, Dainty nodded.

Gilchrist pressed on. 'What did you find in his personal effects?'

Dainty's mobile appeared in his hand as if from nowhere. He nodded to DI Melton. 'Annie'll bring you up to speed.' Then he turned and walked off, mobile to his ear, just as Jessie exited the forensic tent.

'He seems reluctant to give much away,' Gilchrist said to Melton.

'There's a reason for that,' she said, her accent Glaswegian-hard with the rough rasp of sixty-a-day. Then she added, 'Where're youse parked?'

'Behind Dainty's Volvo. Clydeview.'

'I'll talk. You drive.'

CHAPTER 3

The walk back along the footpath was done at a leisurely pace, like a group of walkers out for a carefree morning stroll. The river haar had cleared, a breeze had picked up, and the sun was doing its best to break through the clouds, but not quite succeeding.

'What did Dainty tell you about Leila Hazazi?' Melton asked.

'That she disappeared four weeks ago. And her case has been escalated to a murder investigation.'

Melton nodded in agreement, then said, 'I'm the SIO for that investigation, and we've been working day and night on it for the last three and a half weeks. Ten of us. And it's not enough. The way things are going, we'd still get nowhere with a hundred of us working our arses off.'

'And you believe Mike Elgin's murder is linked?' Gilchrist said.

'Bet my life on it.'

'So the discovery of Elgin's body could give you new leads, and be seen as a potential break in the case.'

'That's one way of putting it.'

'And another way?'

'The stakes are rising.'

He looked at Melton, waiting for her to expand, but like Dainty she seemed reluctant to share her thoughts. 'Look,' he said, struggling to contain his frustration, 'I got a call from Dainty before six this morning, asking for my help. So, here I am . . . here *we* are,' he added, just to make it clear that Jessie was part of the team.

Melton glanced at Jessie, as if considering whether or not to include her, then said, 'Dainty said you were well in with Jock Shepherd.'

A blast from the past. Big Jock Shepherd, once Glasgow's and many might say *Scotland's* crime patriarch, a name he hadn't expected to hear again. But here it was. A bolt from the blue. But big Jock was long dead, so what was Dainty going on about?

'I wouldn't say I was *well in* with Jock, but I met him from time to time.' A glance at Jessie. 'We both have.'

'His daughter, Arletta, now runs the family business.'

'I'd heard. But in her defence, I believe she's trying to make a legitimate go of it.' He and Jessie had taken a few more steps before he realised Melton had stopped walking.

'In her *defence* . . .?' she said. 'What the fuck's that supposed to mean?'

He was surprised by her anger, the speed with which it had risen, but just as puzzled by the scowl on her face, as if she'd sipped a spoonful of Bitrex and was deciding whether or not to spit it out. He returned her hard gaze with a steady one of his own, and forced himself to keep his tone level – no need to fall out with anyone. Well, not until he knew what was going on at least. 'That she's no Jock Shepherd, is what it means. Nothing more.'

16

That seemed to do the trick, for Melton nodded in acknowledgement. 'Sorry, sir,' she said, showing professional deference to his rank. 'But I hate that fucking bitch, so I do.'

'I've always found it best to keep emotions out of all investigations.'

Her lips tightened for a thoughtful moment, then she said, 'Got it.'

With the momentary flashpoint behind him, Gilchrist said, 'So you think Mike and Leila's murders might lead back to Arletta?'

'We don't. Not directly, anyway.'

He noticed the plural pronoun, the inferred connection to Dainty.

'But we're thinking Leila and Mike were onto something,' she continued. 'And when something goes on in Glasgow, the Shepherds aren't far behind. In fact, they're often a step or three ahead. We pulled a few of her boys in for questioning, shook the branches to see what fell out, but so far . . . nothing.'

They reached Gilchrist's car, and he clicked his fob. He opened the passenger door for Melton, waited until she took her seat, then closed it behind her, conscious of Jessie glaring at him, as if to say, *You never do that for me.*

With a disgruntled grunt, Jessie slumped into the rear seat.

He fired up the ignition, did a slow three-point turn, then eased into Clydeshore Road. 'None of this explains why Dainty phoned,' he said, as he powered up the hill. 'As far as I can tell, it's a double murder investigation in and under the jurisdiction of Strathclyde Police. Nothing to do with Fife Constabulary.'

'That's what we thought,' Melton said. 'Until three days ago.'

He turned onto Dumbarton Road, heading towards Glasgow. 'I'm listening.'

17

'We interviewed Elgin twice,' she said. 'He's Leila's partner, he reported her missing, was the last person to see her alive. So he's our first port of call. We thought he was good for it. So we grilled him. For a total of ten hours. But he stuck to his story—'

'His *story*? You don't believe him?'

'Not at first. But we do now.'

Jessie said, 'Now he's dead, you mean?'

'Fucksake,' Melton hissed under her breath, loud enough to let Jessie know what she thought of her comment. 'Our IT division's been working day and night, chasing up leads from Leila's social media. We don't have her mobile, of course, but our IT boys were able to recover phone records of others, names given to us by Mike, friends of theirs, trying to find out her movements in the hours leading up to her disappearance. Mostly been spinning our wheels, but three days ago we managed to track down one of Leila's . . .' She paused, as if searching for the right word. 'One of her contacts. If she can be called that. Amari Bankole. Used to work as a journalist, too, but got caught in the office with cocaine, and was dismissed on the spot. But Amari and Leila kept in contact.' She half-turned her head, and said, 'You with us so far?' as if to goad Jessie.

'Anyone report Bankole to the drug squad?' Jessie quipped.

'Of course. She claimed the drugs were planted, and was able to convince us, the drug squad that is, that she had nothing to do with them. Her DNA being absent helped win her over. But once we found out she'd spent over an hour with Leila the day before she vanished, a wee reminder of her past close call with drugs was enough to have her chirping like a canary.'

'*Singing*,' Jessie sniped.

'What's that?'

18

'Nothing.'

Gilchrist didn't want Melton to lose momentum. 'What was the purpose of Leila and Amari meeting?' he said. 'Did you find out?'

Melton nodded. 'Amari did a bit of work on the side for Leila. Scratch beneath the surface of Glasgow's professional veneer, and you'll find a stinking underbelly of criminal goings-on. Lawyers, councillors, accountants, and the rest of the fucking elite, back-handers for this, back-handers for that. Brown envelopes everywhere, the greedy bastards. Which was what Amari was good at. Finding dirt on supposedly clean individuals.'

She paused then, as if to take a breath, but a glance from Gilchrist confirmed she was scrolling through her mobile. 'Have you ever come across Ryan Hadwin?' she said. 'Founder and CEO of Hadwin Funeral Services.'

Gilchrist shook his head. 'No.'

A tilt of the head to Jessie. 'How about you?'

'Hadwin Funeral Services?'

A sigh, then, 'Yeah.'

'Based where? Glasgow?'

Melton scrolled through her mobile. 'Six funeral homes in Scotland. Two in Glasgow, two in Edinburgh, one in Dundee . . .' A pause, then, 'And the most recent one in St Andrews.'

'St Andrews?' Gilchrist said. 'Whereabouts?'

'Outside of town. On the Leven Road.'

'I'm not familiar with that. How about you, Jessie?'

'Heard the name, but that's about it.'

'Maybe because it's new,' Melton said. 'Opened less than a year ago. Hadwin bought out some other funeral homes. Word is his goal was to be the biggest funeral service provider in the UK.

Also two more in England – Carlisle and Newcastle – but we're not interested in these. Not at the moment, anyway.'

Gilchrist glanced at her. 'His goal *was* to be the biggest. Has he shifted the goalposts, or has something else happened?'

Melton chuckled, returned her mobile to her pocket. 'Dainty said you never missed a trick.' She tilted her head to Jessie. 'How about you? Any questions?' she said, as if to let her know she was sleeping on the job.

'Yeah,' Jessie said. 'You still haven't told us what any of this has to do with us, other than one new funeral home in St Andrews.'

Gilchrist stepped in with, 'Jessie has a point. So how can we help?'

'Four months ago, Ryan Hadwin went missing. Supposed to be jetting off to sunnier climes for a short break, but never showed up at the airport. Nobody knew nothing about it until his girl-friend phoned his office from Spain to ask where he was.'

'Girlfriend?'

'Divorced wife number two a few years back. The girlfriend thought she was shaping up to be wife number three.' She coughed, and grunted, 'Christ, will they never learn?'

'So . . .,' Gilchrist said, 'what became of Hadwin?'

'As good as vanished off the face of the earth. Likely murdered some place unknown by someone unknown is the best we can come up with. His only son, Grant, was the prime suspect, of course. But he was alibied to the hilt. Clean as a whistle. Couldn't find so much as a speck of dust on him.'

'And the funeral business?'

'Everything was taken over by Grant – mansion in Glasgow, two holiday homes in Majorca, luxury cars, the entire funeral business. The works.' She paused, as if steadying herself for the punchline. 'But here's where it gets interesting. Amari Bankole had found out that Ryan Hadwin wasn't Grant's biological father.'

She paused, as if for effect, which had Jessie asking, 'Do you know who is?'

Melton nodded. 'Tony Dilanos.'

It took Gilchrist a couple of seconds to say, 'Arletta Shepherd's husband? I mean, *late* husband.'

'The one and only. He'd been shagging behind Arletta's back for years. But since the death of big Jock, and then Tony, Arletta's been in charge. Fast forward to the present, and some folk in the Shepherd family don't want the business run by a mere woman. Rumour has it there's moves afoot to pull Grant into the family, because he's Tony's son, albeit illegitimate son, and make him a player.'

'And the significance of this is . . .?'

'That there's about to be a major shift in who runs Scotland's criminal empire.'

'That's a bit of a quantum leap,' Gilchrist said.

'We don't see it that way. It's already started. That's the story that Leila Hazazi and Mike Elgin were working on. That's the story they were about to expose, the story that got them killed.'

'You know that for certain?'

'Not a hundred per cent, but pretty close.'

'And all because Amari Bankole, a woman of questionable character, says so?'

Melton shifted in her seat, as if to better confront him. 'We've got two murders in the space of a month – Hazazi and Elgin. We're investigating Ryan Hadwin's disappearance as a murder, too. We suspect Grant Hadwin's behind them all, but we can't prove it. Which is why Dainty phoned you.'

Gilchrist frowned, and shook his head. 'Other than one funeral home in St Andrews, there's nothing I can use to pull Fife Constabulary in. Budgets are impossible. I'd never get approval for funding. I'm sorry, I'd love to help, but I don't see how.'

'You know Arletta Shepherd. You saved her life a few years back, is what I heard. And Dainty says you're the only policeman she's ever trusted, or would ever trust again.'

Not quite how Gilchrist remembered it. More like a bullet that missed, and not of his own doing. 'I was there when her husband, Tony, was killed,' he said. 'But that's about it.'

Melton nodded, as if giving thought to his words. 'Well . . . that's how you can help. I told you it's already started. Arletta's now missing. Nobody's heard from her for three days.'

A quick calculation had Gilchrist concluding, 'Around the same time Mike Elgin was killed?'

'Exactly.'

'So you think she's dead, too?'

'That's what Dainty wants you to find out.'

CHAPTER 4

It took Gilchrist more than a few seconds to untangle the logic of what Melton had said. 'So Dainty suspects that Grant Hadwin's behind the deaths of Elgin, Hazazi, his father, Ryan – albeit not his biological father – and now, Arletta Shepherd?'

'We don't think Arletta's dead.'

That almost stopped him. 'Why not?'

'We have some . . . *contacts* . . . who've told us she's in hiding.'

'Contacts? You mean family members?'

Melton stared straight ahead.

'Names?' he said.

'It's better you don't know.'

'I thought you needed my help.'

'Dainty doesn't want your investigation to be prejudiced in any way. It's better you go in cold, without knowing who to trust or who not to trust.'

Gilchrist tightened his grip on the steering wheel. Dainty was right. When dealing with criminals who lived or died depending on who they trusted, or who trusted them, one word in the wrong ear, or a friendly look in the wrong direction, could be the innocent signal that got them killed. Dog eat dog didn't cut it deep enough.

'Okay,' he said at length. 'Does anyone know where Arletta might be?'

'We believe she hasn't left the country.'

Jessie said, 'Well that narrows it down.'

'But you don't know for sure,' Gilchrist said.

'No.'

Well. There he had it. A missing person's case as good as any. And even if they did manage to find Arletta, what could she tell them? More than likely not a lot came the logical answer. Because she couldn't know who was after her, or she would have ordered one of her family to take care of the problem, surely. But why go into hiding? Why not just lie low and wait it out? Because it had to be deeper than that. Much worse for her. She didn't know who to trust in her own family. So she'd had no option but to run.

Which told him betrayal ran thicker than blood.

'Take the next exit left,' Melton said.

He hadn't been paying attention to where he was going, only that he was heading east, back into the city centre. He took the slip road, then followed Melton's further instructions to find himself zigzagging left and right and across streets that seemed to blend into a jungle of dark tenements and car-lined roads.

'Park anywhere,' Melton said.

He found a spot next to a Pay and Display meter, then Melton surprised him by slotting in a few coins and handing him a display ticket. 'That gives you an hour,' she said. 'Which should be plenty of time.' She nodded to a tenement building on the other side of the street. 'Second floor. Name's by the buzzer. Bankole,' she said. 'Amari. She's expecting you. Give Dainty a call once you're done. He wants to have a word with you.' And with that, she turned and strode off.

Jessie stood next to him, and watched her go. 'She's a strange one,' she said. 'Do you ever feel like you're being played?'

What could he tell her? That there had to be more going on in this investigation than they were being led to believe? That Dainty was playing his cards close to his chest, too close for his comfort? Instead, he said, 'Let's see what Bankole has to say for herself.'

The entrance to the building was redolent of a heady mixture of Dettol and cat's piss, as if a poor attempt had been made at clearing up someone's mess. The door to Bankole's flat didn't change his opinion that the place was a dump. Peeling paint and dried-up putty on the door frame edged a door that still bore the boot marks of an attempted kick-in.

He pressed the bell and waited.

They didn't have long. Several locks clicked and keys clattered before the door swung open to a tidy Asian woman with black leggings and a flat-chested white T-shirt. Her hair was dyed blonde and tied back in a ponytail that dangled over her left shoulder.

Gilchrist held out his warrant card, introduced himself and Jessie, and said, 'We're looking for Amari Bankole.'

'I am she,' she said. 'Please. Come in.' She stood back, and smiled at each of them as they passed.

The door clicked shut, followed by the hard rattling of keys being turned, locks being secured, leaving Gilchrist with the uneasy feeling of having walked into a trap. The lounge was deserted, high-ceilinged and airy, like a bright oasis in a desert of gloom. Light speckled in through paper blinds. Scented candles gave off the sweet smell of jasmine, and some other fragrance as aromatic as perfume. Two computer monitors stood on a wooden table in the corner, next to three laptops and a keyboard. A dozen or so books lay in haphazard piles on the floor by the legs of the table.

'Would you like tea? Coffee?' she asked from behind them.

Gilchrist turned, shook his head. 'I'm fine, thanks.'

'You, DS Janes?'

Jessie looked at her, as if surprised to hear her name and rank.

'Can I get you tea or coffee?' Bankole smiled. 'Something stronger, perhaps?'

'No. I'm all right. Thanks.'

Bankole turned her attention to Gilchrist. 'Now DCI Gilchrist, how can I help you?'

He almost smiled at her elocution, the words precise and measured, with only the tiniest hint of a Scottish accent. Not what he'd expected. Not at all. Those thoughts flashed through his mind in a millisecond, before he said, 'You were expecting us.'

'Yes. DCI Small phoned me, and said you would like to talk to me.'

Dainty seemed to be pulling more strings than he was letting on. 'I was told you met with Leila Hazazi for an hour,' Gilchrist said, 'the day before she was reported missing.'

'I did. Yes.'

'Why?'

'I do research for Leila and Mike, for whatever story they're working on. We used to meet face-to-face twice a month, but sadly . . . now she's missing, presumed dead.'

'And where would you meet Leila?'

'The Counting House. On the corner of George Square.'

26

Gilchrist didn't know Glasgow well enough to visualise the place, but a nod from Jessie let him know she had it covered.

'After she went missing, did you meet with Mike instead?'

'Not in person. But we spoke by phone.'

It struck him then, that Dainty might not have brought Bankole current with the day's events. 'When did you last speak to Mike?'

'Last weekend.'

'Which day?'

'Saturday.'

'When?' he said, knowing he could check her statement through phone records.

'Just after six in the evening. I can check my records for you, if you need the exact time. I have an app.'

'Please.' He said nothing while she slipped out her mobile and worked her way into whatever app she'd acquired. Dainty hadn't told him when Elgin was suspected of being killed, but if he'd been in the Clyde for three days at least – according to Cooper – then this might help work out his final moments, or even where they could focus on CCTV footage.

'Six-oh-seven on Saturday evening,' Amari announced. 'The call lasted five minutes and forty-one seconds.'

Jessie scribbled it down.

'May I ask, please?' Bankole said. 'Why you are interested in my phone call to Mike?'

Jessie said, 'Because he's dead. Pulled out of the Clyde this morning.'

If Gilchrist thought Jessie's bluntness would shock Bankole, he was mistaken. She stilled for a few seconds, as if trying to assimilate the comment in her brain, then said, 'I didn't know that. Sorry. How sad.'

'Been in the river for three days,' Jessie pressed on. 'So you were probably one of the last people to speak to him.'

'Hmm. Yes. Probably.'

So much for grieving for a friend.

'Grant Hadwin,' Gilchrist said, hoping the change in tack might stir up some reaction. 'You told Leila that his biological father was Tony Dilanos.'

'I did, yes.'

'How did you find that out?'

'Through his DNA.'

'No. What I mean is, what caused you to look into Hadwin's paternity?'

'Leila asked me to.'

Gilchrist felt frustration stir. Was Bankole being deliberately obstructive, or simply obtuse? He forced his tone to remain level. 'But why did she ask you? What did she know?'

'She didn't know anything. Not for sure, anyway. She said Mike had heard a rumour about Tony Dilanos, that he'd fathered a child, and that child was Grant Hadwin. So she asked me to look into it, see if I could find proof. That's all.'

'So . . . just a rumour,' he said, more statement than question.

'Yes.'

'From whom?'

'She didn't say.'

Jessie said, 'Tony's been dead for a while. How did you get his DNA?'

'From his criminal records.'

'These records can't be accessed by just anyone.'

'I know.'

'So how did you manage it?'

She pulled a quick smile that showed small teeth. 'I have ways and means.'

'That's illegal,' Jessie persevered.

She shrugged. 'Arrest me, then.'

That seemed to stump Jessie, but she tried to fight back with, 'We might just do that.'

Gilchrist cooled the moment with, 'So who else knows about this connection?'

'Only Mike. I'm sure.'

'And now he's dead.'

'So you said.' She frowned. 'Do you think that's why he and Leila were murdered?'

'We never said Mike was murdered.'

'I'm adding two and two.'

His glance at Jessie warned her to bite her tongue. 'So before we arrest you for breach of data protection,' he said, 'what else have you uncovered?'

'Depends.'

'Depends on what?'

'On whether you're going to arrest me or not.'

Gilchrist returned her gaze, all of a sudden aware of how precocious she seemed, how secure she felt in her own environment, how her inscrutable face showed no signs of worry or concern. He remembered Melton telling him how the threat of charging her with possession of drugs had her . . . *singing* . . . like a canary. Yet, here she was, facing down his bluff. He couldn't say how he knew, but he felt certain she was holding something back, some piece of information that might provide him with a useful lead.

'Whether or not we arrest you,' he said, 'depends on how much we value what you've found.'

'Not to mention,' Jessie added, 'by withholding vital information, you're obstructing a criminal investigation.'

Bankole looked at Jessie, as if seeing her for the first time, blinked once, twice, then turned her attention back to Gilchrist. 'Mike told me on the phone that he met with Arletta Shepherd last Thursday.'

Gilchrist tried to keep his surprise hidden, but wasn't sure he pulled it off. 'Thursday was two days before he was killed,' he said. 'And about the same time Arletta went missing.' He lowered his head and eyed Bankole over an imaginary pair of specs. 'You need to do better than that.'

'Would a phone number work?'

'Whose?'

'Quid pro quo? I give you Arletta's phone number, then you leave me alone?'

He glanced at Jessie, whose lips resembled a white scar. 'Why didn't you give DI Melton, or DCI Small, the number?'

'They never asked.' A pause, then, 'Deal?'

He nodded. 'Deal.'

CHAPTER 5

Back outside, Gilchrist phoned Dainty. 'DI Melton said I should call you.'

'You get anywhere with Bankole?'

'Might have a lead, but it's too early to say.'

'Want to share it?'

Two could play at keeping cards close to their chest. 'No,' he said. 'It's too flimsy. I'll get back to you if it's worthwhile.'

The line filled with silence for a few seconds before Dainty said, 'You're not holding out on me, are you?'

'Let's say that I want to keep things tight until I have a better handle on what's what.'

Dainty fell silent for another long moment, then he sniffed, and said, 'Okay. Get back to me. We still have a double murder investigation to solve.' And with that, the line died.

Next, Gilchrist dialled the number Bankole had given him. He walked off from Jessie, mobile hard to his ear, concerned that if Arletta heard any background noise, she might think someone was listening in. When the connection was made, the line rang twenty times before he hung up. It didn't dump him into voicemail. Not that he would have left a message, but he would at least have felt confident that the number belonged to a living person, Arletta or someone else.

He searched for Jessie, who was on the opposite side of the street on a call of her own, so he tried the number again. Same result, although he didn't wait as long before he killed the connection. He and Arletta hadn't been in touch for well over a year, so he thought it unlikely that she would recognise his mobile number. And if the number he'd been given belonged to a burner, his own number wouldn't be stored in the memory.

He was about to slip his mobile into his pocket, when he thought of sending a text. He worked his way into Contacts, tapped in the number, then pressed the Message icon. Faced with a blank screen, doubts crept through his mind – for all he knew about the number, he could be sending a text to someone he wouldn't necessarily want to know that he was trying to contact Arletta. So, what to text? Short and sweet was as good a message as any. And not cryptic, but something that would let her know who had texted – an abbreviation of his rank and name, perhaps? Bankole had said Arletta had met Mike Elgin, so he decided to go with that, keep it short and vague, and all in lowercase without correct grammar. For a moment he thought of misspelling *dead* as he tapped in the message, but didn't see any advantage in doing so.

elgin dead dciag

He sent the text, then eyed the screen to see if it was received or read. But nothing showed up, and he had the sense of shooting a message into an empty digital universe. Just then, he caught Jessie slipping her mobile into her jacket, call over. He walked back to his car, clicked his key fob, and slipped behind the wheel.

When Jessie strapped her seatbelt on, she said, 'Would've been nice if you'd held the door open for me.'

'I didn't think you were that type.'

'And what type is that?'

He fired up the ignition. 'The type who want men to traipse after them.'

'And DI Annie Melton is?' She scoffed a grunt. 'I think not.'

He eased out of the parking spot. 'I'll be more considerate in the future. I promise.'

'I'll hold you to that.' She shuffled in her seat. 'Right. Let's try that number. Want me to put it on speaker?'

'Just tried it. Couldn't get through.'

'Rang out? Or disconnected?'

'Rang out. I'll try later.'

'That Bankole bitch'd better not have given us a bum number, or I'll hunt her down and arrest her in person.'

'I think she understood that.' He indicated right, then eased into another tenement-lined street. 'Do you know how to get out of here?'

'Where are we heading?'

'The mortuary.'

'Elgin's body won't have been delivered there yet.'

'I know.'

'Jeez,' she said. 'Don't tell me you're still in love with Queen Becky.'

Gilchrist kept his tone level, but his voice firm. 'You haven't forgotten I'm engaged to Irene, have you? Or that Irene is ill, and

33

not expected to see the end of the year. So no, I'm not in love with Queen Becky. And never will be.'

It took all of ten seconds before Jessie said, 'I'm sorry, Andy. I'm really sorry. I meant nothing by it. I'm just . . . I'm just . . .'

'Just an idiot?'

'Yeah. I'm just an idiot. Sorry.'

'So. Which way are we going? Left or right?'

'Hang on,' she said, and tapped the address for the mortuary into the satnav. 'You want the automatic voice on?'

'No, I prefer yours.'

She chuckled at that. 'You really are a smartass,' she said, then spent the next few minutes directing them back onto the main road.

Traffic was bad, and with the confusing one-way road network, riddled with bus lanes and bus gates, it took Gilchrist almost thirty minutes before he turned off Broomielaw onto Bridgegate. Five minutes later, he managed to find a Pay and Display spot in St Margaret's Place.

As they entered the building, Jessie gave an involuntary shiver. 'This place brings back memories. Most of them bad.'

'You never get used to it,' Gilchrist agreed.

He found Cooper in her office, nothing more than a small room off the corridor. She was typing when he knocked, which caused her to glance up for a moment before refocusing on whatever she was typing. Well, what had he expected? A smile? An offer to take a seat, or *I'll be with you in a moment*? No, Cooper was a woman unto herself, and always would be. He sensed Jessie's unease by his side, and it didn't take long before she whispered something under her breath and retreated along the corridor.

That seemed to do the trick, for Cooper closed the lid of her laptop, looked up at him and said, 'To what do I owe the pleasure?'

Her hair had grown, not quite the sensual shoulder-length strawberry-blonde waves of the past, but no longer the surprise Mary Quant cut that hadn't suited her. 'You examined a body earlier this morning,' he said. 'Pulled from the Clyde. Identified as Mike Elgin.'

'I did, yes.'

'Any thoughts?'

'Only that I'll have the opportunity to carry out a post-mortem once the body arrives, and I'll make sure to send a copy of the report to your Office asap, as requested by Dainty.'

The mention of Dainty surprised him. Not like Dainty to offer to share information so willingly. 'Any other thoughts?'

'Other than, you're already beginning to annoy me?'

He ignored the jibe. 'Death by drowning, is what we concluded.'

'Good for you.'

'We suspect Elgin might have been tasered, not enough to immobilise him, but to send him reeling, which caused him to fall into the Clyde.'

'Do you now?'

This is what he hated about Cooper, her irritating condescension, her hot-and-cold turns of openness and secrecy, her ability to toy with him – her cat to his mouse. He did what he could not to rise to the bait, and forced himself to keep his tone level. 'Do you not agree?'

She frowned at him, then tapped the side of her chin. 'Two small reddish marks here, could have been caused by a taser, or could be something more simple, like shaving cuts—'

'He has a beard.'

'Trimmed, by one of those electric trimmers.'

'Meaning?'

'He could have inadvertently cut himself with its plastic prongs.'

'That's stretching it.'

'I know. But it's good to try to think outside the box.' She inhaled deeply, held her breath for several seconds, and let it out. 'You're right, though. He was attacked. And a taser is a good bet. Does anyone know whereabouts he entered the Clyde?'

'Not yet. They're working on it.'

'I would look for a place on the river's edge that has a metal railing running alongside it. It's only a guess, I have to say.' She stared at him then, as if willing him to ask the obvious question.

He needed to know, so said, 'Why do you think that?'

'Two fingers on his left hand were broken, his pinkie and ring finger, as if they'd struck something by force, such as the edge of a metal railing in an attempt to save himself. Bruising didn't have time to develop because he drowned shortly after falling into the river.'

Playing devil's advocate, Gilchrist said, 'He could've held his hand up to protect himself from his attackers, and had his fingers broken that way.'

'Perhaps,' she said. 'But I don't think so.'

'Why not?'

'I won't know for certain until I've had an opportunity to examine the body, but his collarbone was fractured, too. Which suggests another injury received during the fall into the Clyde. I don't think that would have been inflicted during a frontal assault.' She flickered a victory smile, then said, 'Interesting that you said attackers, plural.'

'Just a turn of phrase. But now it's mentioned, any thoughts on that?'

'No.' And with that, she lifted the lid of her laptop, eyed the screen, and began typing.

He knew Cooper well enough to know she'd said all she was going to say about Mike Elgin's death. So he said, 'Ciao,' and turned from the doorway.

But not before he caught a flicker of a smile from his parting word.

CHAPTER 6

Gilchrist found Jessie standing by his car, mobile to her ear. He beeped his fob and opened the door for her. Without looking at him, she slid into the passenger seat. He closed the door quietly, walked around the front, and was about to open the driver's door, when his mobile rang – ID Jack.

'Hey, man,' Jack said. 'It's been a while.'

He couldn't remember the last time he'd heard from Jack – three weeks, maybe four. Not that it mattered, he supposed. Jack lived his own life, worked as an artist in Edinburgh, and seemed to be making more than a half-decent living as a sculptor of obscure steel figures. More importantly, or so Gilchrist thought, he'd cut back on his drinking habits.

'Hi, Jack. Good to hear from you. How's everything?' he said, feeling the need to tread with care around his son's private life.

'Great.' A pause, then, 'I'm at the airport. Flying out to Sweden in a couple of hours.'

'To see Linna?'

'Yeah. Kristen's letting me spend a week with Linna before she and whatsisface head off for a couple of weeks over Christmas.'

'If you'd let me know, I could've bought her something for you to take with you.'

'No probs, man. Ah, shit, that's another call come in. Got to take this. Hey, listen, catch you when I get back. Have a couple of beers together. That's a promise.'

'Sounds good.'

'Oh, and give Irene my love,' he added, almost as an afterthought.

'Will do,' Gilchrist said, but the line had died.

Behind the wheel, he clicked on his seatbelt.

Jessie said, 'Problems?'

'Not at all. That was Jack. Lovely to hear from him, even if it was just a quick call.'

He had only just pulled away from the parking spot, when Jessie said, 'What a bitch that Becky is. I don't know how you stand her.'

'Professional needs,' he said, and accelerated into light traffic.

'She hates me. That much is clear.'

'Isn't the feeling mutual?'

Neither of them spoke again until Gilchrist had worked his way onto the M8 for the return trip to St Andrews. 'Cooper agrees with us,' he said at length. 'That Elgin was attacked by a taser. And that we should be looking for some place by the river that has a metal railing, because several bones in Elgin's hand and collarbone were broken, most likely as a result of trying to prevent himself from tumbling into the Clyde.'

'No doubt we'll read all about it in her PM report.' She shuffled in her seat to face him. 'Seriously, Andy, have you ever walked along the Clyde? Metal handrails everywhere. She might as well have told us diddly.' Then she settled, and said, 'Does Dainty know about the broken bones?'

'She didn't say, but I thought I'd let you pass on that information.'

Jessie pulled up the car's phone system, tapped in Dainty's number, and when it was answered said, 'Jessie here. Got you on speaker with Andy. Any luck with CCTV footage?'

'Needle in a bloody haystack,' Dainty grumbled.

'Did you know Mike Elgin's fingers were broken? And his collarbone?'

'Cooper mentioned that, yeah, but it's not much of a lead.' A pause, then, 'Any luck tracking down Arletta?'

Something in the way the question was asked told Gilchrist that Dainty knew Bankole had given him Arletta's contact number. Which meant that Bankole must have told Dainty about the number, and told him she'd not been 100 per cent honest. 'Nothing yet,' Gilchrist said. 'Working on it.'

'I'm getting my balls squeezed at this end. Let me know as soon as you come up with something. The shit's piling in front of the fan down here.'

And with that, the line died.

Gilchrist cursed under his breath, then said, 'He's still telling us nothing.'

'You think he's hiding something?'

'I suspect he knew that Bankole had a contact number for Arletta, and must've told her to keep that to herself. But if I know Dainty, he'll have had good reason.' He pulled into the fast lane, upped his speed to seventy. 'Try Arletta's number again. Put her on speaker.'

Jessie did, but like before, it rang out.

He ended the call, and gripped the wheel tighter.

'Want me to try again?' Jessie said.

'No. Get hold of Jackie, and have her trace that number. See who it's registered to.' He didn't expect Jackie would have any luck – the mobile was probably a burner. But as an old friend of his used to say – nothing ventured, nothing gained. He let his thoughts turn over, trying to make sense of what they'd uncovered so far, while Jessie contacted Jackie in the North Street Office.

What did they have? Not a lot, came the obvious answer. But often out of nothing, comes something. At least that's what he would like to believe. Mike Elgin and Leila Hazazi had been working on some undercover story that got them both killed. He was certain of that. Too many coincidences to conclude anything else. Leila was first to be murdered, or at least presumed to be. But without a body, they could be shooting in the dark. Mike might not have been murdered – not directly that is – but a taser attack which caused him to topple into the Clyde and drown, was as good as. And Mike had met Arletta Shepherd a few days before he – *and* she – disappeared.

But if you didn't ask *when* they met, but instead asked – what had Mike told Arletta? – you came up with an enticing answer; Ryan Hadwin was not Grant Hadwin's biological father. And Grant was now the CEO of his father's funeral empire, with plans of his own to expand the business throughout the UK. But the vital connection was the link to Arletta, that Grant's biological father was Arletta's late husband, Tony Dilanos – *allegedly.*

Had Arletta known of Tony's infidelity? Of course, she had. Gilchrist had interviewed her years earlier, and been left in no doubt that she was a smart woman who knew what was what. But had she known of Tony's love-child? – if *love*-child was the correct word. Because Gilchrist's memory of Tony Dilanos was

41

of a cruel heartless man who thought of no one but himself. It was no stretch of anyone's imagination to see Tony forming cliques within the family, separate those who favoured Arletta, then pit them against those who favoured him. Divide and conquer, might have been the name of the game. But Tony had been killed in Dundee, during a failed attempt to have Arletta murdered.

So, what if those divisions still existed within the present family? What if there were family members who still harboured resentment against Arletta, and couldn't stand having a female boss? The critical question might be – what if those family members knew of Tony's illegitimate son, and now saw Grant Hadwin as the rightful heir to the family throne, and their means to dislodge Arletta from the seat of power?

Was that a possibility? Had the discovery of Tony's love-child caused Arletta to fear for her life? Was that why she'd suddenly disappeared? The timing seemed right. But was his reasoning—?

'Earth to Andy? Hello . . .?'

Gilchrist jerked a smile. 'Sorry. I was away in another world.'

Jessie frowned at him. 'Are you all right?'

'Just thinking. What were you saying?'

'Jackie's just got back about Arletta's number. It's a burner, Andy. So it's a no-go.'

Well, what had he expected? Of course it was a burner. Arletta was in hiding, likely in fear for her life – wasn't that what he'd just reasoned? The last thing she needed was to leave a digital trail for anyone to find her. Just then, he noticed a road sign for the exit to the M74 South, the main motorway to England. And if his memory served him, it also connected to the M8, and the road back into Glasgow.

'You've been to Jock Shepherd's house before, haven't you?'

'You know I have.'

'You remember the address?'

'How could I forget?'

'Good,' he said, and flicked on his indicator. 'Enter it into the satnav.'

'Are you serious?'

'Never been more so.'

CHAPTER 7

It was almost midday when Gilchrist pulled his BMW to a halt outside what appeared to be the largest mansion on the street, maybe in the city. Nothing much had changed since he'd last been here. A metal gate still guarded the stone-pillared entrance, which was only opened once approval to enter had been granted from security stationed in the main building a couple of hundred yards up a brick-paved driveway. Two Bentleys, gleaming showroom new, sat nose-to-tail at the front door, and had Gilchrist thinking of Mike Elgin's cufflinks. Had Elgin also been on the take? Was that what got him killed? Or was that unrelated? At the side of the building a black vehicle as wide as a Hummer stared down at them, as if parked in readiness of an explosive getaway. He knew the Shepherd family owned the mansion next door, too, with rumours that an underground tunnel connected both buildings.

Gilchrist pressed the electronic buzzer by the gate, and found himself searching for, and locating, a CCTV camera mounted on a tree some ten feet inside the property. Its black eye never blinked as it took them in. Somewhere deep within the confines of the building, he knew he and Jessie were being scrutinised from head to toe. For all he knew they could be scanning them for hidden weapons.

The intercom buzzed, followed by silence, before Gilchrist realised he was expected to introduce himself. Rather than speak, he held his warrant card up to the CCTV camera – a nod to Jessie had her doing the same – and a few moments later, the locks clicked and the heavy gate slid open on well-oiled wheels.

They were halfway up the driveway when two men material-ised from the bushes to the side, muscled frames doing what they could to burst the seams of made-to-measure suits that Gilchrist knew hid the swell of leather shoulder-holsters. The leader of the two, a man with a shaved head as smooth as a polished dome, said, 'Spread 'em.'

Silent, Gilchrist obliged, feet apart, arms wide, while a wand of sorts appeared in the other man's hand as if from nowhere, then swept up and down, around and through, with quiet exper-tise verging on boredom.

A nod to Jessie had her standing likewise. 'Careful with that, sonny, or I'll nick you for sexual assault.'

But after a quick sweep without incident, the man stood back.

'You're all done,' polished dome said, then winked at Jessie. 'Next time we might have to pat you down.'

'And that'll get you a boot in the balls.'

The man smiled. 'Gonnie show me your handcuffs, please?'

Gilchrist held out his arm to lead Jessie away, before she snapped at the bait.

As they neared the main entrance, Gilchrist kept himself between Jessie and the two Bentleys, just in case she had a mind to key their paintwork. He could almost feel the anger rise from her. When they arrived at the foot of the marble steps, a man

45

appeared from the vestibule and stood facing them, legs astride, arms by his side, as if challenging them to battle their way past. He eyed them in silence, giving Gilchrist the thought that he'd seen him before, although he couldn't recall who he was, or where they might have met.

Gilchrist half-smiled, and said, 'DCI Gilchrist and DS Janes of Fife Constabulary.'

'You're out of your jurisdiction.'

'Let's just say it's unofficial. We're looking for Arletta.'

'Why?'

'To ask her a few questions.'

'About what?'

'That's between me and her.'

'She's no here.'

A pause, then, 'So who's in charge in her absence?'

Silent, the man glared at the pair of them, his hard look leaving Gilchrist in no doubt that he and Jessie were being warned to turn around and walk away. But he was in no mood for hardman semantics, and simply shrugged. 'Would you like me to get a warrant and make this visit official?'

Something passed behind the man's eyes, some shadow that seemed to suck the anger out of them. Then he blinked, and said, 'Freddy's busy. He's in a meeting.'

'Freddy?'

'Freddy Dilanos.'

'Is he related to Tony?'

The man turned, as if Gilchrist hadn't spoken. 'Follow me.'

He led them along a carpeted hallway, into a room of dark wood panelling and framed black-and-white photographs of old Glasgow. The air hinted of cigar smoke, and the ambient warmth of a meeting only recently finished. Without a word, the man backed out of the room, and closed the door behind him.

'Bloody hell,' Jessie said, looking around her. 'This place gives me the creeps.'

Gilchrist let his gaze drift around the room. Not that he was admiring the old world décor, rather he was searching for the tell-tale dot of a CCTV camera, which he found in the top corner by the door. He raised his eyebrows at Jessie, gave an almost imperceptible nod to the wall behind her, and said in a low voice, 'Careful what you say.'

'Gotcha.'

Two wooden chairs, with studded red-leather covers, fronted an oversized mahogany desk with intricate carvings on its front panel. A high-backed swivel chair tall enough to be mistaken for a throne stood behind the desk. Other than an A-2 sized writing pad, the desk was clear of papers. Not even a telephone. But in today's digital age, landlines and desk-top phones had effectively been consigned to history.

The door clicked open, and a short man in a three-piece suit and open-necked white shirt strode in as if he owned the place. For all Gilchrist knew, he probably did.

'I'm Wee Freddy,' he said. 'But don't let that fool youse.' He didn't offer his hand, or step behind the desk, but instead stood facing them. Light from the window cast a soft glow that did little to hide the scars on his face. One of them ran from his forehead to his chin, and looked as if he might have felt the sharp edge of a machete.

'What are youse after?' he growled.

'We were hoping to speak to Arletta,' Gilchrist said.

'As youse were told, she's no here.'

'So where is she?'

'How the fuck would ah know?'

'I thought she was the head of the family.'

'Says who?'

'Isn't she?'

Freddy's lips tightened, and his eyes narrowed, a discernible shift from his somewhat forced politeness to downright ready confrontation, a change that seemed to chill the air and had Gilchrist thinking he might have overstepped the mark – although what that mark was, he was none too sure.

'We believe Arletta's missing,' he tried.

'Missing?'

Jessie stepped in with, 'Yeah. Gone. Done a runner. You know? *Missing.*'

Freddy glared at Jessie, a hateful look that could have raised the *Titanic* and sunk it all over again.

Undeterred, Jessie said, 'With a face like yours, maybe you scared her away.'

'Oh, we got a right fucking comedian here,' he said, then turned to Gilchrist. 'She's no here, and ah've no idea where the fuck she is. So the two of youse can go and take a flying fuck to yourselves.' Back to Jessie. 'S'at clear enough, hen?'

'Crystal,' she said, and made to move to the door.

But Gilchrist wasn't quite finished. The security ape who'd led them to this room had mentioned Freddy's surname. But what was the relationship? 'Didn't know Tony had any brothers,' he said.

'Just shows what youse don't know.'

Which Gilchrist took to be a positive response. 'Younger? Older?'

'Whit?'

'Was Tony younger or older than you?'

Wee Freddy's lips curled into what could be mistaken for a smile. Something glinted in his hand, and Gilchrist's heart skipped a beat. But it was nothing more dangerous than a remote beeper, which resulted in two hardmen entering the room – one tall and gangly with ears that could do with being pinned back; the other muscled and wired, chewing gum and cracking his knuckles as if looking forward to testing them out on someone's bones.

The taller man – big-ears – said, 'All right, boss?' while his eyes assessed the situation, first Jessie, then Gilchrist.

'These two wankers were leaving. See they make it to the front gate.' And with that, Freddy turned and bruised his way from the room.

The short man reached out for Jessie, but she brushed off his hand. 'Lay a finger on me, and I'll have you for assault.'

Gilchrist raised his arm to keep the calm. 'We get the message. We're leaving.'

Give them their due, both men stood back while Gilchrist led Jessie from the room and along the short hallway. They said nothing while he opened the front door and helped her over the threshold. Down the marble steps, past the Bentleys, both men no more than a few steps behind. Not a word was said until they were twenty yards or so from the main gate.

'Wait here,' big-ears said, and brushed past Gilchrist.

Jessie tutted in annoyance. 'What's he up to?'

'Opening the gate,' the short man said.

'I wasn't asking you.'

A shove from behind with a grunted, 'Get going,' had her stumbling forward.

Gilchrist held up his hand again. 'Take it easy, son. We're leaving.'

'Not quick enough. Get going.' Another shove had Jessie reaching for her cuffs, and Gilchrist holding her back.

'Forget it,' he said to her.

She glared at the muscled man, who stood with a chewing-gum grin, rolling his head, as if twitching to give her a right good pasting. Then they were beyond the gate and walking to the car, the sound of the gate sliding shut behind them.

'Bloody hell, Andy, that wee bastard was pressing my buttons.'

'You need to calm down.' He clicked his key fob, then held the passenger door open for her.

'You're full of surprises,' she said, as she stepped inside, and gave a parting glare at the closed gate. But the men were gone.

Gilchrist sat behind the wheel, and fired up the ignition. He waited until they reached the first set of traffic lights before he pulled a folded slip of paper from his pocket. He passed it to Jessie.

'What's this?' she said.

'The tall guy with the ears slipped it into my pocket.'

Jessie mouthed an Oh-my-God, unfolded it with care, then frowned as she read it.

'What's it say?' he asked.

'It's a mobile number.'

'Well let's dial it.'

CHAPTER 8

Neither Gilchrist nor Jessie spoke while the number rang out. When the connection was made after five rings, the line filled with silence.

'Hello?' Gilchrist said.

The connection died.

'Try again,' he said.

That time the phone was picked up on the second ring, once more to silence. 'Hello?' he said again.

Nothing.

He waited in frustration for what felt like a minute, with an odd sense of relief that the recipient hadn't hung up, which told him that he was expected to introduce himself. 'Hello?' he tried one more time, then after a few seconds said, 'This is Detective Chief Inspector Andy Gilchrist of St Andrews CID. Can you please identify yourself?'

'Where did you get this number?'

The voice was that of a woman, but no one he recognised. A glance at Jessie, who gave a puzzled frown and a shake of her head. Back to the call. 'It was given to me by a person unknown.

That's all I'm prepared to tell you at the moment.' The tall man with the ears had clearly taken a chance slipping him the number, and until Gilchrist knew who he was talking to, he didn't want to risk the possibility of putting anyone's life in danger. 'So I'll ask you again, can you please identify yourself.'

'Call back in exactly fifteen minutes,' she said.

The line died.

'Jeez,' Jessie said. 'What was all that about?'

'More to the point, who is she?'

'You think maybe it's Arletta?'

'I've the vaguest memory of Arletta's voice being rougher than that. And older, too. So, no, I don't think it was Arletta. But more than likely someone who knows her.'

'How old would you say she was?'

'You're asking a man to guess a woman's age?' He shook his head. 'That's not in our DNA. Even if it was, we wouldn't dare risk it. How old do *you* think she is?'

'Not a teenager. That's for sure. And not ancient. But still mature. Say . . . thirties to fifties?'

He wobbled his head in general acknowledgement. 'We need to watch the time. She said to call back in *exactly* fifteen minutes. We don't want to screw it up.'

'That gives us time for a coffee, then. You've just passed a Costa's. Pull over. Mine's a skinny latte, and I'll share your blueberry muffin.'

He turned into a side road, searching for a parking spot, but in the end settled for the double yellow close to the junction. 'You'd best be quick,' he said, and handed her a tenner. He watched her cross the road and enter the shop. It didn't look busy, but freshly made coffee could have you waiting ten minutes or more in even the smallest queue. When the woman had said to call back in exactly fifteen minutes, he'd noted the time without thinking. A glance at the dashboard display warned him he had eleven minutes left. Again, he puzzled over the significance of the return call being *exactly* fifteen minutes, and again he realised that he didn't want to create any excuse for his call not to be taken. So he would call back with or without Jessie.

He took a moment to phone the North Street Office in St Andrews and instruct DC Mhairi McBride to find out what she could on Hadwin Funeral Services, and its CEO Grant Hadwin, and if they had anything on its late founder, Ryan Hadwin.

He kept the call short, conscious that time was running out, with no sign of Jessie. But he needn't have worried. She scarpered back across the road, and slid into the passenger seat, out of breath, and blowing hard. 'Am I in time?'

'Still four minutes to go.'

'Jeez. Thought I wasn't going to make it. Some punter was fannying about with an espresso.' She flipped the lid off her cup, still panting. 'I was thinking,' she said, and took a sip. 'That she asked us to call back because maybe she's gone to fetch Arletta.'

He'd wondered about that himself, but he'd made no mention of Arletta on the call, so it might be a stretch to conclude that. On the other hand, why would the phone number have been given to him at all, and in such a risky manner? He'd asked for Arletta at the mansion, so maybe it wasn't such a stretch for big-ears to have overheard, or to have asked others what the police were doing there, and been told. Once again, too many questions.

'So . . .' he said at length, 'if she's gone to fetch Arletta . . . then the number we dialled doesn't belong to Arletta, but to someone close to her.'

'And who now *lives* close to her, too.'

'You think so?'

Another sip of coffee, then, 'I don't know.'

'She's gone to fetch Arletta, you said. Wouldn't she just phone her up? I mean, rather than leave the house, run up the street, knock on the door, and tell her someone's going to call back in fifteen minutes. She'd phone her. Don't you think?'

'I don't know what to think, Andy. All I can tell you is that your coffee's not getting any warmer. Here.' She delved into the paper bag and removed a muffin. 'Cranberry. They'd run out of blueberry. It's all yours. I'm on a diet.'

'Since when?'

'Since I realised that running across the road has me puffing like an old biddy.'

'I'll have it later,' he said. 'Two minutes and counting.'

Jessie took a larger than polite nibble of the muffin before returning it to the bottom of the bag, and saying, 'You know something?'

'Never talk with your mouth full?'

'Smartass,' she mumbled, then cleared her mouth with a sip of coffee. 'I was thinking about what you said back there, about Tony Dilanos not having any brothers.' She glanced at him. 'I think Wee Freddy isn't related to Tony at all. Tony was tall and handsome, while that wee shite has a face that could scare rats. I mean, it's like that movie with Danny DeVito and Arnold Schwarzenegger where they're supposed to be twins separated at birth.' She chuckled at that, then said, 'What's the time? Want me to call?'

He nodded, and said nothing while she tapped the number in again.

The call rang out, and Gilchrist disconnected after twenty rings.

'What d'you think?' Jessie said.

'We try again.'

She did, and this time the call was picked up on the second ring.

Gilchrist said, 'Hello?'

The line lay silent.

'This is Detective Chief Inspector Gilchrist. Who am I speaking to?'

'Are you alone?'

A glance at Jessie told him she'd picked up on it, too – the voice of a woman, but not the same woman who'd answered the call earlier. 'Detective Sergeant Janes is sitting next to me. We have you on speaker. It's safe to talk. No one can hear us.' Again nothing, but with it the niggling worry that not being by himself might be enough to make her hang up. He tried once more. 'Who am I speaking to?'

'Did you send a text earlier?'

'Not to this number.'

'What did it say?'

'Hang on. Let me check.' He removed his mobile, worked into Messages and read it out. 'Elgin dead,' he said, then spelled out, 'dciag.'

'Who gave you this number?'

'I don't know the man's name, but he was . . . let's just say he was *distinctive* looking.' He felt reluctant to expand on that, worried that he really didn't know who he was talking to. So he said, 'I'd never met him before, but he slipped the number into my pocket when we were being escorted from your home.'

He thought he caught the sibilant sound of a whispered curse, which told him that he'd guessed correctly when he mentioned *home*. He had Arletta Shepherd on the line – he was sure of that – and he could tell from the shiver in her voice that she was scared for her life—

'Did you speak to anyone?'

'Wee Freddy Dilanos,' he said. 'The new boss.'

'He's no Dilanos,' she hissed. 'And he's no boss.'

'Well everyone did as he said.'

The line hung in silence for so long that he thought they'd been disconnected. Then a clattering noise rattled the speaker, as if the phone had been dropped, and another woman's voice, the one who had answered the first call, said, 'Do you remember where we last met?' then added with a rush, 'Don't say it.'

Gilchrist glanced at Jessie, who looked just as confused. Who was this woman? When had they supposedly met? And even just as baffling, *where* had they last met? 'Well,' he said, struggling to find some way to keep the conversation going, because he was certain that if he answered in the negative, the line would be disconnected. 'It's . . . eh . . . it's been a while—'

'Tonight. Midnight. Come alone.'

He stared at the speaker when the line died.

'Shit,' Jessie said. 'What does she mean? Do you know her?'

He shook his head, thoughts crackling through his mind like sparks. The woman knew him, that much was certain, but who she was, and where they'd last met, he'd no idea – until gradually, through the thinning fog of his memory, he thought he saw the outline of a face he recognised.

CHAPTER 9

For reasons he found impossible to explain, Gilchrist kept his thoughts to himself, not willing to share them with Jessie on the drive back to St Andrews. Not that he didn't trust her; rather, he wasn't sure if he was thinking of the right woman, or that his rationale was even in the right ballpark.

Natalie Foster. That was the name he remembered, and the woman he suspected of having answered the first phone call. Natalie was Arletta's cousin – her mother had been big Jock's sister – and had acted as go-between for Gilchrist and Arletta when Arletta's husband, Tony Dilanos, tried to kill Arletta in a failed attempt to take control of the family business. This was not long after big Jock had passed away, and the Glasgow underworld was looking for a new leader. But the business being inherited by Jock's daughter had not been the most popular of takeovers, and when Arletta had suspected Tony was intent on eliminating her, she'd gone into hiding, in fear for her life.

Was this what she was doing again? Was the criminal under-world about to undergo another seismic shift in leadership? And all because Amari Bankole had uncovered the fact that Grant Hadwin, the new CEO of Hadwin Funeral Services, was the illegitimate son of the late Tony Dilanos?

Was that seemingly innocent fact sufficient enough to set in motion a murderous plot to shift the power in a criminal family – a family that had supposedly been trying to go legit ever since the death of its founding patriarch, big Jock Shepherd? And if so, what power did Freddy have over those controlling the family in Arletta's absence? If his theory was correct, where would Grant Hadwin fit into the scheme of things? Once again, far too many questions and not enough answers. So sharing those convoluted thoughts with Jessie was not the way to go. Not at that moment anyway. Instead he had Jessie coordinate research efforts through the North Street Office.

He had just driven past the Powmill Milk Bar and was accelerating hard along the A977 when Jessie ended a call, and slapped her mobile onto her lap.

'Can't quite work out what that Grant Hadwin's up to,' she said, 'but whatever it is, he's in it up to his hairy armpits.'

'I'm listening,' Gilchrist said.

'Right. Here's what Mhairi and Jackie have found so far. They didn't come up with much on Hadwin, other than minor stuff – parking tickets, speeding, that sort of thing. But they found some stuff on Ryan Hadwin, the father, or not the father, depending on how you look at it, around the time he disappeared four months ago.'

'That's a worrying coincidence,' Gilchrist said. 'But keep going.'

'Apparently there were a number of complaints made to the police over suspicions that the ashes of loved ones were not the ashes of the ones they loved, but were the ashes of some other ones' loved ones, if you get my meaning.'

'Who made the complaints?'

'One of Hadwin's employees. A guy called Wafic Saliba.'

'Anyone else?'

'Not that we know of.'

'So Wafic Saliba's a whistleblower,' he said.

Jessie shuffled in her seat to face him. '*Was* a whistleblower. Not long after Saliba made the complaints, he didn't turn up for work one day, and he's never been seen or heard of since.'

'Anyone look into his disappearance?'

'His co-worker, Sam Fishel, was interviewed and gave a written statement, which said that Wafic had complained about being homesick and been talking about returning to Beirut, and must have decided to leave on the spur of the moment, and just got up and left.'

Gilchrist pulled out to overtake a slower car. 'And that was it? End of investigation?'

'Don't think it even made it to an investigation.'

'Which Office handled the case?'

'Glenrothes.'

He thought about it for a long moment. 'So Ryan Hadwin's business is reported to the police for allegedly not handling crematory ashes correctly. Then the person who made the complaint – Wafic Saliba – vanishes. Never to be heard of again? Correct?'

'Ten out of ten.'

'Did Glenrothes find anything?'

'According to Mhairi, an inspection found the company records and procedures to be meticulously detailed. But with

Saliba gone, and no complaints from the public, that was it. End of. Case closed.'

'Did no one follow up on Saliba's disappearance?'

'Not after Sam Fishel's statement.'

'So who's the common denominator in this?'

'Sorry?'

'Who's the one person who benefits from it all? Ryan Hadwin disappearing. Saliba disappearing. The complaints against the business disappearing.'

'Grant Hadwin,' said Jessie.

Gilchrist nodded in silent agreement. 'Who – according to Bankole – just happens to be the biological son of none other than Tony Dilanos. Which frightens Arletta Shepherd so much that she goes into hiding.' He paused for a moment, to let these facts filter through his system. Then he glanced at Jessie. 'What do you think?'

'I think Grant Hadwin might be worth talking to.'

'Agreed.'

They found Grant Hadwin's place of business on the outskirts of Glenrothes. A bold sign in large Victorian-type scroll stated the name – HADWIN FUNERAL SERVICES – below which its motto – WE TAKE CARE OF THOSE YOU CHERISH MOST – seemed to underscore the sensitive and personal nature of the business.

Gilchrist pulled into an empty car park that fronted a single-storey building faced with planks of composite wood to give the impression of a company conscious of the needs of the environment. To the left, an eight-foot-high chain-link fence surrounded an area littered with smoothed-granite headstones. Some adorned with sculpted angels, birds, roses, stood upright as tall as a man.

Others squatted on the ground like abandoned stone boxes. A padlocked gate guarded the compound, and in the far corner a wooden hut for an office suggested the stone business was managed as a separate entity.

'Are they closed?' Jessie said, as she opened the car door and stepped outside.

'There's additional parking round the side.' Gilchrist nodded to several cars parked by the corner of the building, almost out of view. 'Someone's here.'

Jessie pulled her jacket tight to her with a shiver, and looked around. 'This place gives me the creeps. I mean, listen to it.'

Gilchrist frowned. 'What do you mean?'

'There's nothing. Not a sound.' She tilted her head. 'Do you hear any birds?'

'In the distance.'

She stood still for a moment, head cocked, then said, 'Bloody hell, Andy, you could hear snow falling, so you could.'

At that moment, Gilchrist's mobile rang – ID Dainty. He took the call, and walked to the back of his car.

'We've found the spot where Elgin was attacked,' Dainty said, without introduction. 'Saturday. Just after midnight. Finnieston. Close to the Squinty Bridge.'

'Are you able to ID the attacker?'

'*Attackers*,' Dainty emphasised with a hiss. 'Two of them. But no. Footage is clear as shite. I don't know why they bother putting those cameras up when they're next to fucking useless. All we can tell is that there's two of them. Can't even tell if they're male or female.'

'Males, I would say. Mike Elgin wasn't a small man.'

'Maybe. We've got a team reviewing other cameras, to see if we can track where they went, or even where they came from.'

Dainty coughed hard, as if pulling up phlegm. 'I'll let you know soon as. How about you? Any luck finding Arletta?'

'Depends what you call luck,' Gilchrist said, then paused for a moment. He didn't want to give too much away, because he wasn't sure what he was considering was pertinent to the enquiry, or whether it could send them up the wrong path. 'What do you know about Wee Freddy?' he said.

'What the fuck? Wee Freddy? How did you—?'

'We met him. Didn't get anywhere. In fact, we were escorted from the place at his instruction.'

The line fell silent for so long that Gilchrist thought they'd been disconnected. Then Dainty said, 'Watch yourself, Andy. Freddy's wee in name only. Heartless fucker, so he is.'

'He said his name was Freddy Dilanos, that his brother was Tony.'

Dainty choked a laugh. 'He's no Dilanos anything. Freddy Reid's his name. In and out of Barlinnie most of his life. And definitely not to be messed with.'

'Reid?' Gilchrist said. 'That rings a bell.'

'Aye, a fucking alarm bell. You remember Bully?'

Something flipped over in Gilchrist's stomach at the mention of the name. Bully Reid, the only criminal who'd ever scared him, *really* scared him, and now locked up in Barlinnie for the foreseeable. 'How could I forget,' he said.

'Bully and Freddy are related,' Dainty added. 'Freddy's mum is Bully's sister. Which makes Bully his uncle. But with that fucking lot, for all anyone knows they could be father and son.' Another cough. 'I'll have Annie send you copies of the CCTV footage. Once you've had a chance to look at it, give me a buzz. Later.'

Gilchrist held onto his mobile, his mind spinning. If the Reid family were somehow associated with the Shepherds, that blew the Dilanos–Hadwin father–son relationship into a whole new stratosphere.

CHAPTER 10

The reception area of Hadwin Funeral Services was panelled throughout in light maple wood. Chamber music, almost too quiet to hear, played in the background. The air was thick with jasmine fragrance and something more clinical that Gilchrist couldn't place.

The receptionist, a narrow-shouldered woman in a black skirt and white blouse, with shoulder-length blonde hair and a black root line, which looked as if it could do with a comb-through, pulled herself to her feet and patted down her front, as if dispersing crumbs.

Her lips jerked into a smile that failed to reach her eyes. 'How can I help you?' she said, her smile dropping at the sight of Jessie's warrant card.

'Grant Hadwin available?' Jessie said.

'I'll see if he's in.' She reached for the phone, tapped a couple of numbers, and said, 'There are two policemen at the front desk.' She tightened her lips, then nodded, and hung up. 'He'll be with you in a few minutes.'

She returned behind her desk, and was about to sit down, when Gilchrist said, 'Is Sam Fishel available, too?'

She frowned, and said, 'That's me.'

Aah, Gilchrist mouthed. 'Sam . . . as in Samantha?'

'Sam for short. Yes.'

'Were you questioned by Glenrothes police on Wafic Saliba's disappearance?'

'I was. Yes.'

'What can you tell me about his disappearance?'

She huffed her lips. 'Nothing more than I've already told the police.'

'We've read your statement,' he lied. 'So what made you think Wafic had returned to Beirut?'

'That's where he was from. He said he was homesick.'

'Were you surprised when he left without saying goodbye?'

She shrugged. 'Not really.'

'You were his co-worker, right?'

'Yeah.'

Gilchrist made a point of looking around the reception area. 'So what did Wafic do here?' he said.

'He worked mostly in the back office. And in the stone business. Jack of all trades, really. Driver, too.'

Gilchrist smiled to show he was harmless. 'Heavy lifting? That sort of thing?'

She nodded.

'Have you tried to contact him since he's left?'

'Don't have an address for him.'

'Tried his mobile?'

Her eyes flickered left-right-left, and Gilchrist knew the next words out of her mouth would be a lie. 'It just rang out,' she said. 'I think he got a new SIM card.'

'So you remember his mobile number?'

She grimaced, made a show of shaking her head slowly, as if struggling to recall.

'That's all right,' he said. 'We'll find it when we check your phone records.'

Jessie stepped in with, 'Can you give me your mobile number?'

'Why?'

'Duh . . . We need it to check your phone records.' Jessie stared at her, pen poised over her notebook. 'So what is it, then? I don't have all day.'

'I don't think I have to give that to you.'

Jessie nodded, put her pen and notebook away, then reached for a silver cardholder on top of the reception desk and removed a business card. 'No problem,' she said. 'Here it is. Sam Fishel. Assistant Funeral Director. Aw, that's nice, so it is. And there they are, your mobile and office numbers.' She pocketed the card with a smile and a wink.

Gilchrist said, 'Anything else you can remember about Wafic's disappearance that might help us in our enquiries?'

Fishel was saved further embarrassment by the sound of a door closing and footsteps striding along the corridor. Then a tall man entered the reception area, broad smile, dentist-perfect white teeth, short black hair, dark funereal suit, white shirt and a dark tie to match the hankie in his top pocket. Gilchrist thought his trousers were too tight, but who was he to say?

'Grant Hadwin,' the man said, shaking Gilchrist's hand, then Jessie's. 'Apologies for keeping you waiting, but I had to finish some . . . some business.' He grimaced to show how hard it could be dealing with bereavement, then held out an arm. 'Why don't we go through to my office. We can have a seat. Would you like tea? Coffee?'

'We're fine,' Gilchrist said. 'We won't keep you long.'

'Sure. No probs. Follow me.'

Hadwin's office was plain and simple. A couple of framed certificates on the wall informed anyone who was interested that he was registered with the National Association of Funeral Directors, and had received a Diploma in Funeral Arranging and Administration. He took his seat behind a wooden desk, then held out both arms as an invitation for Gilchrist and Jessie to take the two seats opposite.

'Right,' he said. 'How can I help?'

Jessie leaned forward. 'We were just talking with Sam out there about Wafic Saliba.'

Hadwin nodded, as if he was interested.

'He was a past employee of yours, was he not?'

'He was indeed. And a good employee, too. Such a surprise when he went home.'

'Was it?' Jessie said. 'That's not what Sam said. She said he'd been homesick for ages, and told her that he wanted to return home to . . . where was it . . .? Syria, I think.'

'Lebanon,' Hadwin said, eyes narrowing, lips pulling tight, as if to let them know he wasn't going to be taken for a fool.

'Oh, so it was. Silly me. And you haven't heard from him since, have you?'

'No.'

'Got a mobile phone number for him?'

'No.'

'Don't you keep records of all your employees?'

'Yes.'

'So . . .?' Jessie showed the palms of her hands, as if to say, Where are they?

'Funny you should ask that,' Hadwin said, as if seeing an opportunity to take control of the interview. 'We normally keep records for at least seven years, as mandated by HMRC. But for some reason . . .' He held out his own palms, and shrugged his shoulders. 'Wafic's records are missing.' He raised his eyebrows and shook his head as if at the absurdity of it. 'Unbelievable,' he added.

'You do realise that obstructing a criminal investigation is an offence.'

'Oh, I do, but you're free to go through all our records any time you like.'

'Might just get a warrant to do that,' Jessie said, which received a victory grin from Hadwin.

'No need for a warrant,' he said. 'You have my permission to examine all my records. Anytime. At your leisure, of course.'

'Of course,' said Gilchrist, leaning forward to let Jessie know he'd take it from there. He could almost feel the heat of her anger, and needed to keep her on the sideline. 'How many employees do you have here now?' he asked.

'Including part-timers?'

'Sure.'

'Four full-time, and three part-time.'

'Including yourself?'

'Five full-time, then.' A quick smile to show he was still the boss.

'Has Wafic's position been filled?'

'Part-timers only. We were getting ready to replace him anyway.'

Jessie said, 'Thought you said he was a good employee.'

'When he put his mind to it. But his timekeeping wasn't what it should be.'

'And you've got records of his hours?'

'Used to. But . . .' Another show of his palms. 'As I said, his records are missing.'

'Amazing, isn't?' she said. 'Were the records as badly kept when your father ran the place?'

To Gilchrist's surprise, Hadwin didn't rise to Jessie's bait. Instead, he said, 'My father was an honourable man, with exacting moral principles, and a commitment to succeed in life and in his profession in the funeral service second to none, something I strive to achieve on a daily basis since taking over the business.' He placed both hands flat on the desk, as if to ensure they could not be bunched into fists. Then he leaned forward, eyed Jessie first, then settled his gaze on Gilchrist. 'And before you ask, the allegations levelled against him for criminality associated with the business were proven to be unfounded.'

Not strictly correct, Gilchrist knew, as the man had never been charged, and the case, however strong or weak it was, had never gone to court because of his disappearance.

Hadwin sat back in his chair. 'Anything else you want to know?'

Gilchrist pushed to his feet, conscious of Jessie's eyes on him. Then, before he could stop her, she said, 'What can you tell us about Arletta Shepherd?'

'Who?'

'You heard. Arletta. Shepherd.'

Hadwin pursed his lips, shook his head.

'Married Tony Dilanos,' Jessie pressed on. 'Before he was shot dead.' She jerked a smile. 'You know Tony?'

Another grimace, another shake of the head. 'No. Sorry. Can't help you.'

69

Gilchrist stepped in with, 'Okay, I think we're done. Thanks for your time. If we have any more questions, we'll come back to you.'

'Of course.' Hadwin stood, too, and opened the door.

Gilchrist said, 'Before we leave, can you tell me where you were last Saturday night, around midnight?'

'Of course. Had an overnight stay at the Old Course Hotel in St Andrews. Had a late meal in the restaurant, so we would've gone to bed about midnight, or shortly after that.'

Gilchrist thought the answer too quick, the smile that accompanied it too smarmy. But he nodded, and said, 'We?'

'Excuse me?'

'You said *we* . . . would've gone to bed about midnight.'

'Oh.' He grinned. 'Me and my girlfriend. One of many.'

'Of course,' Gilchrist said, then followed Jessie from the room.

CHAPTER 11

Gilchrist waited until he and Jessie were belted into his car, and he was reversing from the car park, before he said, 'Penny for your thoughts.'

'Me and my girlfriend. One of many. Christ, I bloody hate plonkers like that. What a fanny. And that smile of his?' She shuddered. 'I wouldn't let him touch me with a ten-foot barge pole. No. Make that a twenty-foot barge pole.'

'Do you think he was telling the truth about Arletta?'

'Do I look as thick as he thinks I am? I mean . . . Jeez . . .' she said, as if she'd run out of words, then gushed, 'And he knows Tony Dilanos was his father. I know he does. And that's a fact.'

'Knowing, and proving, are two different things.' He accelerated onto the main road, pushed his speed up to fifty.

'Anyone tell you that you always drive too fast?'

'Mostly you,' he said, and let his speed drop. 'Hadwin's not telling the truth. I agree with you on that. But let's start with the Old Course Hotel. Have Jackie check out his alibi and see if he spent the weekend there with his girlfriend of the night.'

'Will do. But don't expect a result. His alibi'll check out. He answered too quickly, like he'd been waiting for someone to ask him that. I can barely remember what I did last night, let alone several days ago.'

Gilchrist said nothing, while Jessie phoned the Office and got through to Mhairi. He found his mind struggling to make sense of their meeting with Hadwin. The man hadn't been what he'd expected. After meeting with Wee Freddy and the others, he'd somehow expected Hadwin to have been little more than a street-smart hardman, someone who'd landed lucky by taking over the family business. What he hadn't expected was for Hadwin to be politely spoken, well educated, and so at ease in a police interview, with all the answers ready to fall off the tip of his tongue. He'd *answered too quickly*, wasn't that what Jessie had said? As if he'd been prepared. Or perhaps more correctly, as if he'd been *expecting* the police to interview him.

Which begged the question – why? Because he was up to his ears in criminal activity, and knew much more than he was letting on, came the answer. Which also told Gilchrist that Jessie was chasing clouds, that Hadwin's alibi would check out, that they would find nothing untoward in the business – other than Wafic Saliba's missing records – and certainly nothing incriminating against Grant Hadwin, biological son of Tony Dilanos, sole owner and CEO of Hadwin Funeral Services, and possible godfather-in-waiting to the Shepherd family, because all the loose ends had been wrapped up tighter than a Gordian knot, and every last crumb of evidence swept clean.

Jessie was about to end her call, when Gilchrist said, 'Ask her to look into Samantha Fishel. I'm not sure I trust her.'

Jessie did that, and when she ended the call, said, 'I've been thinking.' A pause, then, 'It's not Arletta you're meeting at midnight tonight, but the other woman, right?'

'It wasn't clear who I'll be meeting,' he said. 'Might be Arletta. Or it might not.'

'Didn't she ask if you remembered where you met last time?'

'She did, yes.'

'Well . . . if my memory serves me, Arletta didn't turn up, but Natalie did.'

She looked at him, as if waiting for confirmation. But the truth of the matter was that he'd met neither of them as he'd intended, but instead been directed to a sandwich shop in which he'd been left an envelope with incriminating photographs.

He shook his head. 'She didn't show, is what I remember.'

'But it wasn't Arletta who didn't show, is what I'm getting at. It was Natalie.'

'I suppose,' he said, not sure where Jessie was going with this.

She studied her mobile, tapped the screen, and mumbled, 'It's in here somewhere.' A few more taps and some screen scrolling. 'Here it is. Lauder Road, Edinburgh.'

The name rang the faintest of bells, but he couldn't place it. 'I'm listening.'

'That's where Natalie lives. Or where she did the last time you and me visited her.'

It came back to him slowly, like morning mist clearing. The detached stone house, the white Mercedes sports car, the soft top down in the summer warmth, the taut meeting with Arletta, the tension between them softening when she realised he was on her side.

'Want me to plug the address into the satnav?' Jessie said.

What did they have to lose? Any possible contact with Arletta, came the answer. But what if they just drove past the address, reconnoitred the area, so to speak, just to see if anything had changed, maybe even find out what's what?

'She might've moved home,' he tried.

'When did that ever stop you?'

'Okay. Plug it in. And get Mhairi to check the Land Registry, just in case.'

He'd travelled to Edinburgh often enough to know the A92 connected with the M90 south. From there it was a relatively short drive to the city outskirts. But once in Edinburgh, he knew he would have no option but to work through town traffic, at whatever speed the city centre permitted.

He was approaching the Forth Road Bridge when Mhairi called back.

Gilchrist put the call on speaker. 'What've you got, Mhairi?'

'Natalie Foster's still living at that same address, sir. Or at least, the property's still in her name. Jackie wasn't able to confirm whether it was rented out or not, at such short notice. Would you like me to get back to you on that, sir?'

'That's fine, Mhairi. We're going to do a drive-by, and check it out. How about Sam Fishel? You find anything on her?'

'Yes, sir. She has twenty-eight hours of community service still outstanding from an ASBO last year. She was found guilty of vandalism and threatening behaviour.'

Gilchrist knew Antisocial Behaviour Orders were not granted lightly, and that there had to be good cause for doing so. 'What did she vandalise?'

'Someone's gravestone, sir. Cracked it into several pieces with a sledgehammer.'

He caught Jessie's eyebrows rise, and her lips form a 'Wow'. 'And the threatening behaviour?' he said.

'Swinging the sledgehammer at anyone who came near her. But apparently she was so drunk that she slipped and split her skull. She was cuffed and taken to hospital for treatment. She pleaded guilty at trial, and was given eighty hours community service, which she's currently still serving.'

Jessie said, 'And here was me thinking she was the perfect receptionist.'

'There's more, sir.'

'Let's have it, Mhairi.'

'Ten years ago she spent six months in a young offenders' institute for possession of an illegal substance.'

'Which was?'

'Ten grams of ecstasy. She denied any intent to sell, and claimed they were for her own use. Because of her age, and the fact that she had no previous history, the judge went lightly on her.'

'How old was she?' Gilchrist asked.

'Sixteen, sir.'

'And nothing since then, other than the ASBO?'

'Not that we can find, sir.'

He was about to hang up, when he said, 'Who was her solicitor in her drug trial?'

'I have it here, sir.' The line sounded as if the phone had been dropped, then Mhairi came back with, 'KDH Legal Services, sir. But they're no longer in business.' A pause, then, 'Apparently it was a three-man partnership that fell to pieces when one of the partners was accused of stealing a client's money.'

Gilchrist knew Mhairi well enough to know she wasn't telling him this for the good of his health. 'We're listening,' he said.

'Turns out, sir, that the partner who was accused of stealing the money was Daryl Hadwin, brother of Ryan Hadwin—'

'And uncle of Grant Hadwin,' he said. 'What's he doing now? Is he still around?'

'He is, sir.'

'You have an address for him?'

He wasn't surprised when she said she had.

CHAPTER 12

As luck would have it, Daryl Hadwin's place of business was in Edinburgh, in an attic office off the Royal Mile. Entry was gained through a door at the bottom of a cobbled close, up a winding flight of concrete stairs to an unlit landing, which in turn led to a steep and narrow spiral staircase, at the top of which Gilchrist and Jessie were confronted with a blue wooden door. Chipped paintwork exposed any number of historical coatings of paint.

'Jeez,' Jessie said, struggling to catch her breath. 'If this guy works here five days a week, he must be as thin as a whippet.' She pulled in another lungful. 'Bloody hell, I think I lost half a stone crawling up that lot.'

'No more muffins for you,' Gilchrist said.

'Just ring the doorbell, will you?'

Gilchrist did.

A buzzer crackled and a woman's voice said, 'Name please.'

'DCI Gilchrist and DS Janes to speak to Mr Daryl Hadwin.'

'Do you have an appointment?'

'No.'

'Well he's not in.'

Jessie stepped forward. 'Listen you, if you think I've clambered all the way up these bloody stairs just to be told he's not in, you've got another think coming. Now open this door before I come back with a warrant and break it down and arrest you for obstructing a police investigation.'

To Gilchrist's surprise, the lock clicked.

Jessie pushed the door opened and stomped inside. 'Right. Where is he?'

The receptionist, a teenager with acned skin, purple hair and a gold nose ring, stared at her with eyes opened wide enough to give the impression she'd never seen police officers before. To Gilchrist's left, a man shuffled from behind a desk stacked with haphazard piles of papers, letters, files.

'Hold on, hold on,' he grumbled. 'What's this about a police investigation? Have you found him?'

Gilchrist held out his warrant card. 'Found who?'

'Ryan. My brother.'

Up close, the man's clothes smelled of last night's dinner. His breath reeked of garlic and the weekend's hangover.

'We haven't found Ryan,' Gilchrist said. 'We're here on another matter.'

The man shook his head, then turned and trundled back to his desk. 'For a moment there,' he said, 'I thought, perhaps . . .'

Gilchrist waited until he had shuffled himself back into his chair, before saying, 'Tell me about your brother.'

The man looked at him, as if puzzled to see him standing there. 'What's there to tell? He's missing, presumed dead.' He let out a heavy grunt as he adjusted his chair. 'I'd always hoped he'd be found alive, but now . . .' His voice trailed off to a defeated sigh.

'Now you don't believe that?' Gilchrist said.

Hadwin shrugged.

Gilchrist walked to the desk, cleared a corner, and rested his butt on the edge. 'Why?'

Hadwin shrugged again. 'We used to be close, you know. We'd keep in touch, have a few pints, play the occasional round of golf, that sort of thing. But over the years, we drifted apart. It was the wives, you know. Once they fall out, that's the end.'

'But why don't you believe he'll be found alive?' Gilchrist persisted.

'Because he's been gone too long, that's why. And that son of his. Grant. Far too keen to take over the business. Jumped right in with both feet. As if he'd been ready for it. Haven't heard a word of sympathy from him. Ryan might have been his father, but he was my brother, too.'

Gilchrist let a few moments pass, then said, 'So what d'you think happened to Ryan?'

'Nothing. I refuse to believe he's dead.'

A contradictory answer if ever there was one. Gilchrist glanced at Jessie, a sign to change tack, let her take over.

'What do you know about the complaints filed against your brother?' she said.

Hadwin raised his eyebrows, and shook his head. 'Bullshit.'

'No ashes given to the wrong person?'

'Never.'

'No fiddling the books? Stealing jewellery from the dead? None of that?'

Hadwin grimaced, as if he'd sipped bitter wine. 'No. No. Ryan wasn't like that. He was as honest as the day was long.'

'Then why were complaints filed against him?'

'I've no idea.' He hung his head, defeated.

Gilchrist slid off the desk. Time to cut closer to the bone, find out what Hadwin knew about Grant's heritage. 'How about Ryan's ex-wife?' he said. 'Do you keep in contact with her?'

'Meghan?' He shook his head. 'When Ryan first went missing, we spoke a few times. But not since.'

'What did Meghan say about her ex-husband's disappearance?'

'Said they'd had an argument, that they were going through a bad patch. That he'd left her before. But always came crawling back.' He shook his head. 'First I'd heard of it. I never really trusted her.'

'Why not?'

'Only my opinion. But she'd been shagging behind Ryan's back for years.'

'Any names?' he asked, wondering if Tony Dilanos might come up.

'Was never privy to any of that. But she ended up with Tom.'

'Tom?'

'Tom Byrd. Her live-in partner now. Didn't take long for him to move in. And once Meghan started dingying me, I just gave up on her.' He grimaced. 'Best to keep the peace at home.'

'What about Ryan's girlfriend?' Gilchrist tried.

'What about her?'

'The one in Spain, who reported him missing. Did you speak to her?'

'No chance. As I said, Ryan and I *used* to be close. Never got to meet any of his girlfriends. Of which I believe there were many,' he added with a courtroom flourish. Then he pulled himself upright and placed both hands on his desk. 'So. What's this about a police investigation?'

But Gilchrist wasn't finished. He hadn't reviewed the case files yet. 'What did you tell the police about Ryan's disappearance?'

'Nothing. I was never interviewed.'

'Didn't you tell them of your concerns?'

'Of course, I did, but they weren't interested.'

Gilchrist nodded. Without any evidence of foul play, and with an alleged history of Ryan leaving then *crawling back home*, substantiated by his wife, the police wouldn't take his disappearance seriously. Adults fall out with each other, go off on their own. Some even start new lives without telling family or friends. That's what the police would conclude. Especially if Meghan showed no concern. Even so, if Gilchrist had been involved, he would like to believe he would've followed up more diligently. But none of this was getting him any closer to solving Mike Elgin's murder, or finding Arletta Shepherd for that matter.

He raised his eyebrows at Jessie, in an any-more-questions look.

'Did Ryan ever tell you that Grant wasn't his son?' she said.

Might as well go in with the boot, Gilchrist thought.

Hadwin stared at Jessie, as if struggling to understand what she'd asked. 'You're the second person to ask me that,' he said at length.

'Who was the first?'

'I can't remember her name. Lea, maybe?'

'Leila?' Jessie tried.

'Could be.'

'And what did you say? When she asked if you knew that Grant wasn't Ryan's son.'

'I told her that I didn't know, and she was talking shite.'

'And did you know?' Jessie persisted.

81

'Yeah.'

A quick glance at Gilchrist, then, 'Did you meet her, this Leila?'

'Just for a few minutes. She seemed troubled, distracted, as if she couldn't keep her mind focused for any length of time.' He frowned for a moment, as if a thought had just come to him, then said, 'One thing she did tell me, which I also didn't believe, was that Ryan had gotten himself into debt.'

Gilchrist said, 'Who with?'

'She didn't say. Just that he'd been gambling online.'

Gilchrist frowned. Online betting nowadays was for fools. Because of the speed and ease with which bets could be placed, a bad run of luck could rack up hundreds in a matter of minutes, even thousands. 'Did she say how much debt?'

Hadwin shook his head. 'I've known Ryan all my life, and there's no way he was a gambler. I told her that. But she just smiled at me like I was stupid or something. Which was when I told her to piss off.'

'Did she mention anything else, anything that might help us locate him?'

'No. Not a thing.'

Gilchrist glanced at Jessie, but she looked as defeated as he felt. He handed over his business card, thanked Hadwin for his time. 'If you think of anything else, please contact me anytime,' he said, and followed Jessie from the office.

CHAPTER 13

Jessie buckled her seatbelt. 'You think he's telling the truth?'

Gilchrist fired the ignition, and pulled away from the kerb. 'Why wouldn't he? What's he got to gain by lying to us?'

'Stop us from investigating him and his business, for a start.'

'Only if he's got something to hide.'

Jessie seemed to give his words some thought, then said, 'He knew his brother wasn't Grant's father.' She shook her head. 'I don't know. How would he know that? I mean, it's not something his brother would boast about it, is it? "Hey, you'll never guess,"' she mimicked in a deeper voice, '"but that dead-beat son of mine isn't my son after all." Jeez. What a screwed-up family.'

Gilchrist indicated and turned right through a green light. 'These days, screwed-up families are par for the course.'

'Maybe it makes sense after all,' she said. 'Maybe his brother's gay, and got married just to keep up appearances. Happy families and all that. Good for business—'

His mobile interrupted Jessie. A glance at the screen told him it was Mhairi calling back. 'Put it on speaker,' he said.

Jessie did, then said, 'What d'you have, Mhairi?'

'We've just confirmed Grant Hadwin's alibi. He did spend Saturday night at the Old Course Hotel. Jackie's got CCTV footage of him and his girlfriend in the hotel lobby just after four in the afternoon. Then again later in the restaurant. They left the hotel at nine-ish, and went into town. We tracked them to a couple of bars, then back to the hotel just before midnight. So on the face of it, sir, he's clean.'

'Were you able to identify his girlfriend?' Gilchrist said.

'Yes, sir.' A pause, then, 'She's Sam Fishel.'

'I bloody well knew it,' Jessie said. 'It was written all over that smug coupon of his. Shagging the employees.'

'That proves nothing,' Gilchrist said.

'It proves he's a sleazeball, is what it proves.'

'Let's try and stay focused, shall we?' he said, louder than intended.

Jessie whispered something under her breath, then stared out the window, as if finding interest in a group of pedestrians huddled kerbside, ready to cross the road. Gilchrist finished the call by having Mhairi continue to look into Hadwin and his funeral business, then turned his attention to the satnav and the stop–start drive through town to Lauder Road.

Natalie Foster's house hadn't changed much from how he remembered it. If anything, the hedge that ran behind the boundary wall was wider, taller, denser, as if effort had been made to restrict passers-by from viewing the lawn and the front of the house. The paved driveway lay deserted, and looked as if it could be brought back to life only with a proper power washing. Weeds sprouted

84

like green strips of complaint between the pavers. All this he noticed in a slow drive-by. Not too slow to bring attention to his car, but fast enough to visually engage in the property and its surroundings.

He rounded the corner at the end of Lauder Road, drove on for a hundred yards or so, then pulled to a halt.

'Did you see anything?' he said.

'Nobody's home. I'd say that much. But it's more than that. It looks deserted. As if no one's been there for a while. Want to drive back and try the doorbell?'

He shook his head. 'Not a wise move. Might scare her off.'

She turned to face him. 'I've been thinking.'

'Go on.'

'I think Arletta's not living *with* Natalie, but living close by. She has to.'

'You don't know that.'

'No, hear me out. You're the king of logic, so how about this?' She shuffled in her seat. 'Natalie tells you to call back in exactly fifteen minutes. Why fifteen minutes? Because that gives her time to phone Arletta and tell her you're trying to contact her. Fifteen minutes also gives Arletta plenty of time to put on a pair of shoes and make her way to Natalie's. So what I'm thinking is, that Arletta doesn't live fifteen minutes away. No. She lives closer than that. Only a few minutes away. She has to. No, no, don't shake your head. Think about it. She doesn't want to risk you calling back and Arletta's not there. So there has to be plenty of fluff built into the fifteen minutes. Right?'

'I'll give you that,' he said. 'But Arletta could be staying at Natalie's—'

'No she isn't. She wouldn't risk it. If she's hiding in fear of her life, then staying with Natalie would be putting both their lives at risk.'

'So what're you saying?'

'That Arletta's staying in one of these houses we've just driven past.'

Gilchrist puffed up his cheeks, then let it out. There were so many holes in Jessie's logic that her whole theory could be leaking like a burst sieve. She'd even said so herself that she thought Natalie's house had looked deserted, so there was every likelihood Natalie hadn't been home when he'd made that initial call. She could be anywhere in the world, not in the outskirts of Edinburgh, and probably was. But on the other hand, what had he been hoping to achieve by driving past her home? What was he really reconnoitring? Besides, she'd offered to meet him at the last place they'd met, or hadn't met, depending on the interpretation.

He gritted his teeth. 'Okay . . . let's say that your theory's correct, and that Arletta is staying in one of those houses. You're not suggesting that we knock on all of their doors to find out, are you?'

'Of course not. That would be stupid.'

He nodded. 'Yep. I agree.'

'What we do is, you drive up and down the road, not too fast, and not too slow, while I take photos of the cars in every driveway.'

'Arletta won't have driven here in her own car, Jessie.' He hadn't meant to say it with such cynicism, but the words were out before he could stop himself.

'That's what I'm banking on,' she said.

He stared at her for a long moment, puzzling over her widening smile as she watched his penny finally drop.

'That's very clever,' he said.

'I know it is.' And with that, she fiddled with her mobile, as if content with the smug knowledge that she'd scored a brownie point in her favour, maybe even three.

CHAPTER 14

Jessie took a total of twelve photographs with her mobile, and sent them straight to Jackie with a request to check ownership against the registration number plates. It hadn't taken Jackie long to come back with a result. Mhairi phoned as Gilchrist was easing his car through the busy junction in Cupar town centre.

'Any luck?' he said.

'Only one rental car, sir. A silver Toyota Corolla.' She read out the registration number and the address at which it had been parked – Lauder Road, six homes down from Natalie Foster's address. 'Rented from Europcar in Stirling last Saturday morning.'

Gilchrist glanced at Jessie. The timing fitted. And Stirling was between Glasgow and Edinburgh, so the travel route fitted, too. Which made sense, because Arletta wouldn't have risked renting a car in Glasgow. Somewhere neutral – Stirling fitted the bill – was safer.

'Do you have a name?' he said.

'A Mrs N. Richards.'

'And duration of rental?'

'Open-ended, sir.'

Again, it made sense. Arletta wouldn't have used her own name, he was sure of that. And with her being on the run, and no idea for how long, an open-ended car rental worked, too. So, it looked like Jessie was right. Maybe they were onto something.

'How about CCTV?' he said to Mhairi. 'Check the rental office for footage around the time the car was rented. We might be able to make a positive ID. And find out how the rental was paid for. If it's open-ended, it's almost certainly a credit card. Get card details, and see if it's still being used. And find out what you can on a Mrs N. Richards. The name must mean something.'

'I'm on it, sir.'

When Gilchrist ended the call, Jessie said, 'Believe me now?'

'Would I ever doubt you?'

She chuckled. 'But how did she get from Glasgow to Stirling?'

'She wouldn't have driven there.'

'Maybe taxi?' she tried.

'Too easy to trace.' He gripped the steering wheel, and accelerated up the hill out of Cupar. 'If you step back a moment, and ask how she left her home in Pollokshields without making it look like she was running away, you might come up with the answer that someone helped her.'

'Big-ears?'

'As good a guess as any, I'd say.'

'So he drives her into the city centre, then drops her off?' She shook her head. 'That doesn't work. That leaves her having to get a train or a bus, which would leave a trail.'

Gilchrist nodded. 'I don't think Arletta trusts too many people,' he said. 'So I'm thinking that maybe she left from home herself, on the pretext of going for a coffee, having her hair done,

89

something that wouldn't raise eyebrows, or look suspicious. Maybe she drove into town, parked the car, then hired a taxi, maybe two, and made her way to Stirling where she hired another car under a false name.'

'Sounds a bit too much like James Bond.'

'If what we're thinking is right, then this is a woman who's running in fear for her life. And she's experienced. She knows what's what. And more importantly, who's who.'

'Someone to help her?'

He pursed his lips. They were missing something. He felt certain of that. Using a credit card to rent a car, or buy a train ticket, left a digital trail. He'd met Arletta years ago, not long after big Jock Shepherd had passed away, and the impression he gathered at the time was that she was street-smart, a woman who knew how to look after herself and hell mend you if you dared take her on.

So why use a credit card?

Because she hadn't, came the logical answer. She'd had someone help her. Someone who was just as street-smart as she was. Natalie Foster had helped Arletta before. And was helping her again. Was she who had spoken to him on the phone earlier? Was she who he was supposed to be meeting tonight at midnight at the same place they'd met? Or, now that the name Mrs N. Richards had popped up out of the blue, was Natalie out of the picture, and someone else in the frame? Christ, he felt as if his head was spinning with it all.

'Get onto Mhairi again,' he said. 'Find out who Mrs N. Richards is. I'm willing to bet that the N stands for Natalie.'

'Quite the quantum leap.'

'I know, I know.' He gritted his teeth, hissed out a curse. 'You ever felt that someone was taking the mickey out of you?'

'More often than I care to think.' She turned to face him. 'Why? What's got you fired up? You look as if you're ready to chew nails.'

He forced himself to slacken his grip on the steering wheel. Irene often told him that he was easy to read, that he wore his emotions on his sleeve, that he would never make a good poker player. He tried a smile, but it felt all wrong.

'Sorry,' he said. 'Just thinking.'

'Anything you'd care to share?'

He wasn't sure if his logic was sound, or if his mind was simply taking him down the wrong road to a dead end. Only one way to find out. 'Arletta's too smart to leave a digital trail,' he said. 'She'd never use a credit card.'

'She'd never use her *own* credit card, is what you mean to say.'

'No. She'd use cash. No trail that way.'

'How about the open-ended car rental, then? Would she pay cash for that?'

Shit. Jessie had a point. A credit card was likely to have been used for that. As if on cue, Mhairi called at the moment.

'We've got CCTV footage from the rental office, sir. Can't make a positive ID, but it looks like Arletta Shepherd.'

'How did she pay for the rental?'

'She didn't, sir. She was with someone. A woman who put the rental on *her* credit card. We've confirmed it was a Visa card, with the Royal Bank of Scotland.'

'Was the name on the card Mrs Richards?'

'Yes, sir.'

'You find anything on her?'

'Jackie's cross-referenced bank and credit card details, and the card's brand new. It's only been used once before. Eight pounds

91

sixty-four in Costa Coffee in Stirling that morning. A bank account in the name of Natalie Richards was opened ten months ago, with an initial deposit of two hundred pounds, but has never been used since. DVLA records confirms that Natalie Richards does have a driving licence, but the address on it is non-existent. Jackie can't find anything on the National Births Records that matches the name to a birth date. So we don't really know who she is, sir.'

'Natalie, you said.'

'Yes, sir.'

He glanced at Jessie, who frowned at him, as if to say that having the same first name proves nothing. Well, he had to agree with her that it didn't prove that Natalie Richards was a pseudonym for Natalie Foster. But it did prove that Arletta Shepherd was doing all she could to leave no trail. Which also told him that she really was hiding in fear for her life. But what to do with what he'd uncovered? That was his dilemma.

Organise a team to make an arrest at the house in Lauder Road? On what grounds? He was sure Dainty could come up with something against Arletta on which they could hang an arrest warrant. But that could rip the lid off a can of maggots, which he might not be able to shut again. It took him no longer than a few seconds to work out that his best move was to do nothing at that moment, but to go with the arrangement agreed earlier by phone.

He would meet this woman, whoever she was.

At midnight tonight.

CHAPTER 15

By 7 p.m. that evening, Dainty had confirmed they were no further forward in identifying Mike Elgin's killer. Nor had there been any progress in the hunt for Leila Hazazi. Mhairi and Jackie had found nothing more on Grant Hadwin or Sam Fishel, and after advising Dainty of his concerns over the disappearance of Wafic Saliba, Gilchrist was told in that abrupt way of Dainty's that: *Without a fucking body no resources can be assigned to the case. We've got enough on our fucking plate, Andy, without adding to the shit-pile by chasing fucking ghosts.*

Gilchrist felt as if the investigations were grinding to a halt. With no other leads, he'd instructed his team to call it a day, and to gather in the Office first thing in the morning for a case briefing, with the hope that a good night's sleep might result in fresh ideas for moving forward. He'd kept the knowledge of his midnight meeting from his team, and importantly, or so he thought, he'd kept it from Dainty, too. He couldn't explain why he felt it better to keep Dainty in the dark – for just a day or so longer. Perhaps it was something to do with the sense he had that Dainty was also withholding information from *him*. Jessie was the only one who knew of his imminent midnight meeting, and in an attempt to stay one step ahead, he'd asked her to run the rental car's registration number through the ANPR, and keep him up to date with its movements.

The automatic number plate recognition system had become an indispensable tool for police in tracing stolen vehicles. Using existing CCTV cameras updated with software that could read letters and numbers, vehicles could be located and followed in real time, or their routes tracked in recorded footage. Of course, he could have it all wrong, that the rental car he was asking Jessie to track was nothing to do with Arletta Shepherd at all, but simply an unlikely coincidence.

But if you didn't believe in coincidence, where did that put you?

Outside looking in, was as good an answer as any.

Before heading home, Gilchrist decided to make a last-minute phone call. He couldn't explain why he felt the need to phone, or why he found himself holding his breath and staring out the window into night's dark shadows waiting for the connection to be made. His lungs took an involuntary intake of breath when the call was answered with a curt, 'Hello?'

'Becky,' he said, trying to sound authoritative. 'It's Andy. Andy Gilchrist.'

A pause, then, 'To what do I owe the pleasure?'

And with those emotionless words, he knew it had been a mistake to call, that he had misread his own subconscious feelings. His mind fumbled for something to say. 'I haven't received a copy of your PM report yet.'

'That's because I sent it to DCI Small, from whom I suggest you request a copy.'

He didn't feel it appropriate to remind her that she'd promised earlier that she would forward a copy of the PM to him, as requested by Dainty, once again leaving him with the feeling that he was being kept in the dark.

'Did you find anything out of the ordinary?' he tried. 'Anything worth knowing?'

'Nothing more than I told you earlier.'

'Okay. Yes. Right. Well. I'll eh . . . I'll talk to Dainty, then.'

He was about to end the call when Cooper said, 'I'm sorry, Andy. I'm sorry to hear about Irene. I had no idea.'

He held onto the phone, and said nothing.

'If there's anything,' she said. 'Anything I can do.'

He waited for her to say more, but after a long moment's silence realised she'd said all she was going to say. He knew there was nothing she could do, that her offer was nothing more than a condolence. But he said, 'Thanks, Becky.'

'Sure, Andy.' A pause, then, 'Ciao.'

And with that the line died.

He held onto his mobile for several quiet seconds, before slipping it into his pocket. He scanned his office, then stepped to the door with a mind to have a pint in the Central.

He entered the bar from the College Street entrance, to be hit with the ambient noise of a busy town pub. Chairs clattered. People shuffled. Glasses chinked. Voices shouted and called above the din. He found a space at the corner of the bar, and managed to squeeze in and order an 80 Shilling. He removed his mobile. It was far too noisy to make a call, but he accessed Messages, surprised to find he had two texts from Maureen.

His daughter was never one for keeping in regular touch, or for sending lengthy texts, so he found himself grinning as he read them. The first had been sent at 14:04 that afternoon, a longer than normal message saying she was taking a few days off and would be driving up to St Andrews that evening with a friend, and would he like to meet them in a pub in town. The second had been sent at 17:12, short and sweet, which was more Maureen's style.

In the Criterion

He hissed a curse, annoyed with himself at having missed her texts. For a moment, he thought of simply abandoning his pint, and walking to the Criterion, just around the corner – well, two corners, if you wanted to be pedantic – and catch up with her there. But his pint arrived then, and a glance at his mobile – 19:34 – warned him that after two hours in the Criterion, Maureen could be well on her way through her second bottle of wine or, against all odds, left the pub and gone to whichever hotel she'd booked into. So, he took that first sip of beer, drawing it down a good inch or two, then tapped a text message of his own.

Just got your texts. In the Central. Want to join me?

He pressed Send, and no sooner had he taken another sip, than his phone beeped.

On our way

That went well, he thought. He looked around for some place where the three of them could sit, or at the very least, stand together. But the bar was heaving. He was about to carry his pint in search of a quieter spot when a couple, two stools to his left, threw scarves around their necks, slipped arms into jacket sleeves, and pushed away from the bar. He took quick possession of their stools. And just in time, too, for he caught Maureen shuffling her way through a crowd at the near corner, a tall man of Black ethnicity close behind her, hands on her shoulder.

She came up to him and gave him a tight hug and a light peck on each cheek, leaving him to say, 'How did you get here so quickly?'

'We'd already left the Criterion, and were on our way here. When I hadn't heard from you, I thought you might be having a pint in the pub closest to your Office.'

'That's smart thinking.'

'It's not rocket science, Dad.' She turned to her side. 'I'd like you to meet Ty.'

Before he could say anything, Ty stepped forward, all six foot something of him, with shoulders out to here, hand reaching for his. 'An honour, sir.'

Gilchrist returned a hard squeeze with one of his own. 'Nice to meet you, Ty.'

Ty showed a perfect set of white teeth, gave a tiny nod, and released his grip. Then a wallet appeared. 'Can I get you anything, sir?'

'No. Let me. I'm still on my first.' He turned to Maureen. 'The usual?'

'Which is?' she said.

He pursed his lips, pulled them into a tight smile to let her know she'd caught him out once more, that he should have known better. 'Sorry. What would you like?'

'The usual,' she said, and let out a squeal of laughter at her own joke. She fell into Ty, who wrapped an arm around her shoulder, pulled her to him, and pressed his lips to the top of her head. Maureen beamed, and hugged closer.

Gilchrist had a sense that he was witnessing the birth of a new daughter, someone who could now, at long last, put the black memories of her tortured past behind her. If asked, he would have to say that he was more than pleased. Not to mention a sense of fatherly relief, which he hadn't realised he'd harboured until that moment. Of course, his cynical side might convince him that he was simply witnessing the result of a young couple having spent two hours loosening up in a bar, and looking forward to an intimate evening together.

'How about you, Ty? What are you having?'

'Water for me, please. Sparkling, if they have it.'

He hoped he kept his surprise hidden. Then he eyed Maureen. 'Red or white?' and felt a spurt of disappointment shift through him when she said, 'Sauvignon. Large, of course.'

'Of course.'

They spent the next few minutes organising stools – Gilchrist making sure Maureen was comfortably seated, and Ty refusing to take the stool offered to him by Gilchrist. Then, drinks in hand, and round-robin chinking glasses over and done, Gilchrist said, 'How long are you here for?'

'Saturday,' Maureen said. 'Had some days I had to use or lose.'

'If you'd told me, I could've had the cottage ready for you. Heat turned up. Sheets on the bed. Some food in.'

'No probs, Dad. We're staying in a caravan in Kinkell Braes. Ty's sister's.'

'Well, next time let me know. You're more than welcome.'

'Thanks, Dad.'

He could tell from the tone of her response that his offer was likely never to be taken up, so he considered it best to change tack. 'So how are you enjoying life in the Force?' He'd often wondered if he should have tried to discourage Maureen from joining the police, but painful experience had taught him that she was a woman who knew her own mind. Once it was made up, hell mend you if you tried to interfere.

'That's how I met Ty,' she said.

He thought her answer evasive, but didn't press. Instead, he turned to Ty. 'You work in Strathclyde, too?'

'IT Division.'

'Ever come across DCI Small?'

'Dainty? Of course. Who hasn't?' He gave another wide smile. 'A force to be reckoned with.' He took a sip of water. 'I heard you were down there this morning. Giving your penny's worth on Operation Headstone.'

'Is that what it's called?'

Ty nodded. 'Someone always comes up with an operational name that's meaningful in some way.'

Gilchrist thought he knew the answer, but asked anyway. 'Because of the link to Ryan Hadwin and Hadwin Funeral Services?'

'And also his son, Grant. Yeah. Dainty's got a bee in his bonnet about him.'

'Linking him to the Shepherd family?'

'Yeah, and then some.'

'Then some?'

Ty glanced at Maureen, as if seeking her opinion on whether or not to bring Gilchrist into the fold, so to speak. He probably knew he shouldn't have spoken so openly about an ongoing police operation, and for just a moment seemed unsure of himself.

Maureen had her glass to her lips, and offered him no help.

Gilchrist said nothing, too, just took a sip of his pint and waited for Ty's response. He thought it interesting that he'd learned more about Dainty's thoughts in the last few minutes than he'd been made privy to all day.

Ty coughed, cleared his throat, then said, 'Maybe best if you have a chat with Dainty on that.'

'Of course,' Gilchrist said, and downed his pint, determined to speak to Dainty in the morning.

CHAPTER 16

When Gilchrist returned to Irene's home – a three-storeyed house in South Street into which he'd temporarily moved – he was surprised to find her daughter, Joanne, sitting in the lounge. Her blonde hair hung around her shoulders in an untended fashion, as if she hadn't bothered to brush it in several days, and he thought she looked paler than he'd ever seen her. As he walked towards her, she pushed to her feet and offered him a tired smile. He glanced at Irene in her bed by the front window, positioned there so she could watch passers-by on South Street. She lay on her back, head on soft pillows, eyes closed, asleep.

Joanne gave him a light hug.

'How is she?' he asked.

'Asleep. The tuck-in service hasn't arrived yet.'

The social care team would normally have been and gone by now, but occasionally they were delayed by some unforeseen – often unfortunate – circumstances. 'I didn't know you were coming,' he said. 'You should've called.'

'Thought I should pop round and see Mum, while Mo and Ty had a couple of pints with you. I'm catching up with them later.'

Mo and Ty. A matched pair. A couple known to others, but not to him. Until earlier that evening. He hadn't asked how long they'd been together, never even given it a thought, just assumed they'd only just teamed up, if that was the correct term.

'Have you met Ty?' he said.

'A few times, yeah.'

He mouthed an Aahh, but didn't feel he had the right to dig deeper. For all he knew, Mo and Ty could be married. Christ, was he always the last person to be advised of familial pairings? Recently, his son, Jack, had split from his partner, Kristen, but Gilchrist had found out about it only when he'd been informed that Jack was about to be charged by the Swedish authorities for kidnapping his own daughter. Well, with that in mind, maybe it was better just to be kept in the dark.

At that moment, Irene stirred, and let out a quiet moan.

Gilchrist walked over to her, leaned forward, and pressed his lips to hers. 'How are you?' he asked, taking hold of her hand and giving it a gentle squeeze.

'What time is it?'

'Just after nine.'

'Oh. I must've been asleep for hours. I can't . . . I need . . .' She pushed the sheet back, raised her head from the pillow. 'Can you give me a hand, please?'

'Of course.' He knew better than to object to her requests, and eased her up and over so that she sat on the edge of the bed, her feet resting on the floor. He kneeled down and slid her slippers onto her feet. When she lifted her gaze, her lips parted in a wide smile as she recognised Joanne standing behind him.

'Darling,' she said, and reached for her.

Gilchrist stepped aside while Joanne inched forward, eased her mother to her feet, and helped her shuffle to an armchair in front of the fire. Several minutes were spent making sure she was comfortable and wrapped up warmly in a blanket, with a woollen shawl draped over her shoulders to ward off any wayward chill.

Irene flapped a hand on the arm of the chair, inviting Joanne to sit. Then she said, 'Andy,' and tapped the other arm. 'Come and sit with me.'

Gilchrist did as asked, and shuffled his butt onto the edge of the armchair. It felt odd sitting there, the three of them, he and Joanne perched on opposite arms, Irene in the middle holding each of their hands, the heat from the fire warming their faces. He felt Irene squeeze his fingers, and he gave a gentle squeeze back.

'I've been thinking,' she said, 'that now is the time.' Joanne made to slide off the arm of the chair, but Irene tightened her grip. 'No, Joanne, I need you to hear this.'

'I can't,' Joanne said, her eyes welling.

'I know, darling, but I must.' She lifted her gaze to Gilchrist. 'Andy and I have talked about what I would like to do. But only when the time is right.' She took a deep sigh, then let it out. 'And the time is now right.'

Joanne looked at Gilchrist, her eyes pleading, and he found himself diverting his gaze. How could he help her? What could he say? This was her mother's wishes. Not his. Oh, dear God, never his. But still Joanne's gaze bored into him. Was she pleading for a reprieve from her mother's illness? Was she pleading for an explanation as to how it had all come down to this, that her mother had decided to take control of her own life, that there was nothing she, Joanne, nor anyone else, could do to make her change her mind. Never mind that assisted suicide wasn't legal.

Gilchrist was saved by Irene saying, 'I know how you feel, Joanne, but listen, please, darling, this isn't about you. It's about me. And it's about me when I still have my wits about me, to know what I'm asking to be done. You do understand, darling, don't you?'

Joanne shook her head, tried to pull away, but Irene still held firm.

'I don't want to be a burden to anyone, darling. I don't—'

'Mum. Please. I can't let you.'

'I'm afraid it's not up to you.' She turned to look at Gilchrist, at the same time as squeezing his hand. 'Are you still okay with it, Andy?' she whispered.

He thought back to the times he and Irene had spoken about this moment, how she didn't want to be a burden to anyone, or be placed in a home only for her family savings to be sucked dry by the weekly payments, exorbitant rates that once had her questioning whether or not she would be better off booking into a five-star hotel for the duration. She explained how she wanted to die on her own terms – with dignity – how she knew with pained resignation that her time on this Earth was coming to an end, and how happy she'd been to have met him, and how wonderful it was to have spent the last years of her life with him. And wasn't it so much of a pity that they hadn't met years earlier?

He'd agreed to help her. Of course he had. He would stand by her, follow her final wishes, do what she'd asked him to do. Which was all very well and good at the time. But now, as he stood with his feet on the edge of that precipice, looking into the darkness of the future to come, he understood with unbounded clarity the immeasurable difference between talking . . . and doing.

He returned her searching gaze, gave her a gentle smile, and a nod of reassurance. He would be there for her. Just as he said he would. He would help her end her life. He would assist her in administering the final drinks, swallowing the batch of over-the-counter pills, enough drugs in her system to ensure that when her mind and body were overcome with the weight of it all, and she closed her eyes, she would be closing them for the last time. He would stay with her to the very end, he promised her that, holding her hand and talking to her, loving her all the way to the moment of her passing. She would not leave this world alone. She had nothing to doubt about his willingness to see it through. He assured her of that. But that was then. And . . . dear God Almighty . . . this was now.

Assisting someone to take their own life would be breaking the law. There was no getting around that. But during his career, he'd broken the law before, mostly in pursuit of securing a result in some investigation. He'd done so by overcoming the internal argument that what he was doing was for the good. And now he was about to break the law once again. For the good. For Irene. But as he looked deep into her eyes, trying to reassure her that she could rely on him, that he had the strength and the mental wherewithal to see it through, he found himself struggling with the reality of what he was being asked to do.

How could he hold Irene's hand, knowing he was helping her end her life? How could he give her strength in those final moments when his heart was breaking, his steely resolve was melting, and the last thing he ever dreamed of or wanted was to lose the woman he loved? How could he possibly do that? How could he?

He was saved once more by Joanne's pained voice whispering, 'When, Mum?'

Irene looked up at him, seeking an answer.

'Soon,' was all he could say. 'But not tonight.'

Irene squeezed his hand, and pulled it to her, to press it against her face.

He forced a smile, and prayed she couldn't sense the tortured hurt in his being.

CHAPTER 17

Gilchrist phoned Jessie a few minutes past eleven o'clock. 'Anything?' he said.

'Car's on the move,' she said. 'Last sighting was on the M90 northbound.'

'Were you able to confirm who's driving?'

'Jeez, Andy. No, is the short answer. But I can tell you that there's no passenger, not in the front anyway. Unless they're lying flat on the back seat, or hiding in the boot. But why would they do that?' She paused for a moment. 'So, best I can tell, whoever's coming to meet you is coming alone. You want me to keep tracking it for you?'

'Why don't you call it a night. I'll see you in the morning.'

'I'll ask you one last time. Are you sure you don't want me to come along with you tonight? Just in case something happens?'

'Nothing's going to happen. Trust me.'

'Don't I always?'

'Goodnight, Jessie,' he said, with stern finality. He ended the call, hauled up his collar, and strode along South Street towards the cathedral ruins and the harbour and stone pier beyond. The wind had died, and a light rain had come and gone, leaving the streets and pavements glittering with the beginnings of a winter's frost. Overhead, stars glistened in a black sky. A gibbous moon fluttered through tattered clouds.

By the ruins of Culdee Church overlooking the cliffs and the stone pier, he stood for several minutes, breathing in the cold air, revelling in the freshness from a stirring sea. Waves shunted against rocks, splashing as if by the side of a pool, then as if by whim, clapping the stones that protected the pier with swathes of spray that rose skywards like mist. It looked like the wind was picking up, the clouds thickening.

He made his way down the steep Pends pathway, taking care not to slip on the ice, then strode onto Shorehead. There, the wind was calmer, the kelpy smell of the sea stronger. Fishing boats, anchored for the night, shifted and shuffled against the harbour walls, wooden hulls against rubber fenders, bumping and creaking. Somewhere in the distance, he heard the night cries of gulls in distress.

The stone pier lay dark and deserted. This was where he'd been instructed to meet Arletta Shepherd years earlier. But as it turned out, the location was changed in the heartbeat of a phone call, and he'd been instructed to collect a sealed envelope from the sandwich shop close to the footbridge over the Kinness Burn. Now, at that time of night, the shop was closed, and it seemed to him that the stone pier was as good a place as any for a midnight meeting.

He adjusted his leather jacket, tugged the collar closer to his neck, doing all he could to keep out the November chill. Then he stuffed his hands into his pockets, walked towards the pier, his peripheral vision eyeing the dark shadows around him, seeking out places from where someone could spring out and attack him. And as he eyed the length of the pier, its solitary stone finger reaching for darker deeper waters, he struggled to brush off a shiver of fearful anticipation.

He arrived at the end of the harbour wall, and stepped onto the pier. A quick look behind to assure himself that he was alone – well, as far as his night vision would permit. The sound of his footsteps seemed lost in the chill of the night, the bustling sea to his left with its never-ending motion, its constant splashing and butting against the stone wall. Spindrift rose like mist, only to vanish as soon as it appeared. To his right, the relative calm of the harbour, its waters a good twelve feet below him.

Halfway along the stone pier, with no one in sight, and no movement of any kind on the shorehead behind him, he began to have doubts. Had he misunderstood where he was supposed to meet? Did he have it wrong? He removed his mobile and checked the time – eight minutes before midnight. He was early, and wouldn't expect who he was meeting to be on time, although he half-suspected them – or her – to have him in sight, just to be sure he was alone.

Several minutes later, he reached the end of the pier. Here, the waves were stronger, the wind brisker, the chill factor higher. He shivered off an ice-like chill, grabbed the handrail, and pulled himself up onto the end of the pier. In the black horizon, he caught the tell-tale lights of a ship passing in the night. Going to where? Coming from where? He didn't know. It seemed such an incongruous sight, a solitary light far away on the distant horizon, while behind him – he turned to face the shore – the land seemed alive with lights that danced and glittered in the cold darkness.

From the corner of his eye, he thought he caught movement from one of the lights. He shifted his stance, and focused on it. Had he imagined it? Were his eyes tricking him? He let his gaze settle on the darkness. No. There it was again. The faintest flicker at the end of the harbour buildings. His phone beeped at that moment, and he realised that what he'd seen was the screen light of someone making a call on a mobile phone.

The number was unknown to him, but he swiped the screen and pressed his mobile to his ear, his gaze focused on the last spot where he'd noticed the faint light. 'Hello?' he said.

'Are you alone?' A woman's voice. Not the one he'd come to believe was Natalie Foster's. He felt sure of that. Maybe Arletta's?

'I'm alone,' he said.

'Can I trust you?'

'You know you can.'

A pause, then, 'We don't have much time. Do you know St Rule's Tower?'

'Yes.'

'Meet me there.'

The light flickered again, then vanished into darkness as the call was ended.

Gilchrist stuffed his mobile into his pocket, and scrambled off the end of the pier. He strode with firm purpose along the stone walk-way, peering ahead, searching for movement, something, anything that might help him locate the woman he was going to meet. He thought he caught a shadow flitting over the crown of Kirkhill close to the cathedral wall, but he couldn't say with certainty.

Nothing for it, but to press on.

He walked hard and fast, hoping against the odds to catch up with the woman ahead. But as he rounded the corner onto

Gregory Lane, she was nowhere in sight. Even though his breath was coming at him in hard bursts, clouding the night air, he resisted the urge to break into a jog. Instead, he kept his head down and power-walked into the night.

He reached the cathedral gates, pushed them open, and entered the quiet grounds. He stopped, let his senses take in what lay ahead. The skies brightened for a moment; the twin spires of the ruined cathedral, the stone monolith of St Rule's Tower, rose into the night sky like some surreal rockets waiting to be launched. He took his time, and trod with care as he made his way deeper into the grounds, keeping his gaze fixed ahead as he approached the tower.

The woman's voice came back to him – *meet me there*. But where was there? He knew he couldn't enter the tower, the entrance blocked by a metal turnstile that prohibited visitors from gaining access without having paid admission. So he was more likely to meet her in the grounds close to, or at the base of the tower itself.

When he reached the entrance to the tower, he checked the turnstile, just in case – locked – then pressed his hand against the wall's surface. It felt cold and damp, the rough stone chilling his fingers. Then he turned, stood with his back against the tower, and eyed the night darkness around him. As his vision adjusted, headstones appeared from the shadows to stand to silent attention. He shifted his gaze to the left, then right. But nothing stirred.

He eased his way along the face of the tower, and peered around the corner. Still nothing. He rounded the corner and ventured farther, until he reached the rear of the tower, half-expecting to find the woman there. But again, nothing. He removed his mobile, tapped the screen to cast an eerie glow over his hands. He knew he was being watched, that she was checking the surroundings to make sure he really was by himself. But surely she must know by now that he had come by himself, that he was alone. After a few seconds, he returned his mobile to his inside pocket, and continued his walk around the tower, all the while looking into the shadows, searching for any sign of the woman.

He reached the front of the tower again, when his mobile beeped.

He removed it, pressed it to his ear. 'Hello?'

'Eyes left,' the woman's voice said.

He did as instructed, his gaze searching the cemetery grounds to his left. But still he saw nothing. Then a shaft of moonlight pierced the clouds for a fleeting moment, and he saw a shape emerge from behind a headstone, then stand still. 'Is that you?' he said.

'Follow me,' she said, then seemed to sink into the shadows as she turned away.

He stepped from the tower, and walked towards where he'd last seen the woman. For a moment, he thought he'd lost her, then he caught movement by the ruins of the old priory, a stone building that sat by itself, and made his way towards it.

He reached the building, an empty shell of some outhouse. There, the air felt still and cold, the interior dark and foreboding. He stood at the entrance for several seconds, knowing that the woman must have a clear view of him, and could see he was by himself.

'I'm here,' she said, her voice echoing from the hollow depths.

He took one step towards her, then froze at the cold press of a gun against the side of his head.

CHAPTER 18

'I'm alone,' Gilchrist said.

'I know you are,' a voice to his side whispered, the voice he recognised as belonging to the woman who had answered that very first call.

'Natalie?' he tried.

'Jacket off.'

'I'm unarmed.'

'I know you are.' The muzzle poked hard. 'Jacket off,' she repeated. 'And no sudden movements, or my finger might twitch.'

'Believe me, I'll go as slow as you like.' With careful deliberation he lowered his zip, eased the front of his jacket open, slid it off his right shoulder, pulled his arm out, then did the same with the left. He dropped his jacket to the ground, and let his arms hang by his side.

'Sweater off.'

Silent, he pulled his sweater over his head, then let it drop onto his jacket.

Something stirred from the depths, a shoe scraping stone perhaps, then the figure of a woman appeared.

'Turn to the side,' the woman said.

He thought he detected Arletta's harder Glaswegian accent from years ago, but the muzzle pressed firmer, as if to emphasise her instruction. Without a word, he shuffled to the side, the gun shifting as he did so, so that it now pressed against the back of his head.

'Arms out,' Arletta – if that's who she was – said.

Again, he did as instructed, and said nothing as she picked up his jacket and sweater, and turned them inside out. His house and car keys chinked together. His mobile phone made a brief appearance before being returned to a pocket. Then his clothes were dropped to the ground, and the woman's hands brushed up and down each of his legs, around and over his crotch, then up to pat his shirt, front, sides and back, then run along each of his arms as if checking out his muscles.

She stood back. 'Get dressed.'

'Not want me to take my shoes off?'

'Don't push it, Andy. You don't mind if I call you Andy?'

'If you don't mind that I call you Arletta.' Then, without turning his head, said, 'And you must be Natalie.'

He thought he caught the shimmer of a smile from Arletta as the muzzle released its pressure from the back of his head. He leaned down to retrieve his clothes, and took his time getting dressed, making sure his keys and phone were where they should be, and once satisfied, said, 'Right. Now we're here. What's this about?'

'I could ask you the same,' Arletta said.

Gilchrist turned to the other woman. 'It was your number I was given.'

Natalie said, 'For safety.'

'Safety from what?' he said.

Arletta stepped forward, so that her face was only inches from his. He could smell the heat from her breath. His night vision had settled, and even though they stood in complete darkness, he could make out her features with some clarity.

'Tell me how much you know,' she said.

He spent several minutes bringing Arletta and Natalie up to speed, starting off with Dainty's request to examine Mike Elgin's body, then being introduced to Amari Bankole who told him of the article Hazazi and Elgin were working on, which led them to Hadwin Funeral Services and in turn to believe that the CEO Ryan Hadwin's disappearance was more than just suspicious, but could be one of a number of murders. What he didn't mention was that Arletta's late husband, Tony Dilanos, was allegedly the biological father of Hadwin's son, Grant. Not that he doubted the veracity of that connection, or that Arletta might have been crushed by Tony's betrayal; rather he wanted to see how forth-coming she would be, which could help determine whether or not she truly trusted him.

When he'd told her all he felt comfortable telling her, he finished by saying, 'And that's about it.'

Without a pause, Arletta said, 'Why did you go to my home in Glasgow?' which sent a reminder to Gilchrist that she was as sharp as a tack, and no pushover.

'To speak to you,' he said.

'But why?'

'Dainty said you were missing.'

'Did he now?' The question was rhetorical, and Gilchrist said nothing while Arletta seemed to give thought to what her next question would be. 'How?' she said.

'How what?' he said, all of a sudden not liking the way this was going.

'How did Dainty know I was missing?'

Gilchrist shrugged. 'You'd have to ask him.'

'I'm asking you.'

'He didn't tell me how he knew. And I didn't ask. But if I was a betting man, I'd put money on it coming from one of his snitches.'

She turned away for a moment, and when she next faced him, he had a sense of her hardening her stance. 'You're holding something back,' she said. 'For this to work for me, you're going to have to trust me. You understand?'

'I do. Yes. But when we met before. In Dundee. A while ago. The day Tony was killed. You were less . . . how do I say it? . . . *distrusting.*'

'That was then. This is now.'

'So what's changed?'

She coughed a laugh at that. 'Nothing's changed. On the surface, that is. But beneath the surface, *everything's* changed.'

'You've lost me.'

Another coughed laugh. 'A man of your intelligence? I doubt it.'

She fell silent then, as if waiting for him to tell her what he was missing. But all he could think of saying was, 'Do you trust me?'

'You wouldn't be alive if I didn't.'

He hadn't believed she was capable of killing a police officer. But when it came down to it, if she was hiding in fear for her life, another killing or two was of no significance. 'So tell me,' he said. 'This surface you mention. That's the family business you're talking about. Right?'

She said nothing, just returned his gaze.

116

'So I'm thinking that it's business as usual in some areas. But in other areas, it's not. In fact it's so bad it's rearing up to bite you in the butt. Which is why you're hiding.' Still nothing. He needed to press harder, cut closer to the bone, but for some reason felt reluctant to mention the biological link to Grant Hadwin. It had to come from her. Not him.

Still, he needed to dance around it first.

'Years ago,' he said, 'I put a career criminal behind bars. One of the most vicious men I've ever had the displeasure to meet. He's still inside. In Barlinnie. Likely locked away for the rest of his life.' He paused for a moment. 'Bully Reid. The name ring a bell?'

'Can't say that it does.'

Something in the speed of her reply, the sharpness in her tone, told him she was lying. 'Do you know what I found out about Freddy, who's head of the family in your absence?' he pressed on, wondering if his change in tack would generate a response. But again, nothing. He shuffled his stance, worried that Natalie still held the gun, albeit no longer to the back of his head. 'Well, what I found out was, that Bully Reid is Wee Freddy's uncle. Which I'm willing to bet you didn't know, until you had a meeting with Mike Elgin, and Mike told you.'

Arletta shook her head. 'And here was me thinking you'd solved it all.'

'I'm not finished,' he said, louder than intended. He stepped closer, conscious of a stiffening in Natalie's stance, which warned him that he could no longer beat about the bush. He had to cut to the core. 'Mike also told you that Grant Hadwin was Tony's biological son. Your late husband, Tony, that is.' In the damp darkness, he thought he caught her eyes shimmer. 'Which, as you said, changed everything.'

'How?'

Such a simple question, but a difficult one to answer. 'I'm willing to bet that Grant and Freddy are working together,' he said.

'Why?'

She was either acting dumb, or trying to find out how much he knew. He suspected the latter, and said, 'To take over the family business. A coup to push you out. *Permanently*, if you get my meaning.' He raked his fingers through his hair. 'But what I don't understand is, with you out of the way, why would Freddy entertain Grant coming into the business at all? After all, from what I saw, Freddy seemed to be perfectly capable of running the entire operation by himself. So what has he to gain by bringing in Hadwin?'

He wasn't quite sure which part of his argument had struck a chord, but something had. Arletta turned away, took a step into deeper darkness. Natalie holstered her gun.

Then Arletta stopped, and faced him. 'Hadwin provides a service for Freddy.'

Gilchrist frowned. 'What kind of service?' And even as the words slipped from his lips, he knew what her answer was going to be.

'He disposes of bodies through his funeral business.'

Her matter-of-fact tone was at odds with the seriousness of what she was saying. She wasn't telling him of a disposal service that was about to commence. She was confessing to knowledge of an illegal service that was already in place, one that was up and running. But for how long? All of a sudden Wafic Saliba's disappearance made sense. Leila Hazazi's, too. Even Grant's supposed father, Ryan? Was that what had happened? Grant Hadwin, Wee Freddy's body disposal service provider, had committed patricide, all for the benefit of a criminal business?

'Can you tell me the names of those he's disposed of?' he said.

Arletta gave a derisory sigh. 'So you can arrest me as an accomplice?'

'I wouldn't do that.'

'You might not. But others would.'

'Can you provide proof, then? Something that would let us gather evidence.'

'Of what? You can't recover DNA from ashes.'

'So no burials?'

'Freddy's not stupid. Coffins can be exhumed.'

Gilchrist stopped for a moment, while his mind fired through the logic. Hadwin's company provided the full array of funeral services – collection of the deceased from their home, preparation of the body for viewing if required, selections of coffins and headstones, formal arrangements for burial plots, transportation of the family to and from the cemetery or crematorium, and other associated paraphernalia; flowers, order of service, minister, organist, and the rest. How difficult would it be to slip someone else's body into a coffin for a shared cremation?

But surely it couldn't be as simple as that. Wafic Saliba had been an adult male. Even without knowing his height or girth, it was crystal clear to Gilchrist that disposing of a body in another person's coffin couldn't be done without someone noticing the weight – even if there was sufficient space in a coffin in which to squeeze two bodies. No, if what Arletta was saying was true, then there had to be another way of transporting a body to the crematorium. Stored in the boot of a car? Followed by a midnight drive to the crematorium? But bodies were a dead weight – excuse the pun – so doing so was not a one-man job. And you couldn't just fire up a crematorium in the middle of night without raising suspicion. There had to be some other way. And there had to be more than one person. Two? Three? An entire team?

All of those thoughts and more fired through Gilchrist's mind in a millisecond.

'How long has this been going on?' he asked Arletta.

Even in the cold darkness, he could see her grimace. 'Not long before Grant Hadwin took over his father's business.'

Which made sense. Test the waters by cremating a body or two, then when the time was right, the next body was his father's, then taking over his business. In a morbid way, the pieces were slotting into place. 'How did you find out?'

'You're asking too many questions.' She stepped up to him then, close enough to feel the warmth of her breath. 'Be careful, Andy. That's all I can tell you. Freddy's like no one else I know. He's cruel to the core. And this is just the start.'

'The *start*?' he said. 'Of what?' But she glanced to the side, and at some instruction Gilchrist failed to catch, Natalie stepped from the priory ruins and slid into the black night.

'Don't try to contact me again,' Arletta said. 'It's too dangerous.'

And with that, she followed Natalie into the chilling darkness, leaving Gilchrist alone with his thoughts.

CHAPTER 19

The following morning, Gilchrist rose early and went downstairs to check on Irene. She was sound asleep, her face a sallow white, her breath soft and warm. He took a seat by the side of her bed, dabbed beads of sweat from her forehead, brushed loose strands of hair from her face, then leaned forward and kissed her lips. She stirred for the briefest of moments, her eyelids flickered, before she settled once more into the depths of drug-induced sleep.

He took hold of her hand in both of his, pressed it to his lips, and closed his eyes in the hope that she could hear his thoughts. How could he go through with what he'd promised her? How could he look her in the eye when she wakened, both knowing she would not be here this time next week, in fact in less than a week – only a few days. Sunday evening, she'd decided. That was the day she'd chosen. He'd asked her why? But she'd simply told him that night-time was the perfect time, too, because she'd arranged for him to take Joanne out for an end-of-the-weekend meal, a wee treat from mum to daughter before Christmas. *Because you never know, my darling girl. I might not be here for Christmas.* But now she'd told Joanne of her intentions, how could

121

they both keep up that facade, the pretence of knowing nothing of Irene's plans, and the impossible dilemma of going through with their agreement? He pressed his lips firmer to her hand, felt the nip of tears squeeze from his eyes.

'How can this be happening?' he whispered.

He opened his eyes, and through the blur of tears thought he saw how she'd looked as a young woman, how attractive she'd been. And now? Now it had come to this. She'd asked for his assistance, and without a second thought he'd agreed. After all, it would take some time before the deed needed to be done. Months, he'd reasoned. Maybe longer. And much could be done in the passing of time. And who knew, maybe some miracle cure would be found. But he tightened his lips as reality sank through him.

There would be no last-minute reprieve. Not for Irene. And not for himself. He'd promised he would help her. And help her he would.

Just those thoughts seemed to stiffen his resolve. He released her hand, placed it with care by her side on the bed, and pushed to his feet. He searched for a tissue in his pocket, but had to run a hand under his nose as he walked to the kitchen. He clicked the kettle on, and only then did he open his mobile and check for messages.

One from Mhairi, and two from Jessie.

He opened Mhairi's first – **Report on HFS on desk** – which he took to mean that she and Jackie had looked into Grant Hadwin and his business, Hadwin Funeral Services, as requested, and printed out a report.

Next, he opened Jessie's, which she'd sent in the early hours of the morning – **how did u get on?** – and another, fifteen minutes later – **call me first thing i need to know.** He checked the time on his mobile – 05:45 – thought it was too early to phone, and sent a text instead – will pick you up at 7 – which he thought would let Jessie sleep on and be up in time to read his message and prepare for a day on the road.

He was thinking of calling Dainty, when the kettle clicked, and he turned his attention to making a pot of tea. No, he thought, best not to call Dainty, but to speak to him in person. After all, he now had enough information on Arletta from which he might exhort some quid pro quo response. But what that response was likely to be, he didn't want to hazard a guess.

The car door opened to a blast of cold air. Jessie slumped into the passenger seat, and pulled the door shut. 'Bloody hell,' she said, 'do they ever get the forecast right? If I'd known it was going to be a force ten, I wouldn't have washed my hair. Here.' She unfolded a greaseproof packet. 'Homemade brownie. Chunks of dark chocolate. Thought I'd take some to the Office before that hoover-mouth of a son of mine ate it all. I don't know where he puts it. Could eat for Scotland, so he could. Win an Olympic gold.' She held a piece of what looked like crumbling chocolate cake out to him. 'Try a piece.'

He took it from her.

'What do you think?'

'Good morning,' he said, then bit into it, more for politeness than a craving for all things chocolate.

'It's good. Isn't it?'

He swallowed the mouthful. 'The morning, or the cake?'

'Both.'

He nodded, then licked crumbs off his fingers. 'Definitely the cake.'

'Hah. Told you.' She sat back, and strapped on her seatbelt as Gilchrist slipped the car into gear, then eased down the hill. 'Maybe that's what I'll do when I retire,' she said. 'Open a wee bakery. Better still, bake cakes at home. Sell them around town. Make a fortune, come to think of it. See what they charge in Starbucks and Costa for a slice of cake? Daylight robbery, so it is.'

'You'd have all sorts of stuff to sort out with Health and Safety if you baked at home and sold to local shops.'

'You're too set in your ways. That's your problem. So how did you get on last night? Did she turn up?'

He accelerated onto Bridge Street. 'They did.'

'*They?*'

'Arletta and her cousin, Natalie. Seems they're a team. Natalie provides a safe place for Arletta to hide in, then keeps an eye out for her.'

Jessie frowned at that. 'That can't be news,' she said. 'I mean, if *you've* worked that out, surely Freddy and his hitmen could work that out, too. They'd have turned Natalie's place upside down looking for Arletta.' She looked at him. 'Wouldn't they?'

What Jessie said made logical sense, he had to agree. He'd given some thought to that himself, although hearing it from Jessie seemed to strengthen the logic. 'Well,' he said, 'if you think about it, you have to ask the question – why *haven't* they done that?'

'Good point.' Jessie nibbled at her brownie, then said, 'Maybe they don't want to kill Arletta. Maybe they just want to scare her out of the business.'

'Run her out of town, you mean?'

'Maybe,' Jessie said, then shook her head. 'No. Hounding her out of the business would be unbecoming. Look what she went

124

through with that arsehole of a husband, Tony. After that, she could withstand anything. Besides, she's big Jock's daughter, for crying out loud.'

'And big Jock's dead.'

'Even so, she'd never run away.'

'So she'd rather be killed than run?'

'They won't kill her. Or they would've done that already.'

He was puzzled by Jessie's confident logic, the way she spoke with absolute certainty. He didn't want to mention what Arletta had told him about Grant Hadwin's funeral services providing a body disposal service to Wee Freddy. Not until he'd read Mhairi's report she'd left on his desk. Instead, he said, 'So what're you suggesting, then?'

'I don't know, Andy.' She shook her head. 'How well do you know Natalie?'

'That's a strange question.'

'Not really. Maybe they don't need to kill Arletta because Natalie's keeping an eye on her for them. Maybe Natalie's siding with Wee Freddy.'

He remembered the cold press of the muzzle against his head, the way Natalie guarded Arletta as if her own life depended on it. 'From what I saw last night,' he said, 'that doesn't make sense. Natalie and Arletta are closer than close.'

'Just a bit of lateral thinking. That's all.'

'No, that's good. Any more suggestions?'

'Can't think of any.'

'How about this, then? What if there are more than two of them working together? We know that the guy with the big ears took a huge risk slipping me Natalie's number. Did we ever get his name?'

'Maybe Dainty knows. We'll check with him.'

Gilchrist eased into Market Street, watchful for people dashing across the pedestrian crossing without regard to oncoming traffic. By the time he pulled up outside Starbucks, his mind was made up. 'Best not to tell Dainty that we might have someone on the inside. Not just yet, anyway. Maybe Arletta would be willing to cough up his name.' He handed Jessie a twenty. 'I'll share a muffin with you. Your homemade brownie's got my appetite started.'

'See. I knew you'd like it.'

And with that, Jessie opened the door, and stepped into a stiff breeze.

CHAPTER 20

Alone in his car, Gilchrist dialled the only number he had for Arletta – the contact for Natalie, which big-ears had slipped him on the driveway in Pollokshields. The connection was made right away, but the phone cut off. No transfer to voicemail. Nothing. Just a dead line. He tried again. Same result. He tried once more, taking care to enter the number in case he'd dialled it incorrectly. But again, the line died.

He thought for a moment. What did that mean? Did Natalie and Arletta not trust him? Had they made a point of blocking his only way to contact them? Or was there something else going on? He thought back to Arletta's parting words – *Don't try to contact me again. It's too dangerous.* But too dangerous for whom? Arletta? Natalie? Then a cold shiver chilled his spine. Maybe she was letting him know that it was too dangerous for all of them, himself included. It seemed that he might have to take Dainty into his confidence one more time.

At that moment, his mobile rang – ID Dainty – as if on cue.

'Just the man I need to speak to,' Gilchrist said.

'Where are you?'

'St Andrews, about to head down your way.'

'Don't. I'm on my way up. Should be with you in fifteen.' A pause, then, 'Can we meet someplace other than the Office?'

'Sure. Why?'

'Maybe best that my presence in St Andrews isn't known.'

'What's going on, Dainty?'

'Shit's hit the fucking fan down here. Best if I explain it in person. Where can we meet? Just the two of us. No one else.'

'Inside, or outside?'

'Inside, for fucksake. It always freezes the balls off you up there.'

Gilchrist thought for a few seconds, then said, 'You remember my home address?'

'Yeah.'

'Meet me there.'

The line died.

Less than a minute later, Jessie opened the door and handed him a carboard tray with two steaming cups of coffee slotted into place. Then she clambered inside.

'Got them extra hot with an extra shot. Hope you like it.' She peeled the wrapper off a muffin, oblivious to crumbs spilling onto her lap, then handed him a broken piece. 'Here. Cranberry. Your favourite.'

'Just had Dainty on the phone,' he said, and popped the muffin into his mouth. He followed it up with a sip of coffee – hot hot hot – then stuffed it into the cupholder in the centre console. 'He's on his way up here,' he said, 'and wants to meet. Alone.'

'Did he say why?'

'Only that the shit's hit the fan in Glasgow. Whatever that means. I'll drop you off at the Office. But don't tell anyone I'm meeting Dainty. He thought his visit to St Andrews was best kept quiet.'

'That's odd. Particularly if the shit's hit the fan, as you said.'

Gilchrist eased into Union Street. 'Mhairi's printed out a report on Hadwin Funeral Services. It should be on my desk. I need you to go through that, and let me know if anything jumps out at you. And see if you can find out who big-ears is. How long he's been with the Shepherds. And if he's got form or not. I'll tackle Dainty on it, too, but he might not know him, or if he does, might not be willing to give up a name, so let's tackle it from two sides.' He turned left into North Street, and moments later pulled in front of the Office.

Jessie opened the door, and was about to get out, when she hesitated. 'Want me to give you a call if I find anything important?'

'Only if it's earth shattering.'

She gave him a toodle-doo wave, and he waited a polite few seconds while she entered the building.

Gilchrist hadn't set foot in his own home – Fisherman's Cottage – for almost three weeks. It felt comfortably familiar turning the key and entering the hallway, as if he was returning home from a short break. The hall lay still and silent, quieter than he remembered. Colder, too. A twiddle with the wall-mounted thermostat, and he heard the satisfying click of the central heating switching on.

In the kitchen, he filled the kettle and switched it on. Then he checked out the other rooms, to make sure everything was intact. Back in the living room, mug of black tea in his hand – he'd forgotten to buy milk – and settled into his favourite chair in front of a muted TV, he had a sense that something seemed different about the place. It took him a few minutes before he realised it was the silence.

At Irene's, there always seemed to be an ambient noise of sorts – soft music in the background, TV on in one of the rooms, slippered feet scuffling the kitchen floor, firewood crackling on the open fire, floorboards creaking overhead, distant stirrings from the town outside. Here, in his home, he came to realise that silence was an indicator of loneliness, that without Irene in his life, this is how it would be again. That thought pulled up recollections of recent conversations he and Irene had about end-of-life details no one wanted to talk about.

Irene told him that when she passed she had willed her home and furniture to her daughter, Joanne, but that she'd left all her photographic equipment and files and images to Gilchrist. She'd surprised him by mentioning a small life insurance to be bequeathed to him, too. He'd vehemently resisted at first, but on seeing how set Irene had been, and how his resistance was upsetting her, he'd finally relented.

And then of course, there was this coming Sunday.

Which had his stomach churning, and his heart racing.

He took several deep breaths to force those thoughts away, then placed the mug on the coffee table by the side of his chair, and pushed to his feet. Christ, why had he given in to her demands? Not that she'd twisted his arm. Rather, it had been her quiet persistence, her gentle moulding of his thoughts over time, at the end of which he didn't have it in his heart to refuse her. How could he? He loved her. Which really said it all.

Who would ever allow their loved one to suffer in pain, or to continue living against their will when all hope of life or good health was gone, and that the present moment was as good as it was ever going to be again?

He found himself standing at the back window, looking out over his garden. He'd arranged for a gardener to take care of it. Nothing much. Just cut the grass once a fortnight, trim the edges, water the plants if for any reason Scotland had a week of no rain – an almost impossible thought when he glanced at the dull sky – and tidy up anything obvious; pull out a weed here, prune a branch there. The hut at the bottom of the garden could do with a lick of paint, but that could wait for better weather. In the meantime, he had more pressing matters to take care of. A rattle from the front door announced Dainty's arrival.

As he walked towards the hall, Dainty appeared in the doorway.

'Wasn't locked. Thought I'd let myself in.'

It had been several years since Gilchrist had last invited Dainty to his home, and he stood with modest pride watching Dainty's gaze shift around the room, half-nodding, half-smiling as if surprised by the tidiness of it all.

Then Dainty's gaze shifted to the mug in his hand. 'Could go a cuppa if you don't mind,' he said. 'Milk. No sugar.'

'No milk, I'm afraid. Been staying at Irene's.'

Dainty nodded. 'Black'll do then.'

Gilchrist returned to the kitchen, Dainty behind him, and removed a mug from his mug tree. He topped it from the teapot, and handed it to Dainty. 'Hot enough?'

Dainty took a mouthful. 'Perfect.' He placed the mug on the kitchen counter, then pulled an A4-sized envelope from under his jacket. He peeled back the unsealed top. 'Here,' he said, 'You need to have a gander at these.'

Gilchrist took the envelope and removed a selection of coloured photographs of what was clearly a murder scene. The body was that of a Caucasian male, dressed in a dark suit, white buttoned-down shirt and a black tie as thin as a ribbon. The man was lying on his back in what looked like a small kitchen, evident by the tiled flooring and the base of a washing machine or fridge that crept into the corner of the photo.

'Got an anonymous call to the Office first thing this morning,' Dainty said. 'Voice muffled, saying only that there's a body at this address, then hanging up. We're trying to trace it, but it's a burner.'

Silent, Gilchrist worked his way through the photos one at a time, finding his kitchen stuffy all of a sudden. A close up of the man's broken nose and shattered teeth, lips parted to reveal a black mass of pooled blood that trickled down the side of his face, had him fighting back a nip of bile that threatened to claw its way to his throat. Dark brown eyes, lids half-closed, looked up at him in a sightless gaze.

'Recognise him?' Dainty asked.

'Should I?' Gilchrist glanced at Dainty, puzzled by the intensity of his gaze, a look he'd seen before, a look you might give a lying suspect under hard questioning. It seemed as if Dainty was willing him to spot something. But what, he couldn't say. Back to the image. Still nothing came to him. He flipped through the photos again, hoping to find a clue. But they were all more of the same, although it struck him that the print quality was not the best he'd ever seen. 'What address?' he said.

'Corner of Cadogan and Douglas Street.'

'In Glasgow?'

'City centre.'

132

The address meant nothing to Gilchrist, but as he fingered the images, something about what Dainty had just said niggled. He stopped flicking through the photos and turned his attention to Dainty. 'The *corner* of Cadogan and Douglas Street?'

'Yep.'

'In an office building?'

'No. On the pavement.'

Gilchrist held up the image of the dead man lying on his back on a tiled floor. 'This isn't the pavement,' he said. 'The body's indoors, in a flat or a house.'

Dainty nodded. 'That's what it looks like, yeah. But we haven't found the body, so we don't know where.' He reached for the photos, and took them from Gilchrist. 'We found an envelope at the corner of Cadogan and Douglas. Not this one. Another one, that was tattered and bloodstained, which is being forensically examined as we speak. It looked as if it had been placed there with care, not lying flat on the pavement, but leaning against the corner of the wall. The original photos are also being examined by forensics. These are copies,' he said, and slid them back into the envelope, as if to let Gilchrist know he'd seen enough. 'So,' he said. 'Do you have any thoughts?'

'You've tasked your team to review CCTV footage, I assume.'

'Of course.'

'And they've come up with nothing so far?'

'Nothing definitive. Just a hazy image of a hooded individual walking around the corner, stopping for a moment, then walking on. That's the best we've got. We're trying to retrace his movements before that moment, and track him after. But that's going to take time and manpower.'

Gilchrist walked to the back door, and threw it open. He stood there for several silent seconds, revelling in cool, fresh air that swept away all sense of nausea. 'How long between the anonymous phone call, and someone picking up the envelope?' he said.

'Thirty-one minutes.'

Gilchrist turned. 'After being told there was a body at that corner?'

'Not our finest moment. What can I say? A stick of dynamite up their arses is what some of those dozy bastards need.'

'So in thirty-one minutes, on a Wednesday morning, in Glasgow city centre, how many people would you think walked past that spot?'

Dainty shrugged. 'Doesn't matter. No one noticed it, or picked it up.'

'But that's not the point,' Gilchrist said. 'You're not going to leave an envelope lying on a busy street corner and hope no one touches it until the boys in blue get there. Are you?'

'What're you saying?'

'I'm saying there had to be two of them. One to drop the envelope. And another to watch and make sure it didn't fall into the wrong hands.'

'Fucksake,' Dainty hissed.

'You're spinning your wheels trying to track the hooded guy,' Gilchrist said. 'You'll get him in the end. But that'll take time and effort, as you said. You should focus your initial efforts on CCTV footage immediately after the envelope was picked up. Someone had to be close by, watching. And what about the anonymous call?' he asked.

'What about it?'

'Were you able to locate where it was made?'

'Haven't pinpointed it exactly, but somewhere in Cambuslang. About seven or so miles away.'

'Which would take time to travel in rush hour?'

'I'd say.'

'Which adds one more person to the list. One to make the call. One to place the envelope. And one to watch until it's picked up.' Gilchrist returned Dainty's hard gaze, and frowned. 'Could this be the work of an organisation?'

Dainty nodded. 'That's what we think.' He paused, then said, 'Any other ideas?'

'Just one question. You said the shit had hit the fan. Unless I'm missing something, I don't see where the shit is. Unless . . .' He held Dainty's stare. 'You know who the body is.'

For the first time since entering Gilchrist's cottage, Dainty smiled. 'Jake Cassidy. One of the Cassidy brothers. An up-and-coming family of bad bastards deep into drugs. Originally from the east coast, working on the outskirts of Edinburgh, but now considering expanding their drug-supplying operations into Glasgow. Large family. Six brothers.' He tapped the envelope. 'So the shit-hitting-fan is the Cassidys stepping on some Shepherd toes.' He grimaced, shook his head. 'I wouldn't be surprised if this is one down, five to go.'

CHAPTER 21

'We believe the Shepherd family's behind Jake Cassidy's murder,' Dainty said. 'But again we won't be able to prove a thing. We don't know where the body is. We don't know who killed him. And you can bet your pension on every single one of the Shepherds being alibied to the fucking hilt and beyond.'

'Yes and no,' Gilchrist said.

That stopped Dainty. He glared at him. 'What the fuck does that mean?'

'They didn't have to provide you evidence of a murder. Did they? They could've got rid of the body before anyone knew he was missing.' Gilchrist waited for Dainty to come back at him, and when he didn't, said, 'The way I see it, you've got some members of the Shepherd family – two at a minimum, maybe three – who're risking their lives to provide you with evidence.'

'So why not just phone us up and give us names?' Dainty complained.

'That's a step too far. And they'd be putting their heads on the block if they did that. No, there's still some family honour at play here. They're giving you clues, and leaving the rest for you to do your job and work it out.'

Dainty grunted, lowered his head and stared at the floor for several seconds. Then he looked at Gilchrist. 'You know, there's some sound logic in what you're saying. But there's more to it than that. There has to be.'

'All you've got to go on is the envelope,' Gilchrist said. 'So you need to work around that. Find out who was keeping an eye on it, after it was dropped.'

'By the time we do that, the body'll be beyond recovery.'

'How do you know it isn't already?'

'We don't. But we have to start somewhere.'

'Have any of the Cassidy brothers been questioned?'

'We've got Lothian and Borders doing the initial rounds.'

Which made sense, Gilchrist thought. If the Cassidys were from Edinburgh, it would be seen as stepping on protocol toes for Strathclyde Police to interrogate east coast residents. Best to let the local Force initiate proceedings. But the more he thought about it, the more holes he seemed to find in the assumption that the murder took place somewhere within the city boundaries. For all anyone knew, he could've been killed in England, or anywhere else in the world for that matter, and the photos emailed to Scotland. No, they would have to wait to hear from Lothian and Borders.

In the meantime, they might be able to tackle it from another angle.

'Why Cadogan and Douglas Streets?' Gilchrist said. 'Why there?'

'Why not?' Dainty grunted.

'No, I'm asking, why not somewhere else in the city? Glasgow's a big place. Why drop the photos at that location? There has to be a reason. They're trying to tell you something.'

'Like they're leaving us fucking clues?' Dainty snorted. 'Come on, Andy. Get real.'

But Gilchrist refused to be swayed. 'What's at that junction? Some place that might lead us to a connection we're not seeing. I don't know what. Mike Elgin's murder? Hazazi's disappearance? Hadwin Funeral Services?'

'That's quite the quantum leap,' Dainty said, then frowned, as if some idea had just come to him. 'Fucksake. On the opposite corner, diagonally across the junction is the *Daily Citizen* building. Amari Bankole used to work there. As did Elgin and Hazazi.' And before Gilchrist could speak, Dainty had his mobile out, and stepped into the back garden.

'I want everyone in the *Daily Citizen* building questioned by the end of the day, and that includes cleaners, posties, delivery guys, and anyone else who set foot in the place. And I want every piece of CCTV footage inside and out captured. No, you're not listening. Let me worry about getting the warrants. I don't give a flying fuck how much of a disruption it'll cause. I'll shut the fucking place down if I have to. And if anybody gives our boys any shit, charge them with obstructing a murder investigation. That'll sort the fuckers out.'

Dainty slipped his mobile into his pocket, and almost pushed Gilchrist out of the way as he returned inside. Mobile phone out once again, and he was onto his team, initiating search warrants for the *Citizen* building, and again threatening all and sundry. It was amazing to see the change in the man, as if he'd been some manic depressive who'd been cured all of a sudden, and finally realised what he'd been missing in life.

Job done, mobile returned to his inside pocket, then Dainty said, 'I'm going to visit Lothian and Borders. To keep in touch with what's what. Want to come along?'

Gilchrist shook his head. 'I met Arletta last night.'

Dainty lowered his head, and glared at him. 'You never told me.'

'I'm telling you now.'

'What'd she say?'

'That this is just the start.'

'The start? What's the start? Jake Cassidy's murder? How could she know that?' Something passed behind Dainty's eyes. 'Unless she's involved in it.'

'She's not involved in Cassidy's murder,' Gilchrist said, finding himself perplexed at Dainty's attitude. He'd never seen him so fired up before. Not like him at all. Usually he was circumspect about events, took some time to mull things over. Not like this, rushing into the burning building spraying a fire hose in all directions. 'The start she was referring to,' he explained, 'was Wee Freddy trying to take over the family business, in effect pushing her out. Which is why she's hiding.'

'She thinks Freddy's ordered a hit on her?'

'Almost certainly.'

'So what else did she say?'

'That Grant Hadwin provides a body disposal service for Freddy.' He watched the meaning of his words work through Dainty's thoughts, then said, 'He cremates them. Which tells me that you're never going to find Jake Cassidy's body.'

'Fucksake,' Dainty growled, looking around, as if searching for the answer in the air. Then he glared at Gilchrist. 'He uses his funeral business to clear up Freddy's mess? Is that what you're saying?'

'Suggesting.'

'Saying. Suggesting. Same fucking thing. Don't go all pedantic on me, Andy.' He stomped to the back door again, and stopped on the threshold, as if deciding whether or not to make another call. Then he turned. 'If you know that, why haven't you shut him down?'

'He's already been questioned. Him and his staff. I've got Jessie and others looking into his business.'

'But we've got Jake Cassidy's body now. If it's going to be cremated, you can catch the bastard red-handed.'

'Not as simple as that.' This was the problem with one-track minds. You had to slow them down, point out the obvious, discuss the rationale, before blustering in and blowing to kingdom come and beyond any leads you might have. 'Do you know how many funeral homes Hadwin Funeral Services controls?'

'No. Shock me.'

'Six in Scotland. Two in England.'

'And Jake Cassidy could be cremated in any one of them.'

'If I were a betting man, I'd put money on it being Edendale. That's the crematorium closest to Grant Hadwin's main office. He can keep an eye on operations there.'

Some thought came to Dainty then. 'They could always bury him, I suppose.'

'Coffins can be exhumed. Freddy wouldn't risk that.'

'Right. Edendale it is. You need resources? I'm happy to send a team up to assist in tearing the place down.'

'And if it's not Edendale?' Gilchrist ventured. 'Then we'll have blown our advantage. No,' he said. 'We go slowly on this. Get our ducks in a row. I'll have Jessie carry out more interviews of Hadwin and his staff, just to keep him on edge. Meanwhile, I'd like to have a chat with the head of the Cassidy clan today. Can you set that up for me?'

'Got it,' Dainty said, and stepped outside, mobile once more to his ear.

CHAPTER 22

If Gilchrist hadn't met Arletta and been told that *this is just the start*, he might have shown less interest in Jake Cassidy's murder. But as it turned out, Dainty arranged for him to be escorted to the Cassidy compound by DCI Ross Balder, of Lothian and Borders, who was head of a drug squad that had been trying for two years to nail the Cassidy brothers for drug-related crimes. But the brothers ran their business like a well-oiled machine, and always seemed to be one step, maybe three, ahead of Balder. It hadn't helped that two of Balder's team had recently been arrested for providing inside information to the Cassidys, and were now in custody awaiting trial. But with that revelation, Balder had dismantled his entire team and built a new squad from scratch, whose primary goal was to clean the streets of Edinburgh of drugs, or in Balder's own words – *dismantle the Cassidy empire and put every last one of the bastards behind bars.*

Dainty had forewarned Gilchrist that Balder was not a man to be messed with.

'We'll take a driver and a marked vehicle,' Balder had growled. 'That way we'll get to meet the top man without being strip-searched.'

But the Cassidy compound, as Dainty had called it, was not what Gilchrist expected at all. It turned out to be nothing more than two rows of 1950s council houses along both sides of a quiet street that dead-ended in a hammerhead junction, with one house overlooking the length of the street. The homes had been purchased years ago from the council and sported new front doors and porches, new roof tiles and skylight windows, and extensions that bulged into gardens bordered by eight-foot-high wooden fences. A couple of machine-gun sentry towers in the corners wouldn't be out of place. Brick and cobblestone driveways had replaced front gardens, on which now sat a selection of top-of-the-range BMWs, Audis, Porsches, and in front of one home, a modified Humvee, complete with desert camouflage.

The end house, which backed onto an open field, seemed to be the most extravagant of them all. A yellow low-slung Lamborghini with the roof down, despite the cold weather and threat of rain, was parked nose-to-tail to a silver Rolls-Royce.

'Stop here,' Balder ordered.

The police car pulled to a halt in front of the end house. As Gilchrist stepped out, he noticed men spilling out of the houses farther down the road, as if to form a human barricade across the street to block their exit. Despite the cold, they all wore black T-shirts, matching black jeans and black boots, giving the impression of a well-trained gang of thugs just itching to kick someone's head in.

As Gilchrist followed Balder, he had the unsettling sense of dozens of pairs of eyes watching their every move from behind windows. But Balder strode up the driveway as if he owned the place, warrant card in hand in case anybody had ideas of doing something stupid. Didn't matter how big your criminal family was, or how untouchable you thought you were, killing coppers was bad for business. Still, it didn't hurt to put on a show of strength.

The front door opened when Balder reached the Roller, and a man with shorn hair and a ginger beard that was doing what it could to cover a tattooed neck stepped onto the front step and stood with his arms crossed. Gym-pumped muscles twitched beneath his black T-shirt, and tattoos on swollen forearms shifted and flexed as if willing themselves alive. Gilchrist put him in his early twenties, too young to be head of the family.

'DCI Balder, Lothian and Borders,' Balder snarled, holding out his warrant card. 'And this is DCI Gilchrist, St Andrews CID.'

The man set eyes on Gilchrist, and said, 'You lost your way?' The accent was east coast with a hint of Irish thrown in.

'Is David in?' Balder grunted.

'David who?'

'You know fucking who. Tell him we'd like to have a chat with him.'

'What about?'

'I'm no here to talk to you. Get him.'

'What would you do if I said he's no here?'

'Listen, sonny, we haven't turned up at the front door to be given a lip-load of shite from the likes of you. Tell him we're here on friendly terms. If he wants to change that, then that's fine by me. We'll get a warrant and come back here and arrest his fuck-ing arse. Now go and get him before I lose my temper and arrest you for fucking annoying me.'

One thing you had to say about Balder, he took no prisoners. The young man tried to act cool. He glared at Balder for a few silent seconds, spat a greasy gob on the ground, then turned and trundled back indoors.

No sooner had he slipped inside than an older man appeared at the door; jet-black hair swept back like an oiled cap. Deep-set blue eyes over a square-jaw put him in the close-to-handsome league. But a two-inch scar that ran through his top and bottom lips spoiled the telegenic image.

'Well if it isn't Detective Chief Inspector Ross fucking Balder.' His gaze shifted to take in Gilchrist. 'And who the fuck is this?'

Gilchrist said, 'DCI Andy Gilchrist, St Andrews CID.'

'Oh, Andy is it? On first-name terms are we?' Then his face hardened, and Gilchrist got a sense of how cruel the man could be. 'If anyone mentions the fucking *Partridge Family* it'll be the last fucking thing they say.'

'We're not here to take the piss,' Balder said.

'So what the fuck do you want?'

'To speak to you about your brother, Jake.'

'What about him?'

'He's dead.'

Cassidy stilled, while his eyes died, and his jaw tightened. 'Says who?'

Gilchrist said, 'We believe Jake was killed in Glasgow. Strathclyde Police have opened an investigation into his murder. But we're hoping you can help throw some light on his last movements.'

'Some light? Is that what you're looking for? Some light? Some light like what?'

'What was Jake doing in Glasgow? Who was he with? Who did he last meet? That kind of light.'

'And what's St Andrews CID got to do with Glasgow?' Cassidy said.

'We're looking into possible connections with a criminal element in Fife.'

Cassidy eyed Gilchrist for several seconds, his eyes narrowing as if trying to work out whether he was being lied to or not. 'Well,' he said at length. 'You know what?'

It took several more seconds for Balder to say, 'What?'

'I think you're all fucking at it. That's what. I think you're just trying to trick me into giving away a name or two, so youse can go and arrest some sad bastard.'

'Like I said,' Balder retaliated, 'we're not here to take the piss.'

'And like I said, I think youse're fucking at it.' He sniffed, pulled himself upright. 'Oor Jake was one for the women. That's for sure.' He shook his head, gave a grim smile. 'Off he'd go, looking for his Nat King. He'd disappear for days on end, then come back for a rest, shagged oot rotten.' He sniffed again. 'So I think youse're sticking your noses up your own arseholes looking for fresh air, is what I think.'

Gilchrist tried, 'Have you heard from Jake recently?'

'Like I said. He's off on a fucking shagfest. You no listening?'

Gilchrist slipped his hand into his jacket pocket, which caused Cassidy to jerk into action and reach behind him, and Gilchrist to freeze.

'Hold it,' Balder shouted. 'He's no armed, for fuck sake. He just wants to show you something.'

It took five seconds for Cassidy to release whatever he'd been reaching for, and to stand with his hands by his side again. He nodded. 'Let's see it, then.'

Gilchrist removed an envelope and handed it over, and said nothing while he watched Cassidy slide a multi-ringed hand inside the envelope and remove two photographs. Gilchrist hadn't thought it a good idea to show every photo, just a select couple from which a visual ID could be made.

Cassidy stared at the first one, lips as white as a scar, nose tight, teeth crunching. Then he moved onto the next, and said nothing for what seemed like a minute. Then he looked at Gilchrist. 'Where'd you get these?'

Gilchrist didn't want to give more information than was necessary, so said, 'Turned up at Strathclyde Police HQ this morning. We don't know where Jake's body is. We don't even know *when* he died. We believe it was last night, but we don't know for sure. Which is why we want to have a chat with you about his last known whereabouts. We think Jake's death could be linked to a criminal element in Fife.'

'Whereabouts in Fife?'

'That, I can't tell you.'

Cassidy narrowed his eyes. 'Can't. Or won't. And be careful how you answer that, sonny Jim, because you might just piss me off.'

Balder stepped in with, 'Don't go threatening us. We're here to help. No to take the piss. I told you that.'

'Aye, you did. And I'm telling you to be careful how you answer that question.'

'Fuck sake,' Balder hissed.

Gilchrist said, 'It's not that we *can't* tell you, Mr Cassidy. It's that we *won't*.'

Cassidy reached behind his back again.

'Because it could jeopardise our ongoing investigation,' Gilchrist pressed on, doing all he could to focus on Cassidy's eyes, and not the hand shifting behind his back. 'It's as simple as that. As soon as we have more information, you'll be the first to know.'

'Will I now?'

'Yes,' Gilchrist lied. 'You have my word. But I need you to help us. Give us a name, someone, anyone, who might have been the last person to see Jake alive.'

Something shifted behind Cassidy's eyes, then his lips pulled back to reveal white teeth at odds with the hardman image. 'Dolly Parton,' he said.

'Fuck sake,' Balder cursed again.

'Dolly Dimple is what she is. A right blonde bimbo. With ginormous tits.'

'And her real name?' Gilchrist tried.

'Dorothy McPartin. Dolly for short.'

'Got an address?'

Surprisingly, he had.

CHAPTER 23

DC Mhairi McBride pulled into the car park fronting the head office of Hadwin Funeral Services, and switched off the engine.

Jessie was first out and marched up the pathway with grim determination. She'd taken Gilchrist's call thirty minutes earlier, and his instruction to look into Grant Hadwin with a bit more vigour. 'More vigour?' she'd said, failing to hide her enthusiasm.

'Go easy, Jessie. You know what I mean.'

'You bet.' She ended the call before he could change his mind.

She entered the reception area as Mhairi caught up with her, held out her warrant card to Sam Fishel, the receptionist, and said, 'Is he in?'

'He's with a client.'

'In his office?'

'Yes.'

'That'll do.'

'You can't go in there,' Fishel shouted, as Jessie strode along the hallway.

She reached Hadwin's office, rapped the door hard, and opened it.

Hadwin was seated behind his desk, no one else in the room. He slapped his laptop shut when Jessie burst in.

'Is this what you do when you're not burying folk?' she said. 'Googling porn?'

Hadwin surprised her by smiling, and pushing himself to his feet, arm outstretched for a handshake, as if people exploding into his office was an everyday occurrence. Just then, his desk phone rang. 'Excuse me,' he said, and picked it up. He smiled as he listened, then said, 'No problem, Sam. I've got it.' Then he returned the receiver to its handset with the gentlest of care, and said, 'Why don't you take a seat.' His eyes lit up when Mhairi entered, and he said, 'I believe we haven't met before.'

'Detective Constable Mhairi McBride,' she said, holding out her warrant card.

'Have a seat, have a seat,' he said, then watched her intensely as she sat in the chair next to Jessie. 'Right,' he said. 'How can I make your day?' This aimed at Mhairi.

Jessie said, 'How many burials do you carry out in a week?'

'Depends?'

'On what?'

'On how many people die the week before.' He grinned, pleased with his flippant response. His gaze flickered to Mhairi, as if to check she got his joke.

'And how many cremations in a week?' Jessie said.

'Do you want me to give you the same answer?'

'I want you to stop pissing us around, is what I want you to do.'

'Well, again, it all depends on—'

'Hold it,' Jessie shouted. 'I told you to stop taking the piss.' She glared at him. 'So let me try it this way. How many burials and cremations combined does this funeral home carry out in any given week?'

He shrugged, held out his upturned palms to Mhairi, as if to ask – *How many different ways can I give the same answer?* Then he faced Jessie. 'I think what you're trying to ask,' he said at length, 'is what is the maximum number of souls we can take care of on a weekly basis?'

'And the answer is . . .?'

'Eight to ten per day. Absolute max. So in a six-day week, let's say, fifty to sixty or thereabouts. But no more. We don't do Sundays.'

'There you go. That wasn't too hard, was it?'

Hadwin smiled at Mhairi.

Jessie leaned forward. 'So . . . what's the ratio between burials and cremations in any given week? Roughly,' she added.

Hadwin shook his head, as if puzzled. 'Can I ask you what any of this is to do with anything? I'm not sure I understand why you're asking?'

'We're coming to that.' She smiled. 'So . . .?'

Hadwin returned her smile, but with less enthusiasm than earlier. 'Again, it's difficult to put an accurate figure on it, but nowadays more people prefer to be cremated than buried.' He shrugged again. 'In the past, it was the other way around.'

'So what's the ratio?' Jessie demanded. 'Give or take a few per cent.'

Another shake of the head, a puzzled shrug. 'Say, three cremations for every burial?'

'Asking or telling?'

'Estimating.'

'And what's that as a percentage?'

151

'Seventy-five per cent cremation versus twenty-five per cent burial.'

Jessie glanced at Mhairi. 'He's good at arithmetic, isn't he?'

Mhairi nodded, doing what she could to stifle a laugh.

'I'm not sure I see the funny side of this,' Hadwin complained. 'After all, we provide a caring and personal service to bereaved families at a sensitive and vulnerable time.'

'Is that why you Google porn in your spare time?'

Hadwin tutted, and shook his head. He pressed his hands flat on his desk, and leaned forward as if about to stand. 'Are we through?'

'Not quite. Sit down.'

Hadwin froze for a moment, then sat, with some reluctance she noted.

'So tell me,' Jessie said, 'how many funeral homes in total do you run?'

'Eight.'

'So that's six in Scotland, and two in England,' she said, and watched suspicion creep behind his eyes.

'If you know the answer, why ask the question?'

'To keep you honest.'

He grunted, shook his head, and pushed to his feet. 'I really must ask you to leave. I'm not prepared to be treated like some . . . some fool.'

'Just a couple of more questions,' Jessie said. 'Then we'll be out of your hair.' She returned his gaze. 'Sit,' she said, and to her surprise, he did. She fiddled with her notebook for several seconds, flipping through the pages to keep Hadwin waiting. Then she looked at him. 'If someone dies in Fife, where are they cremated?'

'Edendale Crematorium, mostly. But it depends where in Fife. It's a large county.'

'And if someone dies in Glasgow, which crematorium would they be cremated in?'

'There are a few crematoria that serve the Glasgow area. So it depends where they live.'

'Let me put it this way,' she said, leaning closer. 'Which crematorium would *you* use?'

'Clydevale.'

She sat back. 'And where would you keep a body before its cremation at Clydevale?'

'We have an office in Bearsden, close to Clydevale, where the souls are prepared for burial, or cremation, or for viewing. But sometimes they're kept overnight at the crematorium. After the service has taken place.'

'So if someone died or was murdered anywhere in Glasgow, your company would cremate them in Clydevale, and not one of the other crematoriums. Is that right?'

'Look. I really have to object. Am I under suspicion? Do I need to call my lawyer?'

'Call your lawyer if you want, but I'm just trying to get a handle on how you run your business.' She jerked her lips into an imitation of a smile. 'So . . . Clydevale? Yes or no.'

'There would be no need to transfer the coffin to any other crematorium,' he said, and pushed his chair back. 'Right. That's it. I'm going to have to ask you to leave.'

Jessie nodded, glanced at Mhairi. 'You got any questions for him?'

'None that I can think of, no.'

'Okay, Mr Hadwin. Thanks for your time. We'll see ourselves out.'

Back in the car, Mhairi shivered. 'Did you see the way he kept looking at me?'

'That's because you're good-looking. He thought he was in there.'

Mhairi grimaced, and gave a shiver.

Jessie chuckled, and fiddled with her mobile phone. 'Right, I've got the address in Bearsden. You know how to get there?'

'To Glasgow, yes. Not Bearsden.'

Another few seconds with her mobile, then Jessie said, 'That's it entered into the satnav. Let's go. I've got a funny feeling about this one.'

CHAPTER 24

DCI Ross Balder ordered the driver to pull into the kerb opposite the address in Leith.

'Right,' he said, stepping out of the police car into a cold November wind. 'Let's see what this Dolly McPartin has to say for herself.'

Gilchrist walked side by side with him as they crossed the road and pushed through a door that opened to a small lobby. One lift was out of order. The lift indicator for the other put it at the fifth floor. Balder headed for the staircase. For a bulky man, he was surprisingly agile, and Gilchrist found himself rushing to keep up.

They found McPartin's flat on the second floor. Without hesitation Balder rang the doorbell, and battered the door with the heel of his hand. A flicker of light at the eyehole told Gilchrist that someone was home, and a few seconds later, the door opened and a chain jerked with a loud snap at a short safety latch.

'Dolly McPartin?' Balder said, holding out his warrant card, and introducing himself and Gilchrist.

The woman's eyes widened. 'What d'youse want?'

'To ask a few questions.'

'About what?'

'Best if we do it inside,' Balder said, then leaned forward, his face almost pressing against the door, impatient for it to open.

McPartin released the safety chain, and was almost pushed out of the way as Balder strode past her. Gilchrist followed, resisting the urge to apologise for Balder's brash manner.

In the lounge, Balder turned to wait for McPartin to enter. When she did, Gilchrist watched him take in McPartin's bulging chest. A tight low-neck sweater could have been custom-made to exaggerate her top-heavy figure, while skin-tight jeans over thin legs did little to minimise the damage.

'Do you know Jake Cassidy?' Balder asked, as soon as she entered.

'Yeah. Why?'

'He's dead.'

If Gilchrist was expecting to see shock or floods of tears at the brutal announcement, he was disappointed. McPartin stilled for several seconds, as if having difficulty interpreting Balder's words, then simply said, 'What happened?'

'We believe he was shot. Twice. In the head.'

Still nothing. 'When?'

'Best guess, early hours this morning.'

'This morning?' she said, then frowned. 'I haven't been able to get hold of Jake for two days now. He *always* answers his phone. Even if it's just to send a text that he's too busy to talk.'

Gilchrist said, 'When was the last time you spoke with Jake?'

'Two days ago. I already said that.'

'But when? Morning? Afternoon? Can you remember the time?'

She extracted a mobile phone from a pocket as if by magic, and tapped the screen. 'I texted him on Monday night at nine . . . hang on . . . nine thirty-one. Here it is.' She held her mobile out to confirm the message – **Where r u?** – then said, 'He comes over most Monday nights, but he never showed up on Monday there.'

'And you haven't heard from him since?'

'No.'

Gilchrist held out his hand. 'May I?'

She passed her mobile to him, and he scrolled down the screen to read several more texts to Jake, each one becoming increasingly more frustrated, until the final text sent just before midnight last night – **Fuck u!!!!!** He scrolled back up to retrieve the last message sent by Jake.

'The last message received by you from Jake was on Sunday afternoon at 17:08,' he said, screwing up his face. 'Which appears to be in some abbreviated form.' He showed it to McPartin – **Rnin l8 c u ltr.**

'Running late. See you later,' she said.

Balder said, 'We'll need to confiscate your mobile.'

'And what am I supposed to do until I get it back?' she said, more shocked by that than from hearing of Jake's murder. Well, that's the younger generation for you.

'Get another phone,' Balder said.

Gilchrist tried a softer approach. 'You might not get it back at all, Dolly. It'll be held in police safekeeping for the duration of Jake's murder investigation and beyond. I'm sorry, but you should really look into buying a new phone.'

'Can I claim for costs?'

'You can if you like,' Balder said, 'but you'll likely end up with fuck all.'

'You can't just take people's phones off them. What about all the stuff I've got saved on it? Addresses. Emails. And hunners of photies.'

'You should've downloaded them.'

'What for? They're on my fucking phone.'

Balder shrugged.

'Jesus Christ,' McPartin snapped. 'No wonder everyone fucking hates the cops.'

'I'll pretend I never heard that,' Balder said.

'Pretend all you like. But I said it, and you heard it.'

Gilchrist stepped in like a referee. 'What else can you tell us about Jake?' he said. 'Did he mention anything about meeting someone? Did he seem normal as usual? Or did he seem on edge, maybe worried about something?'

But McPartin appeared too upset about losing her phone to think about answering any questions, so he said, 'I'll have one of our IT guys download everything on your phone onto a thumb drive for you, Dolly. And once that's done, you can collect it from your local police station. That way you won't lose a thing. But we *will* have to hold onto your phone for the time being.'

McPartin glared at Balder, as if willing him to burst into flames. 'See?' she hissed, then turned back to Gilchrist. 'I want a receipt,' she said. 'So no one's gonnie steal my phone off me. All right?'

'Of course,' Gilchrist said.

That seemed to do the trick, for her body seemed to relax, as if all tension had been released. She placed an arm under her breasts, and hitched them up. Gilchrist saw his chance, and repeated his earlier question.

McPartin shrugged. 'Naw, Jake just seemed normal. He didnae seemed to be worried about nothing, you ken? He just took it as he found it, and got on with it. But he was full of it. I'll give him that.'

'Full of *it*?' Gilchrist asked.

'Aye. Full of it. Loved himself. Fancied himself as a ladies' man, you ken? He could chat anybody up. He seemed to get on well with all the girls. Buy them drinks. But he didnae take advantage of no one. He was really nice.' She glared at Balder. 'No like some of youse.' Then back to Gilchrist. 'But when I come to think of it, he did seem a wee bit off recently.'

Gilchrist glanced at Balder, to make sure he was listening. 'A wee bit off like what?'

'Just no himself, you ken?'

'No we don't ken,' Balder growled. 'What the hell are you trying to tell us?'

But McPartin ignored him, as if she were deep in thought, trying to recall some vague event from the depths of her memory banks. 'It was something he said,' she whispered. 'Last Saturday. Down at the club.'

'The club?'

'Aye, Jives.' She grimaced. 'They should change the name to Dives, because that's what it is. A bloody dive. But Jake liked it.'

'So what did he say?' Gilchrist asked, trying to get her back on track.

'It was just in the passing, like. I didnae catch it all. There was too much noise. He was on his phone, shouting. It sounded like . . . Eddy's going to get it.'

'Eddy? Who's Eddy?'

'I don't know. But for a moment, Jake was angry. Really angry. It took him a couple of voddie shooters to calm down.'

'Do you know who he was talking to on the phone?' Gilchrist said.

'No' really. But it was probably that nutter of a brother of his. Davie. He's always giving Jake a hard time.'

Gilchrist glanced at Balder, but he was looking at his watch, as if he hadn't picked up on the significance of what Dolly had said. But if you thought about it, why would he? If you read Eddy as Freddy, then it might make sense. But Wee Freddy being a Glasgow gangster didn't necessarily compute with Balder's east coast sense of gangland.

All of a sudden, the truth of Arletta Shepherd's words struck Gilchrist – *It's already started*. When she'd met Gilchrist, was Jake Cassidy already dead? And had she known? And if so, had the hit on Jake been carried out at the instruction of Freddy? If someone as cruel as Freddy had known that a hit had been put out on him, he wasn't the sort of guy to sit back and wait for it to happen. And with Grant Hadwin and his funeral services simmering away in the background, a pre-emptive hit on Jake, followed by a quick cremation to dispose of the body, was as good a way as any to take care of Freddy's problem.

It's already started.

Had the gangland war of east against west for control of Scotland's billion-pound drug business, with all its money-spinning side businesses, already started? Dainty's words – *the shit's hit the fan in Glasgow* – seemed to suggest that. And photographs of Jake Cassidy's dead body only added to the murderous mystique surrounding up-and-coming boss of bosses, Wee Freddy. But the trouble with gangland warfare was that criminal underlings and their bosses were not the only ones killed in the crossfire.

If Wee Freddy was as ruthless and cruel as Arletta feared he was, then it was only a matter of time before he turned to taking out every single person who was trying to bring him down. No one, criminals and police officers alike, would be allowed to stand in his way. But one thought in particular troubled Gilchrist – Wee Freddy's uncle was none other than Bully Reid, who'd vowed to take his vengeance on Gilchrist for putting him behind bars for the rest of his natural, no matter how long it took, or whether or not Bully was dead when it happened. Gilchrist was familiar with the meaning of *fatwa*, a lifelong death sentence issued in accordance with Islamic law, and seldom overturned. He had no idea of a similar word in Christian Scotland, but he knew enough about Bully Reid's personality to know that his word was no threat, but a promise.

Christ, he thought. Shit hitting the fan in Glasgow could be the understatement of the year. If what he feared was about to happen, then it looked like the shit was about to hit the fan not just in Glasgow, but in Scotland and beyond. And the collateral murder of one of Fife Constabulary's finest could be more or less considered a given.

Gilchrist wiped beads of sweat from his brow at that thought, unable to prevent his hands from shaking.

CHAPTER 25

From the car park, Jessie was surprised by the size of Clydevale Crematorium. The building itself consisted of two chapels, one at either end of a light sandstone building. The gardens of remembrance were as expansive as a football pitch. Cultivated avenues lined with shrubs cut into treed areas as congested as any arboretum, and spread from the crematorium in sylvan paths as slender as walkways.

She stepped into the November chill, and found her gaze morbidly searching for smoke rising from a chimney stack. But the design of the building was such that she was unable to locate any such stack, or indeed any smoke. The car park, too, seemed to have been laid out in modern fashion, with a curved entrance road and wider than normal parking spaces laid out in deceptive curves as if to prevent visitors from facing the crematorium directly. It seemed as if the architects had done everything they could to limit views of the functional body of the place, which was, after all, the legal cremation of deceased people.

'I don't like this place,' Jessie said.

'Never been here before,' Mhairi replied.

Jessie gave an involuntary shiver. 'Gives me the creeps, so it does.'

Just then, a group of people – three women, one male – emerged from a door at the side and walked in solemn silence along a covered pathway, again laid out in a sweeping curve, to stand in a short line. Mourners followed, spilling from the building, some taking time to express condolences with the grieving family, others slipping past to head to their parked cars. At the adjacent chapel, a crowd was gathering for the next cremation.

'That must be the last one of the day,' Jessie said.

Even as she spoke, a funeral cortège of two black limousines and a woman dressed in a black jacket and skirt and holding an ebony-handled walking stick, strode with mournful deliberation in front of the lead limousine. Meanwhile, the car park around Jessie seemed to come alive with people returning to their cars. Doors opened and closed. Engines fired up. Vehicles nudged past. Some mourners stood in groups, chatting together, then dispersing this way and that until one by one every vehicle cleared the parking area, leaving Jessie and Mhairi to stand alone.

Jessie felt a flutter of dampness. She lifted her gaze to the sky, held out an upturned hand. 'Should've known it was going to rain.'

'We can sit in the car until it goes off,' Mhairi suggested.

'Let's see what we can find out about this place,' Jessie said, and with that, headed to the vacated chapel.

Inside, the chapel was high-ceilinged and spacious. Ten rows of chairs, not pews, stretched either side of a gleaming central aisle, all freshly varnished. The air was redolent of fresh paint and oiled wood, and a subtle taste of too many flowers coated the tongue. Rich burgundy curtains lined the end wall, having been closed for the committal service, beyond which the coffin would have been taken away for cremation.

Jessie and Mhairi's footfall echoed in the open space as they strode down the aisle. A sudden shift of clouds outside sent a sunburst through the stained-glass side windows to cast an ethereal glow over the cushioned chairs. For just that fleeting moment, Jessie caught her breath. Then the clouds shifted, the sunlight died, and she felt a shiver flush through her at the sense that someone was watching.

As if on cue, a woman in a black trouser suit entered the chapel through a door behind the raised pulpit, to the side of the curtains. 'Can I help you?' she said.

'Who are you?' Jessie replied.

'The crematorium assistant.'

'Just the person,' Jessie said, and held out her warrant card. 'We'd like you to run us through the cremation process.'

The woman frowned. 'Can I ask why?'

'Yes you can. What's your name again?'

'Lisa. Lisa Sumpter.'

Jessie smiled, then nodded in the direction of the committal curtain. 'Once the curtain closes, that's it, isn't it? The coffin is then lowered into the basement to be cremated.'

'This crematorium doesn't have a basement. We're all on the one level here. Once the chapel is emptied, the coffin is pulled off the catafalque by hand, into the cremation room, which is hidden from public view by another curtain.'

Jessie jerked a smile. 'So you've got technicians to do that?'

'Assistants. There's three of us. But usually only one assistant can handle that.'

'So someone's already taking care of the most recent coffin?'

'Yes. Look, what's this all about?'

'We're at the start of an investigation,' Jessie said, as if that explained all. 'And we need to know how this crematorium works. Can you show us?'

'Well, it's . . . we have another service about to take place. I'm not sure it's appropriate for you to—'

'That's perfect. After you,' Jessie said, and held out her arm as an instruction to be shown the way.

Lisa seemed disinclined to do as Jessie asked, but only for a moment, after which she said, 'Very well. This way,' and led them to the door behind the pulpit.

A few moments later, Jessie and Mhairi were standing in front of what looked like an industrial-sized stainless-steel oven door, some five feet wide by four feet high. All around them, pipes and cables and other mechanical fittings cluttered the ceiling and walls.

'So this is it?' Jessie said, eyeing the steel door. 'Where the bodies get burned.'

Lisa nodded. 'This is it, as you say.'

'Is it on?'

'No.' She turned to the side, took a couple of steps, and opened a door to expose four rows of fixed biers, stainless-steel open shelves with rollers for ease of moving heavy coffins. Coffins sat on three of the shelves. 'We'll start the cremation process after the next service,' she said, and closed the door.

Jessie turned her attention back to the steel door. 'So how does it work?'

'What you're looking at is what's called the cremator, or retort, which is where the bodies are cremated. It takes about an hour and a half to cremate a body, and the inside of the cremator is lined with fire-resistant bricks that can withstand the high temperatures of the cremation process.'

'How high?'

'We normally start the process at seven hundred and fifty degrees centigrade, then run it at around nine-fifty to a thousand. But the bricks are designed to withstand much higher temperatures of fifteen hundred, even as high as two thousand degrees centigrade.'

'That's like some industrial incinerator,' Jessie said, more statement than question. 'So how many coffins do you incinerate at a time?'

'We prefer to say *cremate*, rather than incinerate, which is a more respectful way of describing the process.'

'So how many?'

'Only one at a time. It's vitally important that no remains are mixed with any others by accident. At the end of every cremation, the remains are cleared from the inside using those two metal rakes.'

Jessie eyed two long steel poles standing upright at the side of the cremator. One had a metal head bent at the end for scraping out the ashes, and the other looked like a long-handled brush.

'Would you like me to open the cremator for you?' Lisa said, and without waiting for a reply, stepped up to a control panel and pressed a button, which turned from red to green.

The stainless-steel door slid upwards, causing Jessie to take an involuntary step back from a burst of heat that warmed her face. 'I thought you hadn't done any cremations today.'

'We haven't. That's the heat from yesterday.' She stepped closer and pointed to an opening on the bottom of the cremator floor. 'After each cremation, we scrape the ashes, and they fall through this opening here and are caught in one of those metal containers. The ashes are then taken to the cremulator—'

'The what?'

'The cremulator. It's a machine that pulverises the cremator's remains.'

'So the furnace doesn't burn everything to ashes?'

'The human body often doesn't burn down to dust. Usually crumbled lumps of bones and ash are all that remains. The cremulator pulverises these remains into a fine powder.'

Mhairi said, 'Even the coffin handles?'

'If the deceased is to be buried, the funeral home ensures the coffin handles are metal. If the deceased is to be cremated, the handles are plastic. So, yes.'

'What about metal parts,' Mhairi said. 'You know, hip or knee replacements, that sort of thing?'

Lisa said, 'They're removed before going into the cremulator. Smaller bits of metal, coffin screws, staples, and the like, are sifted out at the end of the pulverising process.'

Mhairi said, 'What about teeth? Do they burn?'

'They usually do, and any fillings, and larger pieces of teeth are pulverised to dust.'

Jessie was keen to get back on track, and said, 'Only one coffin into the cremator at a time, though?'

'Yes.'

'You sure? It would be a tight fit. But if you lay the coffins on their side, you might be able to squeeze them in.'

'We never do—'

'I'm not suggesting you do,' Jessie snapped. 'I'm asking if it's possible.'

'Why?'

'Well . . . is it?'

Lisa shook her head. 'No. The chamber isn't large enough for two coffins. It can take only one at a time.'

'So, it's like a built-in failsafe thingy?'

'Yes, if you want to call it that.'

Jessie frowned, and eyed the depths of the cremator. 'It looks like there's enough room to place another body on top of the coffin, so that the coffin – with the body inside, of course – is cremated together with the body outside on top?'

Lisa put her hand to her mouth, forehead creased like a furrowed field as she scowled at Jessie. 'Are you suggesting that—'

'I'm not suggesting anything,' Jessie said again. 'I'm only asking if it's possible.'

'My God,' Lisa said, and removed her hand from her mouth.

'Well . . . is it possible?'

'I don't know what to tell you. I . . . I . . . suppose it's possible. But it goes against every principle that we as funeral directors hold dear. Who would do such a thing?'

'You'd be surprised,' Jessie said, then added, 'So you could put one body on top of the coffin, and no one would be any the wiser?'

'They wouldn't get away with it,' Lisa demurred. 'It would be noticed when clearing out the ashes.'

'How?'

'At the end of the cremation, the bodies are often left as nothing more than a skeleton, or parts of a skeleton. Many a time I've opened the door and the remains are lying there, arms outstretched to the side. The bones are extremely brittle from being cremated, and fall apart as soon as you try to remove them.

So whoever was clearing the cremator would notice two skeletons, and definitely two skulls.'

Jessie gave that some thought. 'Could you put body parts into some other coffin – minus the skull – and cremate them together?'

'You would still see additional bones. And even if you couldn't, we would know something was wrong before we put the coffin inside the cremator, because of the weight.'

'What do you mean?'

'Every coffin we receive from a funeral home has to be weighed by the funeral home, and the weight recorded on the deceased's records. We would know just by pulling the coffin off the bier that the weight didn't match.'

'You ever get them without being weighed?'

'We would never carry out a cremation without first receiving the coffin weight from the funeral home.'

'Sounds like you have it pretty much sorted. Not a lot'll slip past you.'

'That's the idea,' Lisa said, seemingly relieved by Jessie's comment.

But Jessie frowned. She still wasn't convinced. 'How about this? Is there any way you can compare the amount of gas used in the cremation process to the number of coffins you've cremated that day? Just to make sure no one's slipped in an extra coffin or two?'

Lisa smiled as she gave her professional response. 'The gas usage and the number of cremations are recorded and checked daily, weekly and monthly. Also,' she said, and pointed to a computer screen on the wall, which looked as if it was showing the details of a flow chart, 'the data from every cremation is sent electronically to our head office in Dundee.'

'So there's no way anyone could fluff the numbers?'

'I don't see how.'

Jessie turned to Mhairi. 'How about you? Any other questions?'

Mhairi nodded. 'How many cremations are done on an average week?'

'Difficult to say. We can do up to seven direct cremations in the morning, then a few traditional cremations in the afternoon.'

'On average?'

'Most we've ever done is seventy. So, maybe fifty or thereabouts.'

'You said *direct* cremation. What's that?'

'That's when there's no family present. They maybe can't afford a full service. Or the deceased may come from hospital. Or there's an unknown death, and nobody claims the body. That sort of thing. It's more common than you'd think. We're very respectful in all cases.'

'Are any cremations carried out at night?'

'We're not allowed to,' Lisa said.

'I know that. But are there?'

'No. None.'

'None that you're aware of.'

'Of course not.'

'So if the cremator was turned on at night, who would know? I mean you're in the back of beyond out here. It's not exactly the centre of town.'

Lisa shrugged. 'No one outside, I suppose.'

Mhairi glanced at Jessie, a signal for her to take over.

'So,' Jessie said, 'it's possible for someone to bring a coffin along one night, slip it into the cremator, switch it on, and hey presto, Bob's your uncle.'

'But every single cremation is reported electronically to our head office. They would know something wasn't right.'

'Do you have CCTV working here?'

'Yes. Inside and outside.' Lisa pointed to two cameras mounted high in the corner of the ceiling, which she hadn't noticed until then. 'They're shown on these screens here, and we have another screen in the admin office.'

'Where are the tapes kept?'

'We don't have tapes. The recordings are stored digitally with our head office in Dundee. And before you ask, I don't know how long they keep them. As it's all digital, it could be years for all I know.'

'Who has keys to the place?'

'Me. The other assistants. Bob. The head office, of course.'

'Who's Bob?'

'Bob Cosley. The crematorium director. He's not here at the moment. But he's in charge of this crematorium and three others.'

At the mention of the other crematoria, another thought came to Jessie. 'Who runs this crematorium? Is it Hadwin Funeral Services?'

'No. They're one of a number of registered funeral homes who use our services.'

'So who owns this place? Greater Glasgow Council?'

'No. A privately owned group.'

'Name?'

'The Easterbrook Group. Their head office is in Dundee.'

Jessie was pleased to see Mhairi taking notes. 'You know anyone in the head office?'

'Not really. I get the occasional phone call. But that's about it.'

'Got a name for me?'

'Not off the top of my head, no.'

'Okay. We'll check it out.' A glance at Mhairi told her she had no more questions. She was about to leave, when another thought came to her. 'If you were to lug a coffin in here in the middle of the night, how would you get it in? Is there a back door?'

Lisa nodded.

'Can you show us?'

Without a word, Lisa turned and walked along the side of the cremator to a door in the rear of the building, which she pushed open.

Jessie and Mhairi followed her outside.

Jessie noticed several parking spaces close by, which would be convenient for delivering coffins in the dark of night. But she also saw that the door through which they'd come couldn't be opened from the outside, only from the inside. 'So if you turned up with a coffin in the middle of the night, someone would have to let you in,' she said.

'Yes.'

Jessie eyed the outside of the building, then nodded to the corner of the building to what looked like a construction add-on. 'What's that?'

'The chimney, if you want to call it that. It's where all the cooled and filtered gases from the combustion chamber are vented to the atmosphere.' She nodded to some pipework at the side of the building. 'The hot gases from the cremator are filtered, removing all toxic gases, then pass through those pipes, where they're cooled to thirty-seven degrees before being released into the atmosphere.'

Mhairi said, 'And having been filtered and cooled, that's why there's no smoke.'

'Correct.'

That seemed to do the trick, for Jessie walked inside, back past the cremator and into the cremulator room. She waited for Lisa to return, before saying, 'Thanks,' and handing her a business card. 'You've been really helpful. If anything crops up, let me know.'

Lisa took it, stared at it, and shook her head.

'We'll see ourselves out,' Jessie said. 'Cheers.'

CHAPTER 26

8.34 p.m.
North Street Office, St Andrews

Gilchrist ended the day's debriefing with, 'Okay, that's it for tonight. We'll start afresh in the morning. A quick recap. Mhairi, you and Jackie dig up all you can on the Easterbrook Group. Get onto Companies House, find out the names and addresses of directors, secretaries, shareholders, CVs if you can get them, tax returns, DVLA records, the works. Got it?'

Mhairi said, 'Yes, sir,' while Jackie nodded, her tousled rusty-haired Afro jostling as she did so.

'Jessie, you and I are going to meet Dainty and DI Melton first thing. We need to bring them up to speed with what we've got, but we need to have Dainty share his findings. He's holding something back on this one. And tomorrow morning we're going to find out what that something is.' He eyed the room. 'Anybody got any last-minute questions?' A pause, then, 'Good. I'm heading to the Central for a pint. Anybody want to join me? My treat.'

Jessie said, 'You talked me into it.'

'Anyone else?'

Jackie tried to speak, 'N . . . n . . . n . . .,' but her stammer got her every time, and she shook her head instead.

'Some other time then, Jackie, okay?'

'Uh-huh.'

Mhairi said, 'Can't, sir. Got my long-lost brother up from England. He's promised to take me out for dinner. A rare event, let me tell you.'

'You don't want to miss that, then,' Jessie said.

Mhairi noticed Gilchrist's look of alarm, and said, 'Don't worry, sir. I told him I don't usually eat until later, so he's reserved a table at the Old Course Hotel for nine-thirty.'

Jessie whistled. 'Nice one, Mhairi. I hope he's got deep pockets.'

Mhairi laughed. 'No worries. He's loaded. Works in London as a stockbroker.'

'Any tips he could give us?' Jessie said.

'Yeah. Don't live in Scotland. It rains too much.'

Jessie high-fived her with, 'Touché.'

'All right,' Gilchrist said. 'See you all in the morning. Bright and early. We've a busy day ahead of us.'

Jessie pulled out her mobile. 'I'll see you in the bar. Mine's a G and T. Slimline.'

Gilchrist signalled that he got her order, then strode to his office. He powered down his computer, retrieved his leather jacket from a hook at the back of the door, and picked up his mobile. He skipped down the stairs, pushed through the doors onto North Street, surprised by the stiff chill of the wind. It seemed to have strengthened, and was coming straight off the estuary. He hiked up his collar, and checked his mobile as he turned into College Street – one text from Dainty, confirming their meeting in the morning at Strathclyde HQ in Glasgow.

He decided to give Irene a quick call. He'd already explained to Joanne that he would be home late because of the ongoing murder investigations, and she'd agreed to spend some time with her mum. If Irene was asleep, Joanne would pick up. But he longed to hear Irene's voice, find out how she was keeping, how her day went – my God, as if lying in bed all day, hooked up to goodness knows what, was any way to spend a day.

Rather than enter the Central from the College Street entrance, he walked into Market Street, mobile to his ear. His call was picked up on the first ring with a breathless, 'Hi,' which he recognised instantly as Joanne.

'How is she?' he asked, knowing before Joanne said a word that Irene was asleep, that she'd spent most of her day in and out of drug-ridden consciousness, that Joanne wouldn't want to wake her to take his call.

'She's comfortable,' Joanne said.

He heard the click of her footfall on wooden flooring, and knew she was moving to a different part of the house, out of Irene's earshot. 'Have the tuck-in services been?' he said.

'Come and gone. In and out in no time at all. Seem more keen in keeping the log book up to date than anything else.' She gave a heavy sigh. 'Sorry. That's unfair. It's just . . .'

'I know,' he said. 'It's not personal for them, the way it is for us . . . for you.'

'Andy,' she whispered, and he knew with a sinking heart what was on her mind. 'I'm not sure I can go ahead with this . . . this Sunday. It's . . . I . . .'

'I know, Joanne, but remember . . . it's not about us, it's about what your mum wants. She doesn't want to be a burden to anyone.'

'But she's not a burden. Why doesn't she see that? She knows I'll take care of her for as long as I have to.'

'And that's what you're doing,' he said, trying to keep his tone level. 'Taking care of her. For as long as you have to.' He didn't have to expand on that, the unmentionable fact that Sunday was only a few days away, when their looming promise to Irene would have to be met. 'Think about what your mum wants,' he went on. 'She doesn't want us to see her like this, helpless, weak, knowing she's only going to get weaker until . . . It's not what she wants. She wants at the very least to have some say in . . . in how she passes.'

He held onto the phone for several seconds, listening to Joanne's laboured breathing, her gusts of sniffs and sobs, and felt his heart go out to her. How could he help this young woman? How could he do as her mother had asked them, no . . . *begged* them . . . to do? Was this what he would want for his own children if the roles had been reversed and he'd been able to finagle that dreadful promise from Irene?

'I'm sorry, Joanne.' It was all he could think to say. For a moment, he thought of just heading straight home, forgetting about having a pint. But what would that do? He couldn't do anything more for Irene, or Joanne for that matter, by coming home. In fact, it might be argued that his presence would detract from a private moment between mother and daughter. 'How long are you going to stay with her?' he said.

'I'm thinking of moving into the spare bedroom for the duration.' A pause, then, 'If that's all right with you, of course.'

'Of course it's all right, Joanne. You don't have to ask. Stay as long as you like.'

She paused for a moment, then said, 'Let me think about it.'

'Sure. But come Sunday, we'll need to . . . to stick to the plan.' He let five seconds pass, and when she didn't answer, said, 'All right, Joanne? You know that's what we have to do.'

'I know . . . I know . . . I just don't know if I . . .' She stopped then, and her voice came back in a whisper. 'She's waking up. I'll need to go.'

'I'll be back soon,' he said. But the line was already dead.

He slid his mobile into his jacket pocket, and pushed into the lively din of a Scottish pub. He squeezed his way to the bar, shuffling past couples, apologising left and right, until he was able to rest an elbow on a rounded corner. He caught some football game on the telly high in the corner, highlights of what looked like Man U against Chelsea, but couldn't say for sure. Whatever hunger pangs he'd felt at the Office had left him, and he ordered a pint of Tennent's and a Bombay Sapphire and tonic. 'Slimline, if you've got it.'

He'd taken a couple of sips when he noticed Jessie. She'd come in from the College Street entrance, opposite from where he was standing, and was waving him over, indicating that she had two stools at the bar. Perfect, he thought, and with glasses and bottle of tonic in hand, he worked his way round to her.

'Busy wee place,' she said, taking her drinks from him. She emptied the full bottle of tonic into the gin, and held it up for a chinking, 'Cheers.'

He reciprocated, and took a mouthful of his own.

'God, I needed that,' she said. 'Trouble is, it doesn't last long.' Another sip, and her glass was halfway done. She held it out to the barman. 'Can you put some more ice in that for me. And another gin, too.'

'Here, let me get that,' Gilchrist said.

'Don't you bother.' She shoved his hand away. 'It's my round,' she added, and eyed his pint. 'Ready for another?'

'No, just the one for me tonight.'

She looked at him, held his gaze for a long moment, then said, 'You all right?'

'Yeah. Sure. Just tired.'

'It's Irene. Isn't it.'

He really didn't want to talk about it, and hoped Jessie got the message when he put his pint to his lips with a half nod, and mumbled, 'She's struggling,' then took a slow sip.

'I'm sorry, Andy. I'm so sorry.'

What could he say to that? Nothing, as it turned out.

'I hate to bring this up, you know, with what's going on with . . . but I'd like to have another wee chat with you about Clydevale Crematorium.' She sipped her gin, then said, 'Are you up for talking about it?'

'Sure.'

'If Hadwin's getting rid of bodies for Freddy, then I don't think the crem's the key. It's not possible to get rid of a body that way.'

He grimaced. 'Then why would Freddy team up with him? I don't get it. There has to be a reason, and that reason is for his funeral business. Arletta said so. And there's no reason for her to lie.'

'I hear you, but I don't see how it's done. Everything's recorded. CCTV cameras in all the rooms. Recordings digitally sent to their head office in Dundee. Every cremation is recorded on the computer, and details recorded again at their head office. Coffins are even weighed, for crying out loud. Cremated bodies look like

179

skeletons that crumble to the touch, so there's no doubling anybody up in the furnace. It'd be noticed as soon as you open the door. Gas usage is tallied and checked against the number of cremations on a daily, weekly and monthly basis. Any out-of-sequence cremations would stick out like a sore thumb.' Jessie shook her head, lifted her glass of gin to her mouth, and almost finished it. 'Jeez, Andy, I don't see it. There must be some other way of doing it. But whatever way it's done, it's not being done at the crematorium.'

'At the funeral home, then?' Gilchrist ventured.

'But how? As soon as it gets to the crematorium, it's recorded.'

'Under whose name?'

That stopped Jessie for a moment. 'So, to get rid of a body, they give it a new ID, and send it off for cremation. Is that it?'

'That's too easy,' he said. 'Nowadays it takes days, sometimes weeks, to schedule a cremation. That would mean too much planning. They'd have to either plan the killing way ahead of the cremation, or store the body somewhere, after the killing. Neither of which is Freddy's style, I think.'

'And even then,' Jessie said, 'you've still got the cremation to go through with, with all its checks and balances and recordings and cameras and stuff.'

'How about the direct cremations?' Gilchrist tried.

'It's the same system of checks and balances, but without any family present. And the coffin still has to come from a funeral home, with a death certificate signed off by a doctor.' She stopped for a moment, and raised her eyebrows in suspicion. 'Maybe that's how it's done. Hadwin and Freddy have a doctor in their pocket. Someone who's willing to falsify a death certificate for the sake of a few quid.'

'Or for the sake of not getting a bullet to the back of the head,' Gilchrist said, unable to mask the cynicism in his tone.

'Even so,' Jessie said. 'It's not beyond the realms of possibility, is it?'

Gilchrist held his pint to his lips. Something in the way he and Jessie were discussing the pros and cons wasn't sitting right with him. He couldn't put a name to it, or touch it, or trap his fleeting thoughts. His sixth sense was telling him they were on the right track, that the crematorium was how bodies were being disposed. They weren't being buried. He was sure of that. Coffins could be exhumed. Wasn't that what Arletta had said? But pulverised ashes? Now, there was no coming back from that, no way to link them to Freddy or Hadwin, or anyone else for that matter. But as his thoughts shifted and shuffled through his mind, the slimmest of possibilities began to manifest into some idea, something that could change the course of his investigation.

Dainty held the key. He was sure of that.

And tomorrow he would find out.

CHAPTER 27

6.30 a.m., Thursday

Gilchrist's mobile buzzed from somewhere off in the distance, and pulled him out of a deep sleep. He opened his eyes, confused for a moment as to where he was. He stretched an arm across the bed to feel the sheets cold and not slept in.

Where was Irene?

He came to in a flash, pulled himself upright, switched on the bedside lamp, and as the shadows vanished, reality hit him like a kick to the stomach. What day was today? – as relief swept through him that it was only Thursday, not yet Sunday.

Good God, was this really about to happen?

He swung his legs from the bed, took a few seconds to steady himself. His tongue felt thick, and his mouth as if it belonged to someone else. How long had he stayed at the pub last night? But as his memory swam back to him, he realised he hadn't stayed long, just the two pints – the second one bought at Jessie's insistence – and been home just after nine, which was when he and Joanne opened a bottle of . . .

'Don't tell me,' he grumbled, as he pulled himself to his feet. 'We didn't demolish The McCallan 12, surely.' From the haze of last night's past, he recalled pouring a glass for Irene – *Just a small one, please* – and he'd thought, what the hell, and poured her a goodly measure. But just one, thank goodness. She'd drifted off to sleep not long after that, while he and Joanne retired to the kitchen where they'd had a long heart-to-heart over more than a few hefty measures seated at the breakfast bar. Must have been closer to midnight when he made it to bed, while Joanne, as young as she was, stayed up a little longer to sit for a few more minutes with her mum.

He pulled on his dressing gown and made his way downstairs, and eased into the main lounge where Irene's bed was, careful not to disturb her. She was sound asleep – what else? – and he leaned down to her, and whispered, 'Love you, darling,' and tucked a loose strand of hair behind her ear. She never stirred, not even when he took hold of her hand and lifted it to his lips, all the while struggling to hold back the tears that dimmed his sight.

He'd seen many a victim during his time in the Police Force, and always struggled to display professional dispassion, a necessary part of the job. But now as he listened to Irene's shallow breathing the reality of it all seemed to hit him afresh. Irene was alive now, but in a few more days she would be done with living, she would be gone from this world, gone from her family . . . gone from him.

He gave her hand one more gentle press with his lips, then placed it with care on the bed. He tucked the covers up, making sure they were under her chin just so, the way she liked the covers to be, then made his way to the kitchen.

He couldn't see any evidence of last night's whisky session, and realised that Joanne had cleared everything away. But a quick glance at the drinks trolley confirmed that The Macallan 12 was all but finished. Which at least explained why his head was thumping.

He filled a glass of water and downed a couple of painkillers to see him through most of the morning. He switched on the TV, set it to Mute, and boiled the kettle. Not much on the News. No mention of Jake Cassidy's murder, or of any revenge killings overnight. But he knew within himself, that it was only a matter of time until the Cassidys opened up with all barrels firing.

By the time he stepped outside into the damp darkness of a bitter morning, he was running a few minutes late. He'd arranged to pick Jessie up at seven, but it was only a short drive to her home in Canongate. Even so, he had to wait with the engine running before she trundled down her drive, and almost jumped inside.

'Jeez,' she said, slamming the door behind her. 'It's bloody freezing out there.'

Gilchrist slipped into gear. 'Good morning,' he said, and when she didn't reply, he eased away from the kerb. 'Do you know that people who live in Alaska say it's not the weather that's the problem. It's the clothes people wear.'

'They must be suffering from brain-freeze then. Because it's bloody Baltic out there. It wouldn't matter how many pairs of woolie knickers I had on, that wind would freeze the whats-its off you.'

'Woolie knickers?' he said, and chuckled. 'Really?'

'A turn of phrase,' she grumbled. 'You drive. And it's your turn to get the coffees.' She opened her satchel and removed a brown paper bag. 'Jenny made these,' she said, and peeled back the top to reveal two slices of what looked like chocolate cake so dark it was almost black.

'Jenny?' he said.

'Robert's girlfriend. He stays over at hers most of the time now. I'm thinking they might get married. But having said that,' she added with some emphasis, 'they had a huge argument the other day. *Huge.* I've never seen Robert so upset. Anyway, they seem to have made up, and it's all okay again. For the time being.'

Gilchrist grimaced. He hadn't seen Jessie's son for a year or so now, knew only that he was making his way in life, working in construction with aspirations to become an author of comedy books. Now and again, Jessie would brighten their day with one of Robert's jokes, but being completely deaf from birth, with no hope of ever hearing, had to be an enormous challenge for any woman to take on. 'The cake is Jenny's way of saying sorry,' he offered.

'If it is, she knows how to get to my heart. Although it should be Robert's heart she's getting to.'

'It's the younger generation. They seem to work to a different set of rules.'

'Rules? What rules? As far as I see, anything and everything goes, and usually does.'

Nothing more was said until Gilchrist pulled into the kerb on Market Street and switched off the engine. 'The usual?'

'Go on, then.'

He had just entered Starbucks when his mobile buzzed – ID Dainty. He stepped back outside to take the call.

'Another set of photies turned up this morning,' Dainty said without introduction.

'Same as last time?' Gilchrist tried. 'No body? Just photographs?'

'Yeah, but this is sending us a message.'

Gilchrist pressed his mobile hard to his ear. 'I'm listening.'

'One of Freddy's men,' Dainty said. 'But it's not retaliation by the Cassidys. He's one of ours.'

'I thought you said he was one of Freddy's men.'

'He was. But he'd turned. He'd been feeding us inside info for months.' Dainty let out a whispered curse, then said, 'He was close to Arletta. So Freddy's making a statement. He's letting Arletta and the rest of the gang know that he's no longer waiting.'

'Which means?'

'Which means that he's taken over. The dynamics of Scotland's criminal underworld has just been turned upside down. And I mean turned right fucking upside down.' A pause, then, 'You know Freddy's uncle's Bully Reid, don't you?'

Gilchrist felt the hairs on the nape of his neck rise. 'I do, yes.'

'We're hearing that Bully's pulling the strings from inside the Bar-L. And that's not the worst of it. Two months ago, Bully's long-time cellmate and personal minder, Slim Jim, was released on parole.' Another curse. 'Should never've been let out, but that's today's parole boards for you. Thick as fucking mince. But there it is.'

Gilchrist wasn't sure what the *it* was that Dainty was referring to. He'd never heard of Slim Jim, so the name meant nothing to him. But if he had anything to do with Bully Reid, he could only be bad news. 'Slim Jim?' he said. 'Should I know him?'

'Slim by name only. Fat as fuck. Hence the piss-take on the nickname. He might be fat, but he once tried out for Britain's strongest man, and got thrown out for sticking the head on one of the judges. It took three of them to pull him off. Nothing came of it. Rumour has it he told the judge he'd cram his head up his arse if he reported him to the police. The judge took him at his word, and dropped it pronto.'

Gilchrist's head spun. Too much information, too quick, too soon. He couldn't take it all in. 'So where's Slim Jim now?'

'Down here, causing havoc.'

'I don't understand.'

'You will when you get here.'

With that, the line died, leaving Gilchrist to mull over the danger in Dainty's words.

CHAPTER 28

Strathclyde Police HQ, Pitt Street, Glasgow

The first thing that struck Gilchrist was that Dainty didn't look well. Heavy bags as loose as testicle sacs blackened his eyes and suggested he hadn't slept since they'd met at his cottage. The second was a Black woman in a black T-shirt, off to the side, with toned biceps that looked as if she'd got her money's worth at the gym. The third was an air of tension, so tight he swore he heard it crackle as he and Jessie entered the room.

Dainty said, 'Have a look at these, and tell me what you see,' and slid a Manila folder across the desk to Gilchrist.

He caught it. 'Mind if we sit?'

'Sure.'

Gilchrist did, and waited until Jessie had shuffled herself comfortable before opening the folder. He caught a sharp intake of breath at the first of a pile of photographs that showed in technicoloured close-up the slashed throat of some murder victim. The next image showed the open wound and the man's chin, as if the photographer was pulling away from the victim. The next, farther away still, to show the man's bloodied mouth, opened to a set of dishevelled teeth reddened from blood that oozed from the edge of his lips.

Two images later, Gilchrist said, 'Shit.'

'Recognise him?' Dainty said.

Gilchrist turned the image to Jessie, who nodded in recognition. 'I'd recognise those ears anywhere,' she said. 'He works for Freddy.'

'*Used* to work for Freddy,' Dainty corrected.

Gilchrist said, 'He was one of the two who escorted Jessie and me from the family mansion. Do you have an ID?'

'Went by the name of TK,' Dainty said. 'Initials only. Don't know why, because his real name is Willie Williams.'

'William Williams,' Jessie said. 'That's enough to make you change your name.'

Gilchrist thought back to the moment he felt TK's hand on his side, and the realisation that he'd just slipped something into his pocket – Arletta's phone number, or more correctly, Natalie's. He lifted his gaze from the photos, and held Dainty's hard look. 'How did Freddy find out he'd turned?'

'That's the sixty-million-dollar question.' A tired shrug, then, 'Hadn't heard from him since Tuesday evening. So we're assuming that's when he was killed, and when these photos were taken.'

Gilchrist hung his head, let out his breath. 'Tuesday was when he slipped Arletta's contact number into my pocket,' he said. 'They must've noticed.'

'We'll never know.'

'So who's heading the investigation into his murder?' Gilchrist asked, and found his gaze shifting to the woman in the black T-shirt, who pushed herself to her feet.

'I am,' she said. 'DI Vivien Macario. Grampian Police.' She slid two business cards over to Gilchrist.

He passed one to Jessie, and said, 'Why Grampian?'

'TK was born in Aberdeen. He used to be one of my snitches.'

Gilchrist sat upright, shot a glance at Dainty, then back to Macario. 'Let me make sure I understand,' he said. 'TK worked for you in Aberdeen, then you sent him to Glasgow and *planted* him in the Shepherds?'

Macario never so much as blinked. 'As I'm sure you're aware, DCI Gilchrist, the Shepherd family's reach is nationwide, and expanding. TK was a valuable asset.'

'Who's now dead,' Gilchrist said.

'Unfortunately, yes. But he knew the risks.'

He'd heard many a cold-hearted comment from criminals and others over the years, but the words that spilled from Macario's mouth seemed the coldest of all. 'Did you provide any safeguards, any backup?' It was all he could think to say.

'We did.'

'And I'm assuming you've started a murder enquiry.'

Dainty stepped in, as if to avoid further embarrassment to Macario. 'We played it low key, and sent a pair of uniforms to Freddy's as soon as we got the photos last night. Just to let the bastard know he's not the only person who knows what's what.'

'And?'

'And fuck all. He's alibied to the hilt, just like we knew he would be.'

'But what did he have to say about TK?'

'Nothing. Said the last he saw of him was when he escorted a skinny detective and his fat sidekick from the premises. Sorry, Jessie. Exact words.'

'And here's me thinking I was losing weight.'

Dainty gave a consolation chuckle, and lowered his head. Macario offered a smile that failed to reach her eyes. But Gilchrist felt they were all missing something, himself included. He nodded to Dainty. 'So where does this Slim Jim come into it? On the phone, you seemed to think he had something to do with it.'

'Can't say for sure if he's involved in this or not, but throat-cutting was what Slim Jim was famous for. He once sliced a guy's throat so bad that the only thing holding his head on was the spinal cord.'

Gilchrist glanced at the victim's photo again, and if asked, he would have to say that disproportionate force had been used to slice TK's throat open. Not quite all the way through to the spinal cord, which didn't necessarily point the finger at Slim Jim. Even so, an image of Bully Reid burst into his mind, and he had to stave off a reluctant shiver, force his thoughts back on track. 'So where's Slim Jim now?' he said.

Dainty shook his head. 'You'd think a fat fuck like that couldn't go into hiding. But that's what he's done. We don't know where the fuck he is.'

Macario said, 'We think we'll have eyes on him by close of play today.'

Gilchrist raised an eyebrow. 'Which is contrary to what Dainty's saying.'

'We have contacts,' she said, then sat back, as if that explained all.

Gilchrist nodded. But his mind was elsewhere. He was missing something. They all were. Something to do with the photos. Not the images themselves, but the way they'd been found. In today's age of digital this, internet that, why print out images at all? Why not just download them onto a thumb drive and mail that to the police? It didn't make sense.

'These photos,' he said, and tapped the folder. 'Where did you find them?'

'Same place. Corner of Cadogan and Douglas Street. Last night.'

'Wednesday,' he said, just to confirm the day. 'And we're assuming TK was killed on Tuesday. Right?'

'Right.'

'And you haven't found his body, have you?'

'No.'

'Because they got rid of it on Wednesday morning, probably by direct cremation.' He looked at Macario. 'How big a team do you have?'

'Six at the moment. Why?'

He looked at Dainty when he answered. 'Get a list of all the direct cremations carried out yesterday morning of coffins prepared by Hadwin Funeral Services. I don't think you'll find anything out of order. They've got a system that seems watertight, and we can't figure out how it's done yet.'

'So why go to the trouble?' Macario said.

'Because it'll let them know we're onto them, so they won't be so keen to murder all and sundry if their disposal method is being monitored.' He frowned for a moment, then added, 'But we're still missing something.' He turned to Macario. 'Was TK the only plant you had in the Shepherd's family?'

'Yes.'

He held up the folder. 'So if it's not TK who's sending you these, who is?'

Dainty narrowed his eyes and returned Gilchrist's firm look. 'I wondered when you'd get round to asking that question. Which brings me to why I needed to meet you today.'

Silent, Gilchrist held his gaze.

'TK's been killed. So we've no one inside the Shepherds any more.' He tapped the folder. 'But these prove otherwise. Someone inside is willing to risk their life providing us with proof of TK's murder. And we don't know who that someone is.' He lowered his head and eyed Gilchrist. 'But one person must. Which is where you come in.'

Gilchrist tried to keep his surprise hidden. 'I'm listening.'

'It has to be someone close to Freddy, but whose allegiance is still with Arletta.' He tapped a finger on the desk, then pointed it at Gilchrist. 'You have access to Arletta.'

'Had.'

Dainty froze. 'What the fuck's that supposed to mean?'

'The phone numbers I have are useless. They're dead. She's gone into hiding.'

Dainty's lips compressed to a scar, before he hissed, 'Fucksake.'

The door opened at that moment, and DI Melton entered. 'Sir?'

Dainty lifted his chin and glared at her. 'Anything?'

'We believe we have an ID on one of the perps who tasered Mike Elgin.'

Melton produced a printout of an enlarged CCTV image, and laid it on the desk. The image had been captured just after midnight – 00:02:43 to be precise – grainy and mostly out of focus of two people wearing hoodies. How anyone could ID an individual from images of that quality defied reason. Another image – not as enlarged – showed them walking alongside a river.

193

Gilchrist knew Glasgow well enough to recognise the bridge in the background as the Squinty Bridge, which put the hooded pair by the River Clyde.

Dainty grunted, and said, 'Anyone we know?'

Melton pointed to the face on the left, then produced another image, much clearer, of an Asian person with cropped hair seated in a restaurant. 'Chika Nagano,' she said. 'Born in Japan. Parents emigrated to the UK thirty years ago.'

'Does he have a criminal record?'

'He's a she, and she's clean. No previous convictions. No DVLA points. Income tax records up to date. Lives by herself in Glasgow, and works in the funeral business.'

Gilchrist almost jolted. 'Whereabouts?' he said.

'She's one of the assistants in Clydevale Crematorium.'

Dainty said, 'Bring her in for questioning.'

Gilchrist pushed to his feet. 'Before we do that,' he said, and picked up the enlarged image then faced Melton. 'How certain are you that this is Chika Nagano?' He grimaced, shook his head. 'I mean, this isn't the clearest of images.'

Melton offered a victory smile. 'Because someone grassed on her.'

'Who?'

'That I can't say.' She removed her mobile, and pulled up a text message – Chika nagano shot elgin – and showed it to Dainty.

'*Shot?* Elgin wasn't shot. He drowned.'

'Shot, as in – fired a taser.'

Dainty grimaced. 'A bit thin for me. How about the phone? Did you find out who sent the text?'

'No chance. It's a burner. It pinged a couple of masts in Kilmarnock, which told us nothing. But we had to follow up to find out if Chika Nagano existed, or if it was just some punter on a hoax. We spent over five hours finding out who she was, and another four before we could ID her. When I found out she worked in a crematorium, that nailed it for me.'

'Bring her in,' Dainty said.

'No need to.' Another victory smile. 'She's already in Interview Room 2.'

CHAPTER 29

Dainty instructed Melton to lead the interview, but insisted on Gilchrist being present, which he was happy to do, having assigned Jessie the task of chasing up Jackie and Mhairi for any information they'd found on the Easterbrook Group.

Gilchrist let Melton lead the way, and followed her into the interview room, which felt overly warm, as if someone had turned up the heating and forgotten to switch it off. Melton sat directly opposite Nagano, leaving Gilchrist to face her attorney, a fierce-looking woman in her fifties or sixties with white hair coiled like springs, clasped either side of her head, as if she couldn't be bothered brushing it, or had realised after decades of failing that it really was untameable.

She looked up from whatever she was studying as Gilchrist took his seat, then slid a business card across the table to him. 'Maggie Doig,' she said by way of introduction, then returned her attention to her notes.

Gilchrist reciprocated with a card of his own, but Doig never so much as glanced at it. To her side, Nagano sat in silence, black hair cropped so short, face so flat, so expressionless, that if he hadn't known, he would've been unable to say with certainty if she was a man or a woman. She stared straight ahead, as if fixated on something over Melton's shoulder.

Then Melton opened her folder, and placed her mobile face down on the table. In a confident tone she checked everyone was ready, confirmed the interview would be recorded, and made a point of making sure the recorder was switched on. Once the formal introductions were over, she read Nagano her rights, confirming she was being questioned in relation to the murder of Mike Elgin. No attempt was made to explain that Elgin hadn't been murdered *per se*, but assaulted by taser then drowned. But Gilchrist kept his tongue on hold, and let Melton get on with it.

'Where were you last Saturday night?' Melton asked.

Nagano stared through her, as if she hadn't heard a word.

'For the record,' Melton said, 'Ms Nagano has refused to answer.' She went on to ask four more questions, to which Nagano never so much as blinked. Each time, Melton added her own comment for the record.

She was about to ask another question, when Gilchrist raised his hand. 'May I?'

'Be my guest,' she said, and scowled at Nagano.

'If I could make a suggestion,' he said to Doig. 'It would be for you to have a word with your client and advise her that refusing to answer any questions at all isn't doing her any favours.'

'She's perfectly within her rights not to answer—'

'I know,' Gilchrist interrupted. 'But that's not the point I'm trying to make.'

'And what point is that?' she snapped.

'From my experience,' he said, 'refusing to answer direct questions, or answering everything with No comment, gives the impression of guilt. It also makes it more difficult, in fact impossible, for us to rule that person out of the enquiry. So . . .' He turned his hands palms up, as if to reveal the simple truth of his logic. '. . . your client can continue to stonewall us, which leaves us with no alternative but to keep her in a cell overnight. Or she can help us by answering all questions truthfully, which . . . if she is indeed innocent . . . could rule her out of our enquiry. Whereupon she would be free to leave.'

'I've already advised my client, advice which I'm disinclined to change.'

God, he thought. What chance did any litigant have with Medusa as their solicitor? He glanced at Nagano and had a sense that she'd listened, that she might have taken on board the possibility that she could walk from here if only she answered their questions.

He turned to her. 'Chika,' he said, then reconsidered his approach. 'Ms Nagano, can you tell us where you were last Saturday night?'

'At home.' She continued to stare at some point over Melton's shoulder, and for a moment, Gilchrist wondered if he'd imagined the words.

'Can you corroborate that?' he said.

'No.'

Doig pushed herself upright. 'I need to have a word with my client,' she snarled.

Gilchrist nodded, and Melton said, 'Interview suspended at ten-thirteen. DI Melton and DCI Gilchrist leaving the room.' She clicked off the recorder, and stood.

In the hallway, Melton said, 'Jeez, I thought we were going to have to waste an hour of our time asking questions like fools. Do you think she'll clam up again after being read the riot act by that *witch*?'

'Witch?'

'All she's missing is a broomstick and cloak.'

They reached the coffee dispenser at the end of the hall, and Gilchrist said, 'Coffee?'

'Just water.' She removed a conical cup from a plastic holder on the wall to the side of the dispenser, and held it under the nozzle. Then she threw it back and replaced it under the nozzle for a refill. 'They don't hold much these cups, do they?'

'Just enough,' he said, and did likewise. He took a sip, and said, 'Would you mind if I took over the questioning when we get back?'

'Go for it. I was getting nowhere.'

Melton's candid assessment was refreshing to hear. Far too often, detectives could be territorial when questioning suspects. 'Okay, here's how I'd like to do it,' he said, and spent a few minutes detailing his plan. Then he looked at his watch. 'They should be ready by now.'

And they were, although the atmosphere in the room seemed to have thickened.

Doig ignored them and stared at her notes as they took their seats, whereas Nagano followed Gilchrist's progress with almost beatific fascination.

Melton clicked on the recorder, announced their return, and that the interview was restarting at 10.24.

Without looking up from her notes, Doig said, 'For the record, I have given my client my advice, which is to answer every question with a No comment. But she's refusing to accept my advice.'

'Would you care to leave the interview?' Melton asked.

'I'll stay,' she huffed. 'Just in case.'

'In case of what?'

'In case you become overly aggressive.' She lowered her head and glared at Melton, and for just that moment, Gilchrist imagined she could snort flames from her nostrils.

He leaned forward, placed his arms on the desk, reducing the space between Nagano and himself, and ignored Doig. 'Ms Nagano,' he began, 'do you live by yourself?'

'Yes.'

'And you said you were at home last Saturday, the night Mike Elgin was attacked.'

'Yes.'

'And no one was with you?'

'No.'

'So . . . no one can corroborate your alibi that you were home.'

'No.'

'We have CCTV footage of you and another person walking by the side of the River Clyde late Saturday night.'

Melton produced a printout of the footage, and turned it so Nagano could see it.

Doig glanced at it, then returned to her notes.

Nagano looked at it for no more than a couple of seconds, then said, 'It's not me. On Saturday night I do my exercises at home, then I have bath, then I go to bed.'

Her accent was a strange mixture of lilting Japanese and soft Glaswegian, and Gilchrist had the toughest time imagining her tackling someone as large as Elgin, even with a taser in hand. She looked so slight, as if a gust of wind could topple her. But he'd been fooled before by frail physiques.

'What kind of exercises do you do?' he asked.

'Aikido.'

'Martial arts?'

'Yes.'

He offered a smile. 'Any good?'

'I am black belt.'

Well, there he had it. Fooled again.

He spent the next fifteen minutes questioning her, showing her more CCTV footage, asking about her work at the crematorium, when she was last there, when she was scheduled to return, all the while looking for some kind of reaction, but in the end getting nowhere. He could have battered her fingers with a hammer, and doubted she would have shown any reaction.

But in a way, it was all going according to plan.

He turned to Melton. 'You have any more questions?'

Melton shook her head.

'In that case,' Gilchrist said, 'the interview is over, and your client is free to leave.'

CHAPTER 30

Dainty was less pleased with the outcome. 'You let her go?' he said. 'For fucksake, Andy, she's the only lead we've got so far.'

'She thinks she's off the hook,' Gilchrist said. 'But she isn't.'

'You don't think she's telling the truth?'

'No.'

Dainty held Gilchrist's gaze for a long moment, then said, 'You're not going to share your thoughts with me, are you?'

'Best not to.'

'Ah, right,' he said, holding up his hands in fake surrender. 'Keep me posted.'

Gilchrist watched Dainty walk along the corridor in that big-man's stride of his, knowing he would head straight for DI Melton and grill her on why she hadn't put up more resistance to letting Nagano go. Not that there was a problem with that, for he knew Melton would stick to her word, and not tell Dainty everything.

He found Jessie outside, on her mobile. She held up two fingers to let him know she would be with him in a few moments. He walked off, and pulled out his own mobile.

Mhairi answered right away. 'Sir?'

'I need you to get Clydevale Crematorium's CCTV footage for the last week, starting on Saturday. But I don't want you to contact Clydevale directly,' he said. 'I want you to do it through Easterbrook's head office. I don't want anyone in the crematorium to know that I'm looking into them.'

'Yes, sir. Is there any particular event you want me to look for?'

He'd given it some thought, and in that strange way the subconscious mind works in the background, an idea had come to him. DI Melton was in no doubt that Nagano had been involved in Mike Elgin's assault, but Nagano's confidence in her answers contradicted that. But if you bypassed the question of – was Nagano telling the truth or not? – and asked what she would have done if Elgin hadn't toppled into the Clyde, but had been killed there and then, you found yourself arriving at a different question – what would she have done with his body? And the fact that she worked as a crematorium assistant gave him the only answer he could come up with – Elgin's body would've been transported to the crematorium where it would've been duly cremated. He hadn't worked out yet how they were able to bypass the crematorium's intensive checks and cross-checks, but an inkling of an idea had surfaced from his subconsciousness, and given hint to a possibility.

'Look for a break in the footage,' he said.

'Sir?'

'Look for a break in the timeline, a gap of several minutes or so, maybe more, that's missing from any CCTV footage.'

'You think it's been tampered with, sir?'

What could he tell her? That it was a ridiculous longshot, a wild idea of his that had come to light out of the darkness? That he could be spinning everyone's wheels and wasting time and money? Instead, he said, 'Yes, Mhairi, but I can't say for sure.'

'I'm on it, sir.'

When he hung up, he turned, surprised to see Jessie close by.

'I got the gist of that,' she said. 'So what're you thinking?'

'I'm thinking that we're missing something. And what we're missing is footage of them doing something at the crematorium.'

'Like what? Stuffing a body into the cremator?'

'That wouldn't work. All the readings are digitally recorded at the head office. So an extra cremation would be picked up by someone at the head office.'

'You think so?' Jessie snorted. 'With today's deadheads? I wouldn't be so sure.'

He let out a sigh. 'I don't see how an extra cremation could be missed, even by deadheads.'

Jessie thought for a few seconds. 'They could give the body some other name, and register the cremation that way.'

'Then they'd need to have all the paperwork to make it . . .' He clawed the air with his fingers. '. . . *official*. Which would require the staff at the funeral home to be involved. A doctor to sign off on the death certificate. Maybe one or two at the crematorium, too.' He frowned. 'Which involves too many people. And if they did it that way, what would they do with the remains?'

'Spread them in the gardens of remembrance.'

Jessie's answer seemed simple enough, and her logic reasonable. But he felt they weren't on the right track. Of course, he could be so far off track himself, he was leading them into a different country. He let out a gasp of exasperation, then said, 'Let's see what Mhairi comes up with. If she finds nothing in the CCTV footage, then we'll need to dig deeper.'

'I heard about that Chika whatshername, that you let her go. I don't think Dainty was too happy. I saw him grilling Melton.'

Gilchrist clicked his key fob, and his car beeped at him. 'Depends on how you define the phrase *let her go*.' He took his seat behind the steering wheel, conscious of Jessie's eyes on him as she buckled in.

'Okay,' she said. 'What's your sneaky mind up to?'

'Oh, I don't know. This and that.'

'Not going to share it with me?'

He eased into traffic, and waited until he drew to a halt at a red light. 'I'm not sure what's going on,' he said. 'So, no, I don't want to share it with you. At the moment. Once I get some feedback from Mhairi.'

Jessie shuffled in her seat, as if making herself comfortable for the journey back to St Andrews. 'If I didn't know you better,' she said, 'I'd say you're thinking of waving that magic wand of yours again.'

'No,' he said. 'And hopefully never again.'

The traffic lights changed and he powered through a green light. He wasn't happy that Jessie knew about his relationship with Dick, how he carried out some work for him now and again, all illegal as hell, which was bound to catch up with him sooner or later if he continued with it. So, no, he'd made a point of getting through this one without Dick. However, he did have another number that might be worth calling. If big-ears, aka TK, was an inside informant, then it was more than likely that he'd sided with Arletta. Which in turn provided the converse argument that Arletta must have known about him.

But had she been in touch with TK?

Gilchrist would need to phone and ask her.

But how could he do that if her phone was dead?

Then he remembered trying to phone Arletta a year ago, only to get through to a dead connection – her SIM card had been removed – and learning later that she often removed it when she wanted no one to contact her. Maybe Natalie did the same.

Only one way to find out.

He would phone the number he had for her, and hope he got through this time.

But he would need to wait until he first dropped Jessie off at the Office.

There was only so much shit he could dump her into.

CHAPTER 31

Gilchrist had just exited the M8 onto the M80, heading north to St Andrews, when his mobile rang – ID Mhairi. He took the call through the car's speaker system.

'Yes, Mhairi. What've you found?'

'That mobile you gave us. Dolly McPartin's?'

'What about it?'

'Well, Jackie's been digging into it, and she's found that last week it made four calls in total to an unidentified number, all in the space of seven minutes. The number's no longer active, so we assume it's a burner.'

'You don't know who she was calling?'

'No, sir.' A pause, then, 'But right before and right after those four calls, she phoned another number, which we've confirmed was Jake Cassidy's.'

Gilchrist frowned, and glanced at Jessie, but she shook her head. Whatever Mhairi was trying to tell them, they just weren't connecting with it. 'So has Jackie been able to trace those four calls?' he tried.

'No, sir. It's definitely a burner. But she's triangulated where the calls were made, and confirmed they were made in the

Shawlands region of Glasgow on Monday night; actually early Tuesday morning, sir, the first one at 01:52, and the second at 01:59.'

'And?' he said, struggling to contain his frustration.

Mhairi seemed to have sensed that, too, for when she next spoke, her tone was less assured. 'It's just a thought, sir, but if McPartin said she hadn't spoken to Jake in two days, then I think she's lying, sir.'

'Why?'

'Well . . . the calls were made in Glasgow, sir, and Cassidy was murdered in Glasgow, and the timing's right, so I'm thinking that McPartin might have had something to do with his murder.'

Now Gilchrist thought he saw it, the significance of the location, Glasgow. And who better to call if you wanted to kill your boyfriend, or more specifically, a key member of an opposing organised crime gang – east against west? None other than Wee Freddy, or someone in his employ. What Mhairi was telling him made sense, but it still required a leap in logic to convince him she was right. Too many variables. Too many ifs or maybes. Just too many open-ended questions. If he ever wanted a long lead, well, there he had it.

'I hear what you're saying, Mhairi, but it's all a bit . . . how do I say it . . .? Open to interpretation.'

'I know, sir. I thought you might say that, sir. But in the debriefing, you said that McPartin was from the east coast. But we've looked into her background, sir, and she was born and raised in the south of Glasgow. No doubt about it, sir. She worked for the Royal Bank of Scotland in the Castlemilk branch for over twelve years. As best we can tell, she only moved to Edinburgh six months ago.'

Gilchrist whispered a curse at the memory of her east coast accent – *you ken this, you ken that?* You didn't pick that up in just six months. He remembered thinking at the time that she was laying it on thick. And if she was able to convince Jake of her east coast upbringing, then she would have been able to lead him up the garden path, so to speak, to his death.

But why would she do that? Was she part of Wee Freddy's organised crime gang? Did she have some grudge to hold against the Cassidys? Or against Jake Cassidy in particular? He had no answers, but knew someone who might be able to find them out.

'Okay,' he said at length. 'That's great work, Mhairi. Let me look into it and get back to you. In the meantime, have you had any luck with Clydevale's CCTV records?'

'Not yet, sir.'

'Get onto that as a matter of priority. I need to have something back by close of play today, no later than five. Got it?'

'On it, sir.'

The line died.

Jessie said, 'Jeez, Andy. That was a bit rough.'

He gripped the steering wheel tight, pursed his lips and kept his tongue in check. He hadn't intended to be so abrupt with Mhairi – she was one of his most loyal and hardworking team members – but he felt as if a noose were tightening around his throat. For a moment, he struggled to catch his breath, as an overwhelming sense that his investigation was opening up not just a can of worms, but an entire field of the bastards, doing what it could to squeeze his chest and threaten his peripheral vision.

'You all right, Andy?'

He gasped for air, struggled to find some words, then blurted, 'I'm fine.'

'You don't look it.'

'I'm fine. Okay? I'm fine.'

Jessie faced the side window for several seconds, then said, 'There's a Costa's just off the next exit. Fancy a coffee? I could do with having a pee, too.'

'Sure.' He checked his speed, caught sight of the imminent exit up ahead, checked his rear-view mirror, then eased in behind a car keeping to an almost debilitating thirty miles an hour. But several minutes later, he pulled into the retail park.

He followed Jessie's directions, listened to her chattering comments. 'Look at that queue. Twenty-four-hour McDonald's. I swear it's like that all day long. And don't you dare mention that gym. I've been meaning to sign up for ages. And you should see Robert. I mean, he's got shoulders out to here. And he doesn't do a minute's worth of exercise. Must be that job of his.'

Gilchrist found a parking space, and switched off the engine.

Jessie opened the door. 'It's not as cold as it looks. Fancy sitting outside? The usual? With a muffin?'

'What else?'

She smiled, shook her head, then entered the café.

Alone again, Gilchrist took the opportunity to make a call. He dialled the number big-ears TK had slipped him, half expecting to hear the disconnected tone. But to his surprise and relief, Natalie picked up on the second ring.

'You shouldn't call this number again,' she said.

'I need to speak to Arletta.'

'She's not here.'

'Can you get a message to her?'

'Maybe.'

A couple exited the coffee shop and walked past him without so much as a glance. Even so, he found himself walking away from the seated area, towards a row of parked cars. Then he turned and eyed the shop windows, cars to his back. No sign of Jessie inside, so she must have gone to the Ladies.

'TK's dead,' he said, at length.

The line remained silent for so long that he thought he'd lost the connection. Then a woman's voice, which he recognised as Arletta's, said, 'Who told you?'

'I've seen photographs.'

'Photographs can be faked.'

'These weren't fakes. It's TK.' A pause, then, 'I'm sorry.'

'You've recovered his body?'

'No.' He waited, mobile to his ear, hoping that his short answer might force her to tell him more. But when nothing was offered, he said, 'I need your help.'

'*My* help? How can I help when youse cannae help yourselves? Jesus Christ, you lot are fucking hopeless.'

'Which is why I need your help.'

The line filled with scuffling, as if the phone was changing hands, then Arletta said, 'Tell that short-arse, Dainty, that he'd better not fuck this one up. Because, if he does, we're all fucked.'

The reference to Dainty silenced Gilchrist, but only for a moment. 'I'm listening.'

'Taco. You got that? *Taco.*'

Then the line died, leaving Gilchrist to wonder if he'd heard her correctly.

CHAPTER 32

Jessie placed a steaming to-go cup on the table, and sat down. 'There you go,' she said. 'Fatty latte. Just the way you like it. And a blueberry muffin, too,' she added, splitting it with her fingers. She lifted a piece, and put it to her lips. 'How come you never put on any weight?' she said, then popped the muffin into her mouth.

Gilchrist sipped his coffee, loving the heat against the chill of the breeze. It might not be as cold as it looked, but it was still November, after all.

'Penny for your thoughts?' Jessie said, eyeing him over her coffee.

He placed his cup on the table, breathed in through his nose. 'If I said the word *taco* to you, what comes to mind?'

'Mexican food. Why?'

He jerked a smile, and nodded. 'That's what I thought.' He took another sip, then said, 'How about *Taco* for someone's nickname.'

'Is that a question?'

'Yeah.' He shrugged. 'Do you know anyone who goes by the name of Taco?'

Jessie frowned, shook her head. 'What've I missed? I've only had a pee and bought two coffees and a muffin.'

He hadn't wanted to pull Jessie into any of his dealings with Arletta, but he really was at a loss. 'I called Arletta again.'

'Thought that number was dead.'

'Was. But now it's not.'

'You spoke to her?'

He was surprised by her tone, as if she'd never expected to hear of Arletta again, let alone for him to have a chat with her.

'What did she say? Come on, I'm all ears.'

'Taco.' He held her gaze as he took another sip.

'Taco? Was that it?'

'As well as being told not to call her number again.'

'Jeez,' Jessie hissed. 'Taco, taco, taco. Maybe it's a place. A Mexican restaurant or something. Or one of those Asian-fusion places that serve everything.'

'Mexico's not in Asia.'

'Ah, right, there you go. I'm hopeless at geography.'

He took another sip, then added, 'She also said that if Dainty screws this one up, then we're all fucked, excuse my French.' He held her gaze, wondering if she would reach the same conclusion he had.

She frowned. '*This* one up? Is that what she said? *This* one?'

'Exactly.'

'So Dainty's screwed one up *before* this one?' She stared off over his shoulder for a moment, then said, 'Is she talking about TK being killed? Is that what Dainty screwed up?'

'I don't know. But maybe. Yeah.'

'Which means that Taco's the nickname of someone close to Freddy. Or at least who has close access to him.'

213

He nodded, not sure of Jessie's quantum leap in logic. 'The same as TK. So putting two and two together, I'd say Dainty knows who that person is.' He lifted his to-go cup and pushed to his feet. 'I'm in two minds whether to call him, or drive back into the city and confront him face-to-face.'

'Call him,' she said. 'Then you've not wasted a journey.'

He clicked his key fob and his car beeped at him. Jessie was right. But a face-to-face gave him the opportunity to gauge a reaction, whereas a phone call didn't. Unless you had one of those WhatsApp or Facetime thingies, which he'd never bothered with. Maybe it was time he upped his digital game. Yet again, at his age, maybe not.

In his car, he dialled Dainty's number and put it on speaker.

As usual, Dainty cut through all the platitudes. 'Andy. Make it quick. I'm going into a meeting.'

From the background noise of clumping feet and echoing chatter, Dainty was walking fast. The click of a door opening, dulled the tone, and Gilchrist said, 'Taco.'

'Say again?'

'Taco.' The background chatter silenced all of a sudden, and Gilchrist had an image of Dainty standing still, cupping his hand to his mobile. 'Who's Taco, Dainty?'

'Fucksake, Andy, who'd you hear that from?'

'Doesn't matter. Who is he?'

'He's a she. That's all I can tell you.' A heavy sigh, then, 'Fucksake, Andy, keep that one under your hat. If word gets out . . . Christ, we'll have more bodies than we know what to do with. I mean it, Andy. Not one fucking word.'

'How do I reach her?' Gilchrist said.

'You don't. End of.' A pause, then, 'You've spoken to Arletta, haven't you?'

'And she told me to tell you not to fuck this one up.'

That seemed to stump Dainty.

After a few seconds of silence, Gilchrist said, 'What does she mean by that?'

The connection died.

Jessie let out a long gasp. 'What the hell was that all about?' she said.

What could he tell her? That he hadn't a clue? That Dainty had access to Taco, but wouldn't share it with him, because of . . .? Because of what? What was Dainty holding back? He knew who Taco was. He knew how to contact her. But who was she? And how could she help? Arletta seemed to think she could. But she'd made it clear he was never to phone her again. It seemed he was going round in ever decreasing circles, getting nowhere. Any second now, he felt as if he could be sucked down the sinkhole.

He shook his head. 'I don't know what's going on. Dainty knows something we don't. And he's not willing to share it with us.'

'So how do we contact Taco?' Jessie said.

'That's the million-dollar question.' He reached for his mobile, pulled up the number on which he'd spoken to Arletta. If he wanted to argue semantics, texting wasn't phoning. He typed in a text message – **Dainty won't id taco. Need help** – pressed Send, then switched on the car's engine.

'Do you think that'll work?' Jessie said.

'You need to stop asking those million-dollar questions.'

He slipped into Drive, and pulled into the travel lane.

CHAPTER 33

North Street Office, St Andrews

At five o'clock on the dot, Mhairi knocked on Gilchrist's door.

'Do you have a minute, sir?'

He looked up from his computer, settled himself deeper into his chair. 'Sure.'

'Maybe best if we show you what we've got in Jackie's office?'

'Of course,' he said, and pushed to his feet. He followed Mhairi along the corridor into Jackie's office, where she looked up as he entered, her rust-coloured Afro wobbling as she struggled to make a space for him by her computer.

'That's all right, Jackie,' he said, and leaned down beside her. 'Right. Let's see what you've got.'

Her fingers rattled across the keyboard, and the screen split into four images. It took Gilchrist a few seconds to realise he was looking at the working rooms of a crematorium. The bottom left of each of the screens indicated the date – two days ago – diametrically opposite, on the top right, the time – just after 1.30 in the early hours of the morning.

'Is this Clydevale Crematorium?'

'It is, sir, yes.' Mhairi leaned forward, and tapped the time indicator on one of the screens. 'Watch this, sir.'

Gilchrist peered closer, his gaze hopping from one screen to the next, time indicators at the edge of his vision, all synchronised to the hundredth of a second. The CCTV cameras had infra-red LED lights around the edge of the lenses for night-time vision, which cast an otherworldly grey stillness over the scenes. Two screens he noted as being in the cremator room; one facing the cremator door, the other showing the door to the admin office and the locked storage room where, as had been explained to him, coffins were sometimes stored overnight on three layers of biers for cremation in the morning. Pipework suspended from the ceiling partially restricted the view, but the door itself was clear. A third camera captured the admin office, and the fourth an area on the outside, which looked like the rear of the building.

'What am I looking at?' he said.

'Keep watching, sir.'

He did, but nothing stirred. Not even the branches of a tree in the corner of the outside camera. Then the greyness lightened on one of the screens, not by much, hardly anything at all, but enough for his peripheral vision to pick it up.

'Wait,' he said. 'What did I miss?' He leaned closer. 'Did the time jump forward?'

'Yes, sir.' Mhairi nodded to Jackie, who clicked the mouse, and the screen froze, then wound back, frame by frame. 'There,' she said. 'Did you see it?'

He did. 'The time skipped . . . what . . . twenty minutes or so?'

'Eighteen minutes, thirty-one and forty-seven hundreds of a second to be precise, sir.' She tapped the time indicator on each

217

of the four screens, again all synchronised. 'Which means that the main CCTV recording unit was switched off for the duration. Then switched back on.'

'Wind it forward to the point where it starts recording again,' he said.

Jackie did, and there it was again, the faintest shifting of the shadows on one of the screens. 'If the recording unit is switched back on,' he reasoned, 'then it would record from that moment, and we would see the person who switched it on walking through the building. Wouldn't we? Where's the main recording unit housed?'

Mhairi tapped the corner of one of the screens. 'Here, sir. Behind that door. But the main unit must been on an automatic timer, because it doesn't pick up movement until later.'

'Or set by remote control?' he said.

'Yes, sir. That's possible.'

He stared at the screens again. 'One of the screens flickered. Something changed. The night seemed to lighten.' He shook his head. 'Or did I imagine it?'

'No, sir.' Mhairi tapped the screen that showed the inside of the admin office. A nod to Jackie, and the time backed up, then moved forward, jumping over the missing minutes to show a shifting of light through the closed blinds of one of the windows.

Then the light seemed to evaporate into the night.

'The change in darkness that you noticed, sir, is from headlights of a vehicle driving away. Show the earlier one, Jackie.'

Without a word, Jackie worked the mouse, and a window in the admin office showed a similar glimmer of light, which seemed to drift off in the opposite direction.

'That's them arriving, sir, driving round to the back of the crematorium. But we don't see them parking the van, or entering the building. The CCTV cameras are switched off at that moment, which tells us that they're most likely set on a remote timer.'

Gilchrist said nothing, as he watched the time indicators approach the moment where the CCTV footage skipped forward. 'They've got it down to a fine art,' he said. 'They drive into the car park at the front of the crematorium, just as the CCTV cameras switch off. But not before they're picked up passing the front window. Then on the way out, they're picked up passing the front window again.' He tapped the screen. 'What about other CCTV cameras that show the car park? That might help us ID the vehicle.'

'They don't show the entrance road, only the car park, so they're really ineffective.'

He paused for a moment. 'Didn't you say it was a van?'

'Yes, sir.'

'So you must've seen it.'

She smiled at that, as if impressed by his reasoning. 'Jackie managed to dig up some other footage from a nearby roundabout,' she said, with a nod to Jackie, who switched the screens like the expert she was. Another image appeared, of a white van manoeuvring its way through the roundabout, then accelerating into the night. Jackie clicked the mouse again, and another screen popped up of the front of the van, then zoomed into a close-up of an out-of-focus number plate.

'We couldn't get all the letters, sir, so we captured it as it cleared the roundabout.'

Another click to another screen, and that time the close-up of a more-in-focus number plate came into view.

'The number doesn't show up on any of DVLA's records, of course.'

'Of course not,' he said. 'The plates'll be fake.'

'But we pulled up DVLA records of a white van registered with Hadwin Funeral Services. Same make, same model, but different registration numbers.' She waited for Jackie to work her magic again, and he felt a smile shift the corners of his lips, as he watched one letter disappear from the number plate, while another letter, an E, became an F, and a number 4 became a 1. 'All done with the application of white tape, sir.'

Jackie clicked the mouse, and two images of the same plate but with different numbers, filled the screen. She looked up at him. 'It's . . . it's . . .'

'It's the same plate,' Gilchrist said. He pulled back from the screen, and stood upright. 'Well done, you two. That's really clever investigative work.'

Mhairi kept her gaze focused on the screen while a smile threatened to part her lips.

Jackie beamed, and Gilchrist put his hand on her shoulder and squeezed. 'If it wasn't so non-PC I'd give each of you a big hug. Well done indeed,' he said, and meant it.

'What would you like me to do, sir?'

His knee-jerk reaction was to instruct Mhairi to apply for a search warrant for Hadwin Funeral Services, and an arrest warrant for Grant Hadwin, maybe even Sam Fishel, too, then to gather a team and interview everyone associated with the business. But the logical part of his brain told him otherwise. What did the CCTV footage actually prove? That someone, or a number of people, drove to a crematorium at night at the same time as the CCTV recorder just happened to power off? No. They had much work to do before any warrants were applied for, and many questions to be answered.

What were they doing at the crematorium? Arletta's words about Wee Freddy and Grant Hadwin's arrangement came back to him – *He disposes of bodies through his funeral business.* Had he just witnessed the disposal of a body? But the cremator hadn't been turned on. That would show up on the records first thing in the morning. He looked at the computer again, his gaze settling on the screen that showed the door to the admin office, and off to the side, the closed door of the storage area, as the framework of some idea began to manifest from the depths of his mind. They hadn't witnessed the disposal of a body *per se.* Instead, had they just witnessed the delivery of a body to be hidden in the storage biers, all primed and set for cremation first thing in the morning?

But how would they do that without alerting the crematorium staff that something was amiss? Had they delivered a coffin, or only a body? It couldn't be a coffin, he felt certain of that, because that would show up on their records as unallocated, or some such thing. But what if the coffin and body were registered under a false name? How would anyone know? It would be logged in, and cremated, just like any other. But there were too many checks and counterchecks in the cremation process. That had been made clear to him.

But what convinced him it was not a coffin being delivered but a body, was the time. Not the time of the delivery after midnight, but the time it now took for a deceased person to be certified as dead, registered as having died, their body then removed to the funeral home to be prepared for burial or cremation; and the longest time of all? – the time it took to schedule a cremation, often more than a week, less than two. Too long to be of any practical use to an organised gang of murderous criminals who could not afford the luxury of time, but who needed to dispose of whoever they'd killed in a matter of days, if not hours.

He stared at the screen again. If his reasoning was correct, then they'd just witnessed a body being delivered. But whose body? He eyed the date on the screen. Four days ago. So it couldn't have been the body of Jake Cassidy. Was Cassidy's body still waiting to be disposed of? He seemed to have too many questions and not enough answers. He pulled his thoughts back to the present, and realised that Mhairi was still waiting for an answer.

'We can't make any arrests,' he said. 'Not at the moment. We need to play it a bit longer. Something was delivered to the crematorium that night, so find out who was working the crematory first thing the following morning. Did you notice any time discrepancy in any later footage?'

Jackie's hair wobbled. 'Nuh-huh.'

'This is the most recent?'

'Uh-huh.'

'So no suspicious activity at this crematorium since this event?' he said, nodding to the computer monitor.

'Nuh-huh.'

Then to Mhairi. 'Have you checked out any other crematoria?'

'No, sir. Only Clydevale. I thought that's what you wanted.'

'Yes, it is,' he said, which was all they could investigate at the moment. He couldn't overload his team by chasing shadows. Maybe other crematoria were being used by Hadwin's firm. But it was too soon to say, and too many manhours – time he didn't have – in which to dig deeper. No, they had to work with what they had, and what they knew, which was that Clydevale was being used by Hadwin Funeral Services to dispose of bodies.

But whose body had they disposed of?

And whose body was going to be next?

He thought he knew, but he couldn't ask anyone to run with him on a longshot. He would have to look into that himself. But if you thought about the statistics, the likelihood that Jake Cassidy's body might still be out there, waiting to be delivered, maybe it wasn't such a longshot after all.

Tonight, he thought, was as good a time as any to check out his theory.

CHAPTER 34

Irene surprised him by offering him a welcoming smile when he entered the lounge. She was sitting up in bed, pillows high against her back, an opened paperback by her side, the tenor tones of Andrea Bocelli quietly in the background, which lent an oddly romantic air to the setting. The thought that she had somehow miraculously recovered flashed into his mind for a nanosecond before evaporating in an instant. There would be no recovery, no inexplicable miracles to question the existence of God. Her inevitable end was imminent.

And they both knew that, only too well.

He leaned down to give her a peck, unable to separate the pervasive hospital smell that seemed to all-encompass her, from the sparkle of life in her eyes. Caring platitudes like *How are you feeling?* were little more than wasted words now.

'Can I get you anything?' he said.

She patted the bed. 'Sit with me a while.'

'Of course.' He flattened the duvet, eased his butt onto the edge of the bed, and took hold of her hand. It felt cold, her fingers hard and bony as nails.

'Tell me about your day,' she said.

'Oh, just the usual. Running about daft. Trying to organise this, sort out that. It's never-ending, is what it is.' He gave her a flicker of a smile. 'A policeman's lot, I suppose, is not a happy one. What can I say?'

She held his gaze, and thought he caught a glimmer of tears in her eyes. 'You always look out for me,' she said, and gave his hand a squeeze. But there was no strength in her grip. 'You always protect me. It's what I like about you. Your consideration of others. Especially those you care for.'

'If I didn't know you better, I'd say you were looking for a compliment in return,' he said, trying to make light of the moment, come up with some other light-hearted quip, but found his voice catching. All he could do was lift her hand and press it against his lips.

She returned his gaze in silence, and in that look he could read her thoughts, sense her pained anguish about a future in which she would not be involved, her worry for her daughter, Joanne, how she would cope, having first lost a brother to suicide, now a mother to cancer. And how could he help her? The answer was – he couldn't.

There was nothing he nor anyone else could do to steer past the unavoidable.

'You know what you could do for me?' she said.

'Anything.'

'I'd love to breathe in some fresh air.'

He glanced at the long sash window, heavy velvet curtains either side. On the far side of the street, the stone walls of the building opposite stood as dark as midwinter, no lights in sight. The faint glow from streetlights below hinted at warming the scene.

She shifted in bed, pulled herself free from his grip.

'Why don't I let some air in, then?' he said, and slid off the duvet.

At the window, he couldn't remember the last time it had been opened. Come to think of it, he had no memory of it ever being opened. But to his surprise, the latches slid aside as if recently oiled. Then two hands on the wooden frame, a firm heave-ho upwards, and the frame cracked open to let in an icy chill.

He glanced back at her. 'Is that okay?'

'Wider, please.'

'You sure?'

'Positive.'

He had to put some effort behind his next shove, to open the frame wider than it had been for years, maybe even ever. But he managed to raise it a couple of feet, and when he turned round, he had to stifle a gasp at Irene lowering her legs to the floor.

He rushed over to her, took hold of her arms. 'What're you doing?'

'Getting some fresh air, like I said.' She pulled an arm free, then reached up for his shoulder. 'Here. Help me up.'

'I don't think this is good for you,' he said, wrapping an arm around her.

'It really doesn't matter if it's good for me or not, now, does it?'

'Well, you've got me there.'

She chuckled at that, a dry rasp that sounded as if it came from empty lungs. He gave a grin of his own to let her know he found the funny side, too, although whatever there was to be amused at, he couldn't say. Catheters were not popular with bedridden women, but Irene had insisted that she be connected to one – so much easier emptying the bag every now and then, as opposed to struggling up and down to the bathroom several times a day. So the only tube he had to take care of was the one connected to the drip stand, which he moved along on its wheels as they shuffled the ten feet or so to the open window.

At the window, he steadied her while they stood still.

She put her arm around his waist and tilted her head to him. He held her in a firm but gentle grip, horrified by how frail she'd become. Her body could have been a skeleton with skin, although her face looked as it always had, bright and alive and full of the false promise of loving and living.

'You know something?' she said.

He hugged her in response.

'You never really appreciate the simple things in life until you no longer have them.' She took a deep breath, her body shivering from the effort. 'It's wonderful. Clean fresh air. Makes you want to go out for a walk and take it all in.'

For a fleeting moment, he thought she was asking him to escort her outside, but even if she had, he knew she could never make it down the stairs.

'I read somewhere once,' she said, 'about a man who suffered from depression his entire life. Until he was diagnosed with a terminal illness and given six months to live.' She sniffed, and another shiver seemed to travel the length of her. 'Only then, did he see the joy in living. It took him until he knew he was about to die, before he could appreciate life. What a sad way to have lived.'

He mumbled agreement, not sure what she was trying to tell him. That only now was she appreciating the most simple things in life? Like fresh air? Like being able to stand by an open window and look at the night outside? Like not being horizontal in bed for the first time in weeks? Or like standing upright, next to the man she loved?

He pressed his lips to the top of her head, and whispered, 'I know this sounds a silly question to ask. But how do you feel?'

She looked up at him, her eyes questioning.

He tried a smile. 'I mean, do you feel good enough for me to disconnect you from the tubes for a short while, and take you outside? We have a wheelchair, don't we?'

'Upstairs.'

'Okay, why don't you go back to bed, and I'll find the wheelchair. Once I've figured out how to set it up, I'll come and get you. Sound good?'

'Too good to be true?' she said, and offered him another smile.

Again, he was struck by her beauty, how even in the poorest of health her face and eyes seemed to belong to someone brimming with life. But as he helped her shuffle her way back to bed, he could tell from her struggle, the weight of her breathing, that the rest of her body was failing her.

He eased her onto the duvet cover, in a half-on half-off sitting position, and propped a pillow tight against her to prevent her from toppling over by accident.

'I don't think I like the idea of being pushed around in a wheelchair,' she said.

'Oh. Right. I suppose it was a silly idea after all,' he said.

'Why don't you find me something warm to wrap up in? Then once I'm all cosy, you can help me down the stairs, and we'll go for a stroll along the road to the Criterion.'

'For a cheeky glass of wine, or two?'

'That would be lovely.' She flashed another smile, but in that moment he could sense her discomfort, see how she was putting on a face for him, that she was only going along with his silly idea to please him.

'You don't look comfortable like that,' he said. 'Why don't you put your feet up?'

'Yes. Okay.' Her voice sounded breathless.

He lifted her legs together, and laid them gently on the bed. Then he adjusted her pillow, and said, 'How does that feel?'

'Much better.'

He held her hands, rubbed his fingers over hers, once again surprised by how cold she felt. 'Are you feeling cold?'

'Just a bit.'

'Let me close the window, then.'

It didn't take him long, less than a minute to pull the frame down, slide the latches over, and fiddle with the velvet curtains to hang them the way they had been. But by the time he turned around, Irene's eyes were closed, her frail body overcome by tiredness.

He made sure she was tucked in securely, her head and shoulders propped against the pillow, not too high, not too flat – but just so. Then he walked around the bed, took off his shoes, and shuffled onto the duvet and lay down beside her.

He took hold of her hand, gave a gentle squeeze.

But there was no response. She was sound asleep.

Within minutes, he joined her.

CHAPTER 35

10.30 p.m.
South Street, St Andrews

Gilchrist woke to the sensation of something moving on his lap. Other than under-the-counter lights in the kitchen, and shadowed light from a lamp in the hallway, the house was almost in total darkness. It took him a moment to recall where he was, then he felt it again. He flapped a hand at his leg, and realised it was his mobile in his pocket; the alarm set on vibrate mode so as not to waken Irene. He rolled to his side, and slipped from bed without a sound.

As he walked to the kitchen, he realised he'd forgotten to tell Jessie of his plans for that evening. He hoped he wasn't too late for her to accompany him. Not that her assistance was essential, but two heads were always better than one.

He tapped in her number, and studied the contents of the fridge while he waited for her to answer. He was about to end the call when she picked up. 'Whatever it is, I can't make it,' she said. 'I've spent the whole night on the toilet. Both ends, which is more information than I want to share.' She coughed at that moment, a choking sound that told him she was likely throwing up. Then her voice came back, pained and breathless. 'Sorry, Andy. Got to go. Nature's not calling. She's screaming.'

'Do you want me to drive you to the—'

But the line died.

He held onto his mobile. He should drive to her home, make sure she was okay. But a glance at the time warned him he was already cutting it fine. He sensed it was too short notice to get anyone else involved in his plan, and it was such a longshot anyway, that he could feel embarrassed asking someone else to come along with him.

Nothing for it, he thought, but to go it alone.

A quick wash and a change into heavier clothing, a final check on Irene and a fluffing of her pillow and a peck to her sweating forehead, and he was on his way.

On the way to his car, he dialled Mhairi's number.

She answered right away with, 'Yes, sir?'

'Sorry to phone so late,' he said, 'but you live not too far from Jessie, don't you?'

'I do, sir, yes. Five minutes.'

He told her of his call to Jessie, how he was not in any position to drive to her home – a white lie, he knew. But what could he do? Without his asking, Mhairi offered to take a late-night walk to her place and check her out.

He thanked her, then hung up.

Outside, the night chill had him tightening his woollen scarf and tugging up his collar. He clicked his key fob, slipped in behind the wheel, and fired the ignition. A flick into gear, a heavy foot on the pedal, and he accelerated into light traffic, faster than intended. But to hell with it. He was running later than planned, and it was a good hour and a half to Glasgow. At that time of night, he wouldn't expect to be held up by traffic, but you never could tell.

He zigzagged his way through town; right onto Bell Street, left onto St Mary's Place, right onto City Road, then left onto Pilmour Links. He braked hard for the mini-roundabout by the entrance to the Old Course Hotel, took the corner with an unhelpful squeal of rubber on asphalt, then settled down for the fast night-time drive south.

He waited until he was through the outskirts of Guardbridge before trying to contact Annie Melton, in the hope that she might be able to replace Jessie on that night's quest. But his call dumped him into voicemail, and he left a message asking her to give him a call if she picked it up before midnight. Any later than that, and he could be considered rude. After all, she wasn't a member of his team, but of another police division entirely, answering directly to Dainty, who was best kept in the dark until he had a better grip on his own thoughts.

By the time he arrived at Clydevale Crematorium – just before one in the morning – he hadn't heard back from Melton, so had no option but to proceed on his own. The place lay in darkness, no more than a black silhouette against a grey Glaswegian sky. He slowed down as he took a first run past the building on the main road, eyes peering into the grey shadows, searching for any signs of life within, the irony of which pulled a smile to his lips – it was a crematorium, after all. But he saw no lights in any of the windows, no signs of movement close by, no cars or vans abandoned in the car park, or parked suspiciously down the side.

Again, the worry that he really was scraping the bottom of the barrel for leads came into his mind, and almost had him shaking his head. This latest theory was so hypothetical it might be considered fantasy.

But, on the other hand, they'd found no record of Jake Cassidy's body having been cremated, and the missing CCTV footage uncovered by Mhairi and Jackie had been recorded before his murder. Which logic dictated – well, more correctly, logic *half-suggested* – that if Jake's body was to be cremated, it would need to be moved from wherever it was hidden to the crematorium under cover of darkness. And bodies being what they were, didn't remain in good shape for long, without giving off noticeable odours. So, Gilchrist had managed to convince himself that Cassidy's body would likely be delivered to Clydevale Crematorium in the small hours of a morning, and in particular, *that* morning.

Christ, when he thought about it, his rationale leaked like a bullet-ridden sieve. Why that morning? Why Clydevale? Why cremate the body at all? And just as importantly, why this time in the morning? Because that was the time noted on the earlier recording. Even so, there were so many holes in his logic that he felt thankful that Melton hadn't responded. And with that thought in mind, he performed a U-turn at the nearest junction, and did another drive-past the crematorium.

Same result. No lights. No cars. No vans. No movement.

He did another U-turn at a roundabout, then parked at the side of the road, some thirty yards from the entrance to the crematorium. He doused the lights. Overhead, a break in the clouds exposed a bright moon that was doing what it could to cast light over the scene. The crematorium building faded in and out of darkness, its dark silhouette rising like some night-time beast, only to vanish again into the shadows.

He lowered the car's window, and breathed in the night chill. The air in Glasgow felt a degree or so warmer than on the east coast, and more humid, too. He could almost taste the rain in the air. A gust of wind ruffled his hair, and brought with it the sound of night-time traffic in the distance. Behind him, in the mirror, some several miles distant, the lights of Glasgow emitted an orange glow into the sky, as if the whole city was on fire.

He found himself sinking into his seat as headlights rose from behind, brightening the road to his side, then darkening into tail lights as the vehicle drove past. It wasn't a van, so he didn't think it would turn into the crematorium. For a moment, he held his breath as its brake lights glowed red. But the moment passed, and the car drove on into darkness. Several more vehicles passed by, brake lights flashing as they neared the entrance. His heart skipped a beat when he caught sight of a larger vehicle in his rear-view mirror, and almost held his breath as it approached. But it turned out to be a Range Rover travelling so fast that his car wobbled in its passing.

He checked the time – coming up for 2 a.m. – and decided to give it until 2.30, having convinced himself that any later was too late, that any unusual activity in the small hours of a weekday morning could be deemed suspicious and draw unwanted attention to themselves. But the truth of the matter, if he was being honest, was that he had an hour and a half's drive home, which would allow him only a couple of hours of sleep before he had to commit to another long day. Besides, this theory of his was about as ridiculous as he'd ever come up with, and was beginning to piss him off.

At 2.18 he'd had enough. Time to call it a day, or more correctly, night. He was about to insert the key into the ignition, when his rear-view mirror reflected brightening light from an approaching vehicle. He eyed it in his mirror, trying to gauge its size – car or van? – then found himself sinking down into his seat again as it neared.

It seemed to be travelling slower than previous vehicles, as if the driver knew he was over the limit and was driving with care. Or was on the lookout for anything suspicious as he neared his destination, which, as it turned out, happened to be Clydevale Crematorium.

Gilchrist held his breath in stunned disbelief as the van's brake lights flickered – long enough for him to confirm it was a close match to the number plate on the van Jackie had captured on CCTV footage earlier – then held steady for a long moment before diminishing to tail lights only as it took a sharp right turn without any indicators flashing, and veered onto the crematorium's entrance road. He watched its lights probe the darkness as it eased through the curved travel lanes, until it took another sharp turn to work its way along the side of the building, where it sank out of view.

All of a sudden, Gilchrist realised the difficulties he faced. Here he was, in the small hours of a cold November morning, in the middle of nowhere, about to confront a vanload of gangsters in the process of transporting a body – almost certain to be a murder victim by the name of Jake Cassidy – to a crematorium for illegal cremation that day. And to make matters worse, they were more than likely armed all the way to their oxters, with no qualms about killing anyone, policeman or not, to avoid being arrested.

He cursed himself for his own stupidity. He'd persuaded himself so convincingly that his theory was nonsensical that he'd given no thought of what to do if, against all odds, it was proven correct. And now, here he was, alone, unarmed and wishing he'd had the courage of his convictions to at least have arranged for backup in the case of an emergency.

But as those thoughts flashed through his mind at the speed of light, he realised, too, that he was in an extraordinary position as a witness to a crime being committed. He had the place, the time, the purpose of the crime, means of transport, and method of disposal. All he had to do was secure irrefutable evidence – a photo of the van, or of the body being moved, or better still, a video of the criminal team in action. With that in hand, he could secure a warrant and shut the crematorium down first thing in the morning, then have a field day making arrests.

He opened the car door and stepped into the cold Glasgow night.

CHAPTER 36

Gilchrist soon found himself wondering about the wisdom of his actions, and for a moment thought of calling off and phoning for backup. But the missing recorded CCTV footage that Mhairi had shown him reminded him that the task of dumping the body in the crematorium building would be over and done within eighteen minutes or so, and by the time backup arrived from nearby Glasgow, the gangster crew would be long gone.

For the second time that night, he decided to go it alone.

Before he entered the grounds, he familiarised himself with the workings of his mobile phone, making sure he knew how to put it on video mode, but importantly, to do so without activating the flashlight. Maureen had once explained to him the quick way to video mode, and he swiped his thumb up the screen just as she'd shown him, then pressed the video icon. And there it was. He held it out in front of him, one eye on the screen, the other on the surroundings. Then he turned and took a quick sweep of the building and car park.

Satisfied that he now knew how to work it, he made his way into the crematorium grounds. He kept to the asphalt surfaces, working deeper into the car park until he reached the front of the building. He stopped for a moment, alert to any sounds. But the night lay as quiet and still as a cemetery. Not a sound. Not a breath of wind. Nothing but the hard beating of his own heart, the warm air from his lungs.

He crept along the front of the building, keeping low, conscious of the CCTV camera mounted high on the far corner. What if he was being watched at that moment by the gang inside? What if the CCTV recording was not on remote shutdown, but those eighteen or so skipped minutes had to be deleted from the control room itself? For all he knew they could be watching him, waiting for him. Then what?

He forced those thoughts away.

It was too late. He was already committed.

He reached the corner where the access road ran along the side of the building to the back entrance, paused for a moment, then tilted his head to the side and risked a quick look.

The van was there, headlights off, tail end hidden behind the building where the driver had reversed and backed it up to the rear door. His hearing picked up scuffling, leather on concrete – more than one person from the sounds of it. He thought he caught a voice or two, but couldn't be sure, and in his mind's eye he saw two men struggling with a body bag as they manoeuvred its dead weight into the building and along the narrow corridor. He waited until the sounds diminished, then slid around the corner and half-walked half-crouched his way to the van, mobile in his right hand, thumb poised to swipe the screen.

He reached the van, and crept around the front to the driver's side. For a moment, he thought of opening the door and removing the keys – that would put them in a right pickle. But the cabin light might come on, and the keys might not be in the ignition, and they likely had a spare set anyway. So all he would have done was alert them to his presence.

He discarded that thought, and edged along the side of the van.

Its back doors lay wide open, and the air held the faint tang of exhaust fumes. He slipped beyond the van, and saw that the rear door to the building was open, the kind that could normally only be opened from the inside, like an emergency door. So they must have had a key to open it from the outside, another clue that someone who worked in the building, one of the crematorium assistants, had to be involved. But if the crematorium was effectively run by Hadwin and his associates, the whole bloody lot of them had to be involved.

At the back door, he stopped and listened.

He could hear voices now, the deep tones of a man, angry, cursing in loud whispers, the higher pitched tones of a woman's voice retaliating. Something clattered to the concrete floor, followed by another deep curse. Perhaps all was not going as planned. A lock clicked, the noise sharp and metallic in the dark interior. Then more shuffling.

He thought of getting closer, entering the building, trying to video them from the end of the corridor. But that would really be chancing it. He still wasn't certain how many there were. Two for sure. Maybe a couple more, for all he could tell. His night-time vision had settled, and in the dim light from the moon he eyed the pipework that ran from the building into a filter unit the size of two double beds on top of each other, then doubled back to the exhaust unit, in effect the chimney. But in the homogenised architecture of dealing with the dead, no one would recognise it as a chimney, and once the noxious gases had been treated, there was no tell-tale smoke.

All of a sudden, the whispers loudened, the scuffling shifted. They were returning to the van. The job was done. No time to lose now. But if he moved back past the van, he might be seen. A quick glance to the side, and he knew what he had to do. If he hid behind the filter unit, he would have a clear view of everyone as they left the building. A clear view of the van, too, as it was leaving.

He stepped off the path, onto a grassed area, one hand brushing the side of the filter unit to keep himself steady as he made his way deeper into darkness, fearful of stumbling. If he bumped against anything in the shadows, he could give his position away. But he reached the far corner of the unit without mishap. The shadows lay in thicker darkness there, and he sank to his knees, held his mobile at face level above the rim of the filter unit, and swiped the screen with his thumb.

Just in time.

Two figures emerged from the building.

The smaller – a woman, he thought – walked to the back of the van, closed the left door first, then the right, turned the handle to secure the lock, then disappeared along the side, to the driver's door. The other, a hulking shadow, remained at the building's back door as if preparing to close it. He grumbled something, a curse maybe, or an urgent call to get a move on. Then another figure exited the building, followed by a fourth, both mid-height and stocky like bodybuilders, presumably the musclemen of the team. Someone grunted again, and the two shorter men walked briskly to the passenger door, leaving the hulking man to close the back door and secure the building.

Gilchrist held his breath as the man turned his way, then stopped for a moment, as if he'd caught sight of him. Then he gave a rattling cough that seemed to vibrate the very air, a sound so deep and fierce that he might have been trying to pull his socks off from the inside. Another cough, more productive that time, then a glob of phlegm spat so hard that Gilchrist could have sworn it ricocheted off the filter unit. A curse, another clearing of the throat, and the man stumbled in the dark along the side of the van.

Gilchrist let out his breath in a long sigh of relief, but kept his focus on his mobile as the van's engine burst into life, clouding the air behind it. He had to make sure he captured everything. Even if the lighting was poor, he felt confident that the IT experts could improve the quality sufficient enough to identify each of the crew. A mechanical clattering of gears as the driver engaged first, then the van eased away and edged its way round the corner of the building. He waited until the sounds of its engine diminished in the cold air before he dared to stand. He thought he heard a door slam, or the wheels mount a concrete kerb, he couldn't say, but when he could no longer hear anything, he pulled himself out from behind the filter unit, and by the light of his mobile phone sent the video he'd just recorded to Jessie.

A few seconds later his mobile lit up with the message *undelivered* next to his text. He tried to send the message again, and received the same *undelivered* message. He put it down to signal reception being poor that far out in the wilds, and slipped his mobile into his pocket, intent on trying to send it once he'd reached his car, or later when reception picked up. Then he made his way along the back of the building, around the side, his mind working through what he had to do first thing at the Office in the morning.

Despatch a uniformed team to the crematorium before any staff arrived, to secure the crime scene and detain all employees as and when they turned up. Plus a team of SOCOs to carry out a full forensic examination of the building, and recover the body of the deceased, whomever that person was – and if he was a betting man, he'd put money on it being Jake Cassidy. Have the IT guys print out high-quality images of each member of the van's team, then apply for arrest warrants, and another warrant to seize the van itself and perform another forensic examination. That would probably lead to more arrests, and would more than likely be sufficient to incriminate the likes of Hadwin and his associates, but importantly confirm the alleged link to Freddy. Hadwin *et al.* might think they were beyond the law, but Gilchrist's video evidence would surely put an end to their murderous association.

At the front of the building, no longer in the shadows, the night seemed brighter, the air fresher. He stepped onto the driveway, heading back to his car, dipping his hand into his pocket for his car keys. He thought he caught movement to his side, as his senses picked up the sound of boots scuffling through grass. He had time only to lift an arm in an attempt to protect his face as a hulking figure rushed at him from the shadows. Then the night flashed white as his mouth exploded, and his world tilted as the driveway rose up to smash against his face with a painful grunt.

His breath left him with a gasping groan as a boot thundered into his ribs.

Somebody cursed as his body jerked from another kick.

One more lurch, then all lay still and quiet.

CHAPTER 37

7.10 a.m., Friday

Jessie drove to the Office in her wee Fiat 500, the journey too short and the engine too weak for its small cabin to have heated up and cleared the condensation from the windscreen by the time she drove through the pend on North Street.

She shivered off the chill and wrapped her scarf twice around her neck as she walked across the car park and into the Office. Whatever had caused her to throw up last night had come and gone. Even by the time Mhairi turned up, she'd felt better. One of those mystery bugs that just breezes in, does its business, then leaves. She felt so much better, although she would have to agree that her stomach felt a tad tender. All that aside, Andy was supposed to collect her from home that morning, but he never showed. She'd called his number twice but got a dead phone, then reasoned that he must have forgotten to charge it – which wouldn't be a first, she had to admit. Still, she missed the luxury of being chauffeured to work in a car twice the size of her own, and ten times as comfortable.

In her office, she powered up her computer, and tried his mobile again.

Same result. Same dead phone.

'Shit, Andy, what're you playing at?' she whispered, then felt a sickening slump in her stomach at the sudden thought that something might have happened to Irene, and he'd switched off his phone while he took care of his personal affairs. 'Bloody hell, don't tell me,' she said, as she went in search of Mhairi and Jackie.

Jackie was already at her desk, printer churning out what looked like reams of reports. She barely looked up from the screen when Jessie entered.

'You heard from the boss this morning?' Jessie asked her.

Jackie shook her head, kept on typing. 'Nuh-huh.'

'Will you let me know as soon as you do?'

'Uh-huh.'

She tried Mhairi's office next. 'Any news from the boss this morning?'

'Not a thing.' Mhairi frowned. 'Didn't he have any appointments? Dentist? Doctor?'

'No. He would've told me. But that's not what's troubling me.' She took a seat next to Mhairi. 'His mobile's dead.'

'Dead, like . . .?'

'Battery removed. SIM card binned. Dead like that.'

'Let me try.' Mhairi produced her mobile as if by sleight of hand, tapped the screen a couple of times, then screwed up her face when she received a dead tone.

'Maybe something's happened to Irene,' Jessie tried.

Mhairi grimaced again, then shook her head. 'He'd let us know. Especially as we're in the middle of this investigation. And he'd be calling in every fifteen minutes for an update. You know what he's like.'

Jessie nodded her agreement. She liked to think she knew Andy well enough to be able to predict his moods on a daily basis, maybe even read his mind from time to time. But not phoning to let her know he wasn't able to pick her up that morning, and now being out of touch completely, was so out of character it was more than worrying, it was . . . Shit. She didn't know what it was like. It just wasn't like Andy.

Something had happened to him, she was sure of it. But what? And how to find out? That was the problem. She couldn't phone Irene for fear of upsetting her if she didn't know where he was. And she didn't want to contact his daughter, Maureen, for the same reason. Trying to contact Jack was a waste of time. It would likely still be several hours before Jack surfaced from his bed. They each had a right to know if something was wrong, of course, but until she knew what that something was, she thought it best to keep her concerns between the three of them only – Mhairi, Jackie and herself.

Mhairi interrupted her thoughts with, 'What're you thinking?'

'I'm thinking something's happened, and we'd better check it pronto.'

'Agreed.'

'Right. Let's talk to Jackie.'

Back in Jackie's office, Jessie said, 'Can you do us a favour, Jackie, and get onto the ANPR for the boss's car.'

Jackie stopped typing, looked first at Mhairi, then Jessie, eyes wide, mouth open in an unasked question. Then she said, 'Uh-oh.'

'Exactly. But let's not jump the gun,' Jessie pressed. 'I'm going to drive along South Street and check out the parking spots.

Maybe there's a simple explanation; his car's broken down or something.' Although that didn't explain the dead phone. 'Mhairi's going to make a couple of calls, see if any other Offices know where he's at, or if he's got any meetings set up.' She lowered her head and eyed Jackie. 'Until we have a better idea of what's going on, we keep this to ourselves. Okay?'

'Uh-huh,' Jackie said, while Mhairi nodded.

'Right,' Jessie said. 'I'll get back to you as soon as I hear anything. And you do the same.'

It took Jessie twenty-five minutes to drive through town, up and down North Street, along the one-way system of Market Street, up and down South Street, along Bell Street then doubling back through the West Port onto South Street again. She drove down Abbey Street and the length of Queen's Terrace, and even ventured up the Scores looking for Gilchrist's BMW, which was when her mobile beeped – ID Mhairi.

She took the call as she turned into South Castle Street. 'Anything?'

'Jackie's located Andy's car on the ANPR, last sighting on Springburn Road just after midnight last night.'

'Which direction was he heading?'

'North.'

Jessie had been born and raised in Glasgow, spent her early years in the Force with Strathclyde Police based in central Glasgow, so knew the main streets well enough to have an image in her mind of where Andy could be driving to. 'Shit,' she said. 'He's heading to Clydevale Crematorium.' Then a thought hit her. 'You said that's the last sighting?'

'Jackie's still working on it, but that's as far as she's got.'

Jessie went with her gut instinct, and to hell with the consequences if she was wrong. And dammit, she couldn't be wrong. 'Have her search for CCTV footage around Clydevale Crematorium. Check out local businesses in the vicinity. They'll have CCTV cameras in the hundreds. And get onto the Crematorium's CCTV system. There's got to be a recording of him somewhere.'

'Jeez-oh, Jessie, you think he's in trouble?'

Mhairi's question stopped her, but only for a second. 'I think he's in deadly trouble. And we need to pull out all the stops on this. Get onto the CCTV control centre in Glenrothes and tell them what's happened. We need their help to access all CCTV footage in the vicinity as a matter of urgency. I'll be back in the Office in a few. I'll have a word with Smiler and bring her up to speed.'

'I'm on it,' Mhairi said, and ended the call.

Jessie pulled to a halt in the middle of the road. She needed to make one more call, and had to search her Contacts to do so. When she found the number, she placed the call, and shifted into gear again, mobile hard to her ear.

'Yeah?'

Jessie always thought Dainty sounded larger on the phone than in real life. 'Jessie here,' she said, as a curt introduction. 'We need your help.'

Give Dainty his due. He was sharper than a tack, and knew from the tone of her voice and the fact she'd phoned him directly, that all was not well. 'What's up?'

'Andy's missing. The last sighting we have is his car on Springburn Road, heading in the direction of Clydevale Crematorium.'

'Fucksake,' Dainty hissed. 'Did he tell anyone what he was planning?'

'Not as far as we know. But I'm pretty sure that's where he went.'

'Fucksake,' he hissed again. 'I told him to be careful around this lot. They're fucking nutters, the lot of them.'

'Dainty,' Jessie said, struggling to keep her tone level. 'Do you think they'd . . .?' She stopped, unable to say the words, voice choked in her throat.

'We don't think at all,' Dainty said. 'We take action. Keep this number free. I'll get back to you.' And with that, the line died, leaving Jessie to wipe tears from her eyes.

CHAPTER 38

Jessie rapped the office door with more force than intended.

'Enter,' Smiler said, her tone more even than Jessie's announcement deserved.

Jessie pushed the door open to Chief Superintendent Diane Smiley's office. She was immediately struck by the cleanliness of the room, and an aromatic fragrance that choked her senses and seemed thick enough to taste. She caught the culprits – a pair of scented candles burning on the window sill – their flames flickering warmly inside frosted glass holders. A Persian rug that had to cost a couple of thousand, maybe more, hosted two wooden chairs in front of her desk, polish glistening, and positioned to within an inch of perfect symmetry.

Jessie had only ever confronted Smiler in her office with Andy by her side, and as she walked towards the seated figure – dyed blonde hair coiffed to perfection, laundered uniform, and white shirt that looked as if it had been removed from its wrapping that morning – all of a sudden she felt out of her depth, as if she had no right to be there. She noticed an overspill of reports and folders stacked ten deep, maybe twenty, on the floor at the side of her desk – a touch haphazard, she had to say. So maybe Smiler wasn't such a neat freak after all.

Smiler's lips moved in a tight imitation of a welcoming grin, arm out to offer Jessie one of the chairs in front of her desk.

'I'd rather stand, ma'am,' Jessie said, surprised by the strength in her voice, a sharp tone that could have come from someone else. 'I won't take up much of your time, ma'am, because we don't have much time, I'm afraid. In fact no time at all.'

A row of furrows ploughed across Smiler's otherwise smooth forehead. 'DS Janes?'

'I'm sorry, ma'am, it's Andy, DCI Gilchrist I mean, he's missing.' She could have cursed at herself at the way she blurted it out. But dammit, they really didn't have time, and she needed Smiler to pull out every single stop she could. And then some.

'Missing?' Smiler said, as if her mind was struggling to comprehend the word.

'We can't reach him, ma'am. He's not answering his mobile. In fact, his mobile's dead. We have a sighting of him on the ANPR heading in the general direction of Clydevale Crematorium in Glasgow, which as you know is currently at the centre of our investigation.' She wasn't sure how up to date Andy had kept Smiler – probably on the outskirts, knowing him – and hoped she hadn't put her foot into some overfilled budgetary pie.

'CCTV?' Smiler demanded.

'Jackie and Mhairi have managed to track him through ANPR, and are now phoning local businesses to secure additional CCTV footage, which we'll send uniforms to bring in. I've also been in contact with the control centre at Glenrothes HQ, ma'am. And been in touch with Strathclyde Police for their assistance.'

'Have you now?'

Jessie didn't care for Smiler's tone, nor the inference that she might have overstepped her authority. But she struggled to keep her emotions in check, her tone level, and said, 'I'm sorry, ma'am, but I hate to say that DCI Gilchrist's life could be in grave danger. We need all the help we can get. And we need it *now*.'

Smiler reclined in her chair, as if to seek respite from Jessie's verbal onslaught, then said, 'Who did you speak to in Strathclyde?'

'DCI Small, ma'am.'

'Major Crimes Unit?'

'Yes, ma'am.'

'Let me give his boss a call. Make sure she fully understands the seriousness of the situation.' She pulled herself forward and reached for her phone. 'Keep me up to speed on this, Jessie. You need anything else, let me know.'

'Yes, ma'am.'

Smiler lifted the phone, and was about to dial when she looked at Jessie and gave her a flicker of smile. 'Well done.' Which was effectively Jessie's cue to leave the room.

Back in Jackie's office, Jessie said, 'Anything?'

Jackie nodded, and tapped her monitor.

Jessie leaned forward, almost shoved her out of the way. 'Sorry, Jackie,' she said, and eased back a tad. 'Let's see what you've got.'

But Jackie seemed unperturbed, as if she were used to being pushed aside. A click of the mouse, and there was Gilchrist's BMW. It took Jessie a moment to collect her thoughts, and say, 'That's at the roundabout near Clydevale, isn't it?'

'Uh-huh.'

'And nothing after that?'

'Nuh-huh.'

'You sure?'

'Uh-huh.'

'So that suggests he's driven to Clydevale Crematorium. And if so, he might still be there.'

'Nuh-uh.'

'What d'you mean?'

Another click of the mouse, and an image of a white van working its way into and through a car park came up on the screen.

'Where's this?'

'Cly . . . Cly . . .'

'Clydevale Crematorium?'

'Uh-huh.'

'And is that the same white van as before?'

Jackie held out her hand and wobbled it.

'Yes and no?' Jessie said, then added, 'Same van as before, but different registration number plate? Is that it?'

'Uh-huh.'

Mhairi entered the office at that moment, her face tight, her look grim. 'Dainty's just off the phone,' she said. 'They've found Andy's car.'

Jessie's breath caught in her chest as she tried to read into Mhairi's words, and forced herself not to think the worst. She wanted to ask if the car was occupied, and if not, had they checked the boot? But her lips refused to move, until she blurted, 'Where?'

'Blair's Scrap Merchants, on the north side of Glasgow, about two or three miles from Clydevale Crematorium.'

'And . . .?'

'The car's abandoned. No signs of Andy.'

A surge of relief as strong as a blast of wind almost rocked her off her feet, then vanished in the aftershock. No body didn't mean Andy was still alive. In fact, it could mean much worse. 'Have they checked inside the crematorium?'

'Dainty says they're doing that right now.'

'And . . .?' she asked again, struggling to contain her frustration.

'Too early to say.'

Jessie could tell from the look on Mhairi's face that, just like her, she was expecting the worst. But what had happened? Why had he gone there? Had he been following someone, then been overpowered? Would they find his body in the crematorium, lying inside a coffin, ready for cremation that morning? Was that why they'd abandoned his car remote from the crematorium? To throw the police off the trail? Without ANPR, no one would have been able to connect him to the crematorium, especially if his car had been abandoned miles away. Or did she have it all wrong? Had he not been at the crematorium at all? Had she given Dainty incorrect information? Were they wasting time chasing shadows, when all the time Andy was somewhere else?

She took a deep breath to steady herself. She felt as if her mind was spinning out of control. Too many questions. But she couldn't just sit there, guessing. She had to drive down to Glasgow and be at the heart of the investigation, and be there when they found Andy. She didn't want to add the morbid thought – dead or alive – but she knew what they were all now expecting to find.

Andy had gone down to Clydevale Crematorium on his own, on a hunch, without telling anyone of his plan, if he did indeed have a plan. CCTV footage of his car heading there, nowhere near Blair's Scrap Merchants, told her that he was more than likely trailing someone to the crematorium, or at least investigating suspicious activity in or around the area. But now his car had been found abandoned, it told her, too, that they really shouldn't expect to recover anything other than his dead body.

'Blair's Scrap Merchants?' she said to Mhairi.

'Yes.'

'So how about this? Andy drove down to Clydevale Crematorium last night to check something out. We don't know what yet. Maybe he was following someone. Maybe he was going down there on a hunch. We don't know. What we do know is that his car was located what . . .? About a mile from the crematorium?'

Jackie said, 'Two . . . two . . .'

'Two miles,' Jessie said. 'But CCTV footage is pretty conclusive that Clydevale was his original destination.' She tightened her lips, not sure if her logic was correct. But she had to get it off her chest. 'His car was abandoned at Blair's Scrap Merchants, miles away, which tells us what?' She looked at Mhairi, then Jackie, and realised that neither of them wanted to suggest the obvious, which was that Andy had been killed at the crematorium, and his body stuffed into a coffin ready for cremation first thing that morning.

Then Mhairi said, 'He's dead, isn't he?'

Jessie didn't want to say she agreed with her, that Dainty and his team would phone them within the hour and tell them the dreaded news. So she forced herself to stay positive. 'We don't know that yet. And until we do, God forbid, we work on the assumption that he's alive.'

Mhairi hung her head, her lips tight, trying to suppress tears welling.

Jackie sniffed, ran a hand under her nose, then stared at her computer monitor, her fingers stilled for the first time that morning.

'I need to get down there,' Jessie said. 'Offer my help.' Although what help she could give was beyond her.

'I'll drive,' Mhairi said.

And with that, she strode from the office, Jessie almost jogging after her.

CHAPTER 39

By 9 a.m., Clydevale Crematorium was closed for business, and the building and car park cordoned off. Two uniformed officers guarded the entrance, with strict instructions not to let anyone through, other than police personnel – no rubberneckers, no nosey-parkers, and especially no media.

One SOCO van was parked at the front of the admin building, another was parked around the side. Scenes of Crime Officers, fully kitted out in forensic coveralls, gloves and bootees, were already hard at it, laying out metal plates, dusting windows, doors and handles for fingerprints, meticulously photographing everything for the record.

Dainty and Melton had already reconnoitred the building and checked it was securely locked – which it was – then searched the surrounding grounds for signs of criminal activity. Other than disturbed shrubbery to the left of the main door, likely caused by an animal – fox or deer – foraging for food, they found nothing of concern.

Dainty and Melton slipped on latex gloves, then entered the admin office. Everything seemed to be in order, nothing disturbed.

Cabinets, desks, filing trays, all as they should be. A quick look into one of the drawers revealed nothing out of the ordinary. He closed it, opened another – much of the same. Together he and Melton walked into the back rooms where bare walls and runs of pipework and cable trays and metal cupboards added a semi-industrial theme to the place.

Dainty's mobile rang. He answered with a curt, 'Yeah?'

'I have Lisa Sumpter here, sir. She says she's an employee, and a keyholder.'

'Send her in. We could do with someone telling us what's going on.' He hung up, then glared at the closed doors of the cremator with a suspicion bordering on hatred. 'Feel the heat from that?' he said to Melton.

'You think it's been on this morning?' she said.

'We're about to find out.' He turned as the door opened, and a young woman entered, dressed in black, face pale and drawn from the shock of finding her place of work heaving with police activity.

'You Lisa?' Dainty said.

'I am, yes. What's happened?'

'We'll get to that,' he said, and nodded to the cremator. 'You know how this thing works?'

'Yes.'

'Has it been on this morning?'

'No.'

'You sure?' He turned to face the cremator. 'It feels like it.' Then he removed a pair of latex gloves from his pocket and handed them to her. 'Put these on,' he said, 'and open it.'

Lisa did as instructed, then stepped up to a control panel on the wall, and with shaking hands lifted the screen and pressed a button. A red light changed to green, and a heavy mechanical sound emanated from deep within the workings.

Dainty, who had been standing next to the cremator door, took a step back with a hissed, 'Fucksake,' as the door slid upwards. He peered into the interior, shielding his face from a surge of heat that threatened to force him backwards. 'Is it usually this hot?'

'Yes,' Lisa said. 'That's from yesterday.'

'How do I know this hasn't been on this morning?' Dainty said, puzzled by the strength of the latent heat.

'If it had, you wouldn't be standing there,' she quipped, seemingly over her shock of moments earlier.

With the door wide open, the interior seemed to be nothing more than dark brickwork, with vents spaced evenly along both sides and the ceiling. The floor was a grey metal-looking surface covered with a sparse dusting of residual ashes, with a rectangular slot cut into it at the mouth of the cremator, neatly placed for the collection of ash remains.

Dainty noted a rectangular-shaped bucket beneath the slot. 'What's in that?' he asked.

'The remains of yesterday's cremation.' She pointed to a long-handled scraper by the side of the cremator. 'The ashes are pulled out using that.'

'So whose ashes are these?'

Lisa reached up for a card slotted to a board, which he hadn't noticed until then, and read off a name and age – a woman in her late nineties – and the date of her death.

'Let's see the ashes,' Dainty said.

Lisa bent forward, removed the bucket, then held it out to him.

'What are these lumpy bits? Bones?' he said, resisting the urge to rummage around the remains.

'Yes. It's mostly ash, but some bones don't disintegrate during the cremation process. They're brittle enough to crush with your fingers. But we use the cremulator.' She carried the bucket to another machine, which Dainty guessed was the cremulator, and positioned it inside with care.

She was about to switch it on, when he said, 'Hang on, hang on. How do we know that's the ashes from one body?'

'There aren't enough ashes for two.'

'How can you tell?'

'Experience.'

Dainty seemed lost for words for once, not even able to spit out a curse. Then he nodded with some reluctance, and stood back.

Lisa switched on the cremulator, then the air seemed to vibrate and a noise like a giant food mixer grinding hard biscuits filled the room. A couple of minutes later, she switched it off, removed the bucket, and let Dainty peer inside.

'Nothing but fine ash,' she said, then went about her business of emptying them via a large filter funnel into a circular cardboard container, all done with the utmost care, he would have to say. Ashes emptied, she put the lid on the container, placed the card with the name and age and date of death onto the lid, then walked into a side room, where she placed it on a shelf, among other similar containers.

Dainty followed her back into the main room, and watched in silence as she pressed a button and the cremator door closed. Once shut, the light changed back to red. He looked at Melton, who nodded to a set of metal doors to her left. 'What's in there?'

'That's where we store coffins, if we have to wait for a cremation to finish. If there are too many cremations in a day, they're
stored overnight, then cremated first thing in the morning.'

'Any in there just now?'

'Yes.'

'Open it,' Dainty ordered.

Lisa removed a key, and opened the door to reveal a set of
three roller shelves, like biers, wide enough to store two coffins
on each shelf.

Dainty stepped forward, and slapped a gloved hand onto one
of the coffins. 'There's four here. Is that normal?'

Lisa shrugged. 'Sometimes.'

Dainty grimaced. 'First thing in the morning, you said. Who's
here to help you carry them from here,' he turned to the cremator, 'to there?'

'Pat and Tam should be here by now.' She shrugged again. 'But
it's not difficult. We use the adjustable bier.'

Dainty frowned. 'Show me.' He tapped one of the coffins.
'This one.'

Lisa walked past him, and took hold of what looked like a
hospital gurney with metal rollers for a bed. She wheeled it over
to the storage area, pressed a button, and the bier rose until it
stopped, level with one of the shelves.

Dainty reached for the coffin he'd selected, gripped it, and
pulled. On well-oiled rollers, it slid out onto the adjustable bier
with no effort. He turned to Lisa. 'Open it.'

Lisa's eyes and mouth widened. 'We . . . we're . . . we can't do
that.'

'Why? Is it screwed shut?'

'No, it's . . . it's not . . . we never do that.'

'Are you suggesting we need a warrant to open this?'

'Well . . .' Lisa looked to one side, then the other, as if searching for someone to give her an answer. Then she said, 'I don't know.'

Dainty nodded to Melton, an unspoken instruction to open the coffin. Then he pushed in front of Lisa. 'Step back,' he said, and grabbed one of six lid fittings – three either side – and started to unscrew it. Melton did the same on the other side, and in a matter of minutes, the lid was ready to be removed.

He faced Melton on the other side of the coffin. 'Ready?' he said, and together they eased the coffin lid up, and slid it to the side, back onto the storage shelf.

Dainty looked inside, at the grey face of an elderly man, eyes weighed down with two coins – an old-fashioned belief to prevent the dead from looking for someone to accompany them to the grave – white shirt, black tie, black suit; as if he were the undertaker of his own funeral. Silent, Dainty shook his head, and together he and Melton replaced the lid and screwed it secure.

They slid the coffin back onto the storage bier, and pulled out another. It, too, was a simple wooden coffin, but with four brass screw fittings for the lid. Something in the way it slid onto the mobile bier warned Dainty that all was not as it seemed. It felt too . . . what did he want to say . . .? too *heavy*? But he kept his thoughts to himself as he and Melton worked in silence to undo the lid.

A nod to Melton, and they eased the lid up and over and onto the storage shelf.

Dainty knew from the tightening of Melton's face that they'd found what he'd dreaded finding. He closed his eyes for a second, and when he looked inside couldn't prevent a hissed curse escaping his lips. He stared at the body parts in stunned disbelief for what felt like minutes. Then his years of experience as a detective kicked in, and he turned his head and shouted, 'Get the fucking SOCOs in here. *Right now.*'

CHAPTER 40

Mhairi pulled to a halt at the entrance to the crematorium, and held out her warrant card to one of three uniformed officers controlling the entrance – a ruddy-cheeked woman who looked young enough to be in her early teens.

'St Andrews CID,' Mhairi said. 'We're looking for DCI Small.'

The officer stepped aside to allow Mhairi to drive through, and as she worked her way into the car park, Jessie said, 'I don't like the looks of this.'

She hadn't heard from Dainty – neither of them had – and had decided not to call him directly. If Dainty found something, he would let them know, she'd rationalised. On the other hand, Jessie began to see the failure in her logic. If Dainty *had* found something – meaning, if he'd found Andy's body – he wouldn't tell her over the phone. He'd wait until they arrived, then speak to her in private, tell her the dreadful news personally.

Mhairi pulled into a parking spot, and Jessie was out the door and jogging towards the admin building, pulling on her latex gloves, before Mhairi pulled the handbrake on. She burst into the office, and stopped, her breath stilled, her heart racing.

The door from the office into the back rooms stood ajar. Four coffins lay open on the tiled floor. The place thrummed with activity. She couldn't make sense of the scene at first – Dainty on his knees, holding what looked like a man's leg in both hands, passing it to one of the SOCOs at his side. On a plastic sheet behind him, two more SOCOs were adjusting body parts like some surreal jigsaw puzzle – two arms, a torso cut into three bloodied pieces of butchered meat, a foot and calf with the knee bone attached.

Just then, Dainty glanced up and saw her. He gave a tight grimace, shook his head, and pushed to his feet. 'It's a fucking mess, Jessie.' He shook his head again as he neared, held out his arm as if to guide her away. 'You don't need to see this. Nobody does.'

'Is it . . .?' Jessie tried, but her voice choked in her throat.

Dainty sniffed. 'It's not Andy. That's all I can tell you. Don't know where he is.' A quick glance behind, then, 'I'm sorry, Jessie, but I don't hold out much for his chances.' He faced her, lips pressed tight, white with anger, or something worse. 'Just when you think you've seen it all.' Another shake of the head. 'You couldn't fucking make it up.'

Still struggling to work it out, Jessie whispered, 'What's the . . .?'

'Best we can tell,' Dainty said, and nodded to the room behind him. 'The coffins are too small to put a whole body in beside the . . . the *occupant*, for want of a better word. So they cut it up and spread the parts about. In this case it's taken three coffins. Haven't come across the poor fucker's head yet, but we're think-ing it's Jake Cassidy.'

As if on cue, a voice from behind shouted, 'Sir?'

Dainty turned, just as one of the SOCOs held up a man's head. 'Found it by the feet, sir.'

For a moment, Jessie thought he was going to pass it to Dainty like some sacrificial offering. Then he said, 'Two shots to the temple. No exit wounds. So I'm thinking soft-nosed bullets to rattle around in the brain cavity. But the pathologist'll confirm.'

Dainty said, 'That's Jake Cassidy. Seen him looking better, right enough.' Then he looked at Jessie, then lowered his eyes as if ashamed of his joke.

The SOCO was about to pass the head over to one of his team, when Dainty said, 'Hang on. What's that? Let's have a looksee.' The SOCO held the head still while Dainty pried the teeth apart, peered inside the mouth, then shoved his fingers into it. It took him a few seconds to remove what Jessie thought was a blood-sodden postcard of sorts.

'What is it?' she asked.

Dainty held it out – a piece of hard card folded over two or three times, and creased tight. He took his time to unfold it, turned it over, then held it up to the light. 'Christsake,' he hissed. 'These are some sick bastards.' Defeated, he held it out to Jessie.

For a moment, Jessie struggled once again to make sense of what she was looking at; a colour photograph, creased into eight sections, but now pressed flat to show a close up of a bloodied amputated penis with testicles intact. Jessie felt her eyes being pulled to the adjacent room with its assorted body parts, and her gaze settling on the lower of the three pieces of torso – the stumps of both thighs with a bloodied centre where the penis should have been. She felt her stomach turn over at the memory of Dainty's words – *I don't hold out much for his chances.* An ice-cold shiver took hold of her as an image of Andy's dismembered body flashed into her mind, only to vanish as quickly as it appeared.

'You all right, Jessie?' Dainty said, retrieving the photograph.

Jessie felt it slip from her fingers. 'I'm fine.' She shook her head, turned and walked from the office. The air felt cold against the flush of her skin, and she caught sight of Mhairi talking to one of the SOCOs. Their eyes met, and in that fleeting moment Jessie was able to answer Mhairi's unspoken question with just a look – It's not Andy, but some other poor soul.

She walked, almost staggered, to a wire fence at the edge of the property, then turned to face the melee behind her. She stood still for a moment, and stepped back to rest against a strutted post. What the hell was she doing here? She'd never wanted to be a police officer in the first place. It hadn't been something she'd dreamed of as a child, but instead found herself applying to join the Force almost by accident, just to spite her mother. And now, here I am, she thought, in the bloody thick of it, trying to sort through the mess from a bunch of murdering psychopaths, and dreading to know what tomorrow will turn up, and praying to God it won't be Andy's mutilated and dismembered corpse.

Her mobile rang at that moment. She thought of just ignoring it, until she glanced at the screen and saw it was Smiler. She took the call.

'Yes, ma'am.'

'An update, DS Janes?'

The formal address had Jessie almost stiffening to attention. She took a deep breath to steady herself, and in as strong a voice as she could muster, said, 'We found a body, ma'am. But it's not Andy, I mean, it's not DCI Gilchrist, ma'am.'

The line swelled with digital silence for several seconds, before Smiler came back with, 'Thank God for small mercies,' then added, 'Have you been able to make an ID yet?'

'Yes, ma'am. Dainty . . . I mean . . . DCI Small of Strathclyde Police confirmed it was Jake Cassidy.'

The line hissed from a gasp of breath, or a whispered curse, she couldn't say. Then Smiler said, 'So it's started.'

Jessie wasn't sure what the *it* was, but thought it best to concur. 'Looks that way, ma'am.'

Smiler coughed, as if to recover her composure, then said, 'Chief Constable McVicar has instructed other regional offices to provide any and all assistance you need, DS Janes. So you have my full backing, too. I believe DCI Small is in charge?' she queried.

'He is, ma'am. Yes.'

'Is he there?'

'Yes, ma'am.'

'Put him on, will you?'

'One moment, ma'am.' Jessie walked back to the admin office, caught Dainty's eye, and signalled for him to take the call. She mouthed *Chief Superintendent Smiley*, but didn't think Dainty understood the lipread. When he reached her, she covered her mobile with her hand as she passed it to him. 'The boss,' she said, and Dainty nodded.

'DCI Small,' he boomed.

Jessie left him to it. In the back room beyond the door, the jigsaw body had taken shape. Jake Cassidy now lay on his back on the floor, like a stitched mannequin, staring blind-eyed at the ceiling. Seeing the body, more or less whole again, did little for her anguish, a heavy sense of foreboding that threatened to well to the surface in tears. Where was Andy? How could they find him? And even if they did, were they too late to save him?

Another glance at the body caused a whimper to escape her lips.

She pressed a hand to her mouth, and sought fresh air outside.

CHAPTER 41

'You are fucked. And I mean *truly* fucked. *Big* time fucked.'

The voice came at Gilchrist as if from a distance, Glaswegian-rough and hardman-deep. He blinked, tried to open his eyes, but his sight was hindered by something. At first he thought he'd been blindfolded, but it took him several seconds of blurred vision and shifting shadows to realise his sight was hindered by swollen eyes. As his senses recovered, other parts of his body stirred alive with aching complaint.

A sharp pain that throbbed in time with his heart could be a knife stabbing the top of his head. His chest felt constricted, as if it couldn't pull in enough air to fill both lungs. His tongue could be cardboard, thick and dry. He tried to run it over his lips, but tasted blood from cuts that felt hard and raw. He turned his head, and a searing pain flashed from his neck to his shoulder, and it took him some time to adjust his position so that the pain was almost bearable.

Where was he? He couldn't open his eyes wide enough, or turn his head to work it out. But he sensed he was in a basement of sorts. The room felt cold and sounded echoey. Shoes shuffling over concrete alerted him to movement by his side, and the warm breath of someone by his ear had him tensing his muscles in anticipation of another blow.

But none came. Instead, he heard a lock turning, a door opening and closing, then the steady clicking of hard shoes on dry concrete.

'How's he doing?' someone said, a man's voice that almost pulled up a name. He'd heard it before, that hard Glaswegian accent. He was sure of that. But for the life of him he couldn't connect it.

'He's coming to.' A pause, then, 'Want me to beat the fuck out of him again?'

'Naw, let's see what he has to say for himself.'

The man's face shimmered before him, zoomed in and out of focus, then steadied into a shape that resembled some surreal painting. He strained to focus, but his eyes failed to work the way they should. They didn't need to beat the fuck out of him again, he thought. The fuck was well and truly beaten out of him already. He tried to say something, clear his throat, but fire shot through his side. One or two ribs had to be broken. Maybe more. He attempted to adjust his position, and choked back a scream. *Christ.* Maybe all of them.

'Are youse awake?' said a voice by his ear.

Gilchrist thought it best to say nothing.

'Ah said . . . are youse *awake?*'

Something hard bit into his shoulder, and a scream locked in his throat.

'Good,' the man growled. 'Ah want youse to feel this. Ah want youse to feel every fucking bit of it, for aw the trouble youse've caused me.' Another squeeze to his shoulder, and Gilchrist passed out. At least, he thought he did, for the man was by his ear one instant, then at his feet the next.

'Here's what's gonnie happen,' another man said, the first voice, the hardman-deep voice that sounded like gravel turning in a concrete mixer. 'We're gonnie ask questions, and you're gonnie gae us answers. And you're gonnie gae us answers that are no fucking lies. Aw right?' Something jabbed his ribs, and fire like a Bunsen burner scorching his skin caused his peripheral vision to darken again.

'Leave him for a wee bit,' the voice by his feet said. The seconds seemed to turn into minutes – or maybe he'd passed out again – before the voice said, 'Who put youse onto us?'

Gilchrist wanted to say something, anything, just to avoid being tortured once more, but his lips seemed stuck together. He managed to whisper, 'Water.'

'Whit's that?'

'Water.'

'Oh I'll gae you water aw right.' And in the next second, a hosepipe appeared in the man's hands as if by magic, and fingers were by his mouth, prising his teeth apart, and the hard edge of a nozzle battered its way to the back of his throat, deep enough to have him gagging. His throat felt as if it exploded from the pressure of water being jetted into it. He coughed, choked, spluttered, his body's natural reaction to the onslaught. Arrowheads of pain fired through every nerve ending in his system. Even when the hose was removed, the fire still burned, and he continued to cough and splutter up bile and vomit that spewed from his mouth like froth, but did nothing to douse the pain. His vision darkened again, and he almost thanked a God he didn't believe in for giving respite from the pain through unconsciousness.

But it was not to be.

His vision recovered from the warmth of the man's breath by his ear again. 'Now that you're well and truly watered, we're gonnie try this again. Aw right?' A pause, then, 'So . . . *who* . . . put youse onto us?'

Gilchrist whispered, 'Elgin,' which seemed to be the only word he could say that wouldn't involve movement of any body parts.

'Whit's that?'

'Elgin,' he gasped. 'Mike . . . Mike . . . Elgin.'

'Youse're a lying bastard.'

Pain fired through his shoulder again, and his scream turned to a whimper as darkness swept in and swallowed him. He seemed to be floating in some ethereal world, with an eerie sense of being given an irreversible choice of death over life. He could hear distorted voices in the background, distant, unintelligible, swaying in and out of reach, the world around him humming with a comforting sensation of numbness. Was he dying? Was he already dead? He couldn't say. All he wanted was to remain in that state forever, let whatever was about to be, just happen. Living was beyond his control. Dying, too.

Then his world erupted, and pain shot through his being again.

He tried to say, 'No,' then forced his lips closed, gritted his teeth as tight as he could.

But he had no strength left in him, as fingers as hard as pliers squeezed his jaw, tore his mouth open, and the rough edge of the hosepipe was rammed to the back of his throat.

He gagged once, twice, then his world blacked out.

CHAPTER 42

Gilchrist came to with a painful groan. He lay still for a moment, struggling to recall where he was, why he felt in so much pain. His stomach spasmed, he coughed, turned his head to the side and spat out bubbles of bile and watery froth. He spluttered some more, and spittle dribbled from his lips. He tried to open his eyes, surprised to find his vision had marginally improved.

He felt hands working on his right arm, fiddling with his shirt. Not hard hands, but soft, like those of a . . .

'We don't have much time,' the woman said, as something stung his biceps. 'That should ease the pain,' she added. Then her hands were by his head, lifting it up. 'Can you move?'

He mumbled something, an incoherent sound that seemed to emanate from the depths of his throat. He coughed, tried to bring up whatever was choking the back of his throat, but spat out blood. Hands moved to his shoulder, and he winced from the pain, but it was nothing like before. Whatever she'd injected him with was definitely working, and fast. Maybe morphine, but he wasn't going to bet on it.

'You need to stand up,' she said, and he couldn't help but catch a sense of panic in her voice. She vanished for a moment, then he felt his legs being tugged, and his feet hit the floor with a force that almost had him toppling over. He reached out for support, found none, until his arm was thrown over a shoulder, and another arm wrapped around his waist, and tugged him to her.

'One step at a time,' she said.

The pain had definitely lessened, but the problem with pain-killing drugs was that they could make you woozy. He did as instructed, and stepped forward, but his leg could've been attached to someone else's body. His foot slapped the concrete. Then again.

But at least he was upright.

'That's it,' she encouraged. 'You'll feel dizzy for a few minutes, but walking'll sober you up. Come on.'

Another tug, and he found himself half-shuffling half-tripping his way towards a door. From the corner of his eye, he thought he saw someone on the floor – an overweight man on his back, his belly as rotund as a pregnant woman's. Blood pooled at the man's head. But he could have been mistaken.

'Keep going,' she said, as she eased the door shut behind them. 'This way.'

He was coming to, finding his sense of balance again, his sense of logic, too. Above them, he heard the sounds of hard footsteps on creaking floorboards, raised voices, swearing, angry, in that strong Glaswegian dialect. But he was too focused on walking – well, staggering – in the direction of another door that promised fresh air and an escape route.

'You're doing great,' she gasped. 'Keep going.' She reached for the door, turned the handle, and wintry air as cool and clean as any he'd ever breathed swept over him. He gulped it in, as if it were life's elixir.

She tugged him to the right, and he almost toppled. But she caught him, held him to her. 'You okay?'

'Just about,' he managed to say, and glanced at their surroundings, saw they were at the back of some mansion, its stone walls, two or three storeys high, rearing up to his side.

She removed her arm, and he felt himself wobble. But she held onto him, steadied him again. 'Needs to be in single file,' she said. 'Can you manage?'

He nodded.

'Follow me. And keep close to the wall. They won't see us from there.' She moved ahead of him, but took hold of his hand from behind her, as if to make sure he wouldn't lose his way. He stumbled after her, making sure he bumped against the wall, and didn't fall the other way, onto the grass. His legs felt heavy, and wouldn't quite obey the instructions from his brain. He tripped once, then again, but on both occasions she managed to support him.

Then they were at the corner of the building, facing the boot of a car, which opened as if by magic at the click of a key fob.

'Get in,' she said, and he half-clambered half-fell into the boot's dark interior.

It smelled new, and even in the darkness, he found himself trying to figure out what make of car it was. A Mercedes? A Bentley? A Jaguar? He didn't know. All he knew was that it was big, with a boot wide enough for him to lie on his back with his legs bent.

The car swayed like a boat on gentle waters as the woman took her seat behind the wheel. Then the engine fired alive, and he heard the click of the gears engaging, the thrum of the exhaust pipe as the car eased forward. He didn't know for certain where he was, but if he was a betting man, he'd put money on it being Freddy's house in Pollokshields. And in his mind's eye, he drove the journey with her, felt the car veer to the right as it cornered the front of the mansion, followed by a short burst of power before it turned left onto the downhill driveway where it drew to a halt at the main gate, engine purring with restless energy, as if it couldn't wait to be out of the place and accelerate along the open road. A man spoke – one of the bodyguards, Gilchrist guessed – voice hard, tone sharp. Then the woman's response, light and cheeky, which pulled a laugh from the man.

Gilchrist held his breath, fearful that they could somehow hear him.

The seconds ticked by, and he found himself struggling to keep calm in the confined space. He breathed out, breathed in, felt a tremor work its way from his legs to his hands. He needed to stretch his legs, and the pain in his chest seemed to be returning. He put his hand to his mouth to prevent himself from coughing, and realised he couldn't keep it back. He would have to cough. But he couldn't. That would give him away. He grabbed his throat with one hand, and squeezed. Then shoved the fingers of his other hand into his mouth and bit down on them, in a desperate bid to avoid coughing.

Another laugh from the man, deep and loud, followed by another quirky comment.

Christ's sake. What was taking so long? All of a sudden, he had an overwhelming urge just to open the boot and make a run for it. He had to get out of there. He just had to. And with that thought, the need to cough left him.

He removed his fingers from his mouth, and fumbled in the dark, searching for a lever or something that would open the boot. Then the thought that there might not be any release lever hit him, and a sense of panic threatened to overpower him. And as it did, he realised the seriousness of the situation he was in. He couldn't draw attention to himself. He had to wait it out, force himself to act rationally. It was the drugs. That's what was affecting him. Nothing more. They were affecting his brain, screwing with his sense of logic.

Then the engine revved, words were spoken, and the car eased forward and rolled to the left as it exited the driveway onto the main road. Gilchrist whispered a word of thanks, a prayer of sorts. But it came out as a quiet sob instead.

CHAPTER 43

The journey didn't last long, less than ten minutes as best Gilchrist could guess. In between stops and starts, he heard the sound of traffic, and tried to visualise where they were. But he had only a visitor's knowledge of the streets of Glasgow, and after a quick left turn, then a right, he was as good as completely lost.

When the car stopped, he heard feet rushing towards the boot, and had to scrunch his eyes shut from a sudden burst of sunlight.

'Holy shit,' Dainty said, then stepped back as two paramedics leaned into the boot and eased Gilchrist upright.

'Can you stand?' one of them said, a chubby woman with curly red hair and a green uniform – far too tight – who was already wrapping a blood pressure monitor band around his arm, while a muscled man with more hair on his face than head, said, 'Let's get you out of there.' Tattooed arms reached in, pulled him upright, then up and over the rim of the boot.

Gilchrist stood still, wobbled more like, then shook his head at a wheelchair being presented to him. 'I'll walk,' he said, and stumbled forward, one leg at a time, until he entered the back of the ambulance.

Despite his best efforts of resistance, the paramedics insisted he lie on his back on the gurney, while they took measure of his vital signs. The woman fussed around him, humming a tune, in between asking him how he felt, where he hurt, checking out his eyes – *follow the light, that's it, and look up, now to the left.*

He did all as instructed, and felt a sense of relief sweep through him when he heard Jessie say, 'You're not listening to me. I'm going to see him. So step back.' Then he heard her clamber aboard and there she was, looking down at him, trying to force her lips into a smile as her eyes ran up and down his body to take in his dishevelled state. 'Shit, Andy, you've gone and got blood all over your shirt.'

He almost laughed, but winced as a stab of pain stopped him.

'Don't tell me,' she said. 'It only hurts when you laugh?'

He tried a smile to let her know he got her joke, then said, 'Who . . .' then had to lick his lips. 'Who . . .' he tried again, '. . . was the woman?'

She turned to the female paramedic. 'I'll look after him for a few minutes.'

'I'm not finished the—'

'Don't piss me off,' she said. 'One minute,' she added, and held up two fingers. She waited until she and Gilchrist were alone. Then she crouched down beside him. 'She's Taco, otherwise known as the woman-whose-name-Dainty-won't-say. You should've seen Dainty. For a small man he truly is frightening when he's raging.' Jessie let out a hard laugh, then said, 'He'd organised an armed team from the Strathclyde's Tactical Firearms Unit, and had top-level clearance to storm Wee Freddy's property and rescue you. But Taco persuaded him to hold off. She told him straight. Wee Freddy would've killed you before they could reach you.'

Gilchrist found his gaze drifting to the open door of the ambulance, searching for Taco, the woman who really had saved his life. He thought he recognised her seated in the back of an unmarked police car, being interrogated by someone in plain clothes.

Jessie interrupted his thoughts with, 'She's a police constable who was fifteen months undercover in Freddy's gang, and put her life in danger. She can't stay in Glasgow any more. Too much info on what's what. She'll need to leave now. She knows that. So Dainty's agreed to have her transferred to some other division down south, where she won't be known.'

'But what about . . . about Freddy?' he said.

'Dainty had it all set up, and as soon as he knew you were safely out, he set the armed team loose. Took them by surprise. No one even knew you were missing. The raid was done and dusted in a few minutes. No one was killed, at least from our side, and last I heard, they had Wee Freddy in handcuffs in the back of an unmarked car screaming blue murder.' She showed some teeth. 'Serves the wee bastard right.'

Gilchrist pulled himself to his feet.

'Hold on, Andy, what're you doing?'

'I need . . . I need to talk to . . . to Taco.'

'Not a good idea. Dainty won't like that.'

But Gilchrist pushed her aside and shuffled from the ambulance.

Both paramedics were on him immediately, but he told them in no uncertain terms that he was going to talk to someone *first . . . then* he would return to the ambulance. 'And believe me, I'm better than I was fifteen minutes ago,' he said, pleased that his tongue was loosening up, and the pain diminishing. He caught

Dainty's eye while he was on the phone. Dainty killed the call, and strode towards him like a lion to its prey.

'What the fuck, Andy? You need to go to hospital.'

'I'd like to ask for your help.'

Dainty frowned. 'Sure. Anything.'

'I want to talk to Taco.'

Dainty looked away, puffed out some air, then came back with, 'Can I ask why?'

'I want to thank her.'

'Already done that.'

'But I haven't.' Gilchrist returned Dainty's stare, with a hard one of his own.

Dainty blinked first. 'Stay here. I'll see if I can free her up for you.'

Gilchrist watched Dainty march to the car in which Taco was being debriefed, in that big-man's stride of his, pull open the back door, and say something out of earshot. Then he turned, and signalled Gilchrist to join him.

Gilchrist concentrated on his stride, trying not to shuffle, but his left leg felt as if it had lost all of its muscle. He reached the car in a slap-footed manner, and Dainty stood back, an invite to slide into the back seat. But not before the detective seated next to Taco exited from the other side and closed the door.

'Just the two of you,' Dainty said to Gilchrist, who nodded, then half-slid half-flopped into the back seat. Taco watched him with a steady gaze, her blue eyes focused and alert. He struggled to find a sitting position that was anywhere near comfortable, and came to realise that he might have a fracture in his shoulder.

When he turned to face her, he said, 'I won't ask you your name.'

'Good. Because I wouldn't tell you.'

He held her steady gaze. 'You were there, weren't you?'

'Where?'

'Clydevale Crematorium. Last night. I watched you. You drove the van.'

She nodded in silent confirmation.

'You dropped the photographs off, too. In Glasgow.'

'Is that a question?'

'Why photos?' he said, not answering. 'Why not a thumb drive? I couldn't understand that.'

'Freddy's paranoid about computers and mobile phones. He's got them all tracked. Didn't trust any of us. Had them checked whenever we got back from a job. I couldn't keep any images on my mobile. So I had to transfer them and print them out, then delete the files.'

Gilchrist nodded. It made sense, in a roundabout way. 'Where's your mobile now?'

Her gaze shifted beyond Gilchrist's shoulder, then she said, 'With Dainty.'

'And it was Dainty who agreed to set you up as undercover in the Dilanos family,' he said, more statement than question. 'So he must've known about the funeral business and the connection to Grant Hadwin. Did he?'

'You'd have to ask him.'

Gilchrist paused for a moment, then said, 'Chika Nagano. You know her?'

'Heard the name. Worked in one of the crems.'

'We questioned her over Mike Elgin's murder. She denied being involved.'

'Of course she would.'

'You think she was involved in any way? Tasered him maybe?'

'I doubt it. She worked for Hadwin. Not Freddy.' She grimaced, wobbled her head, then said, 'But Freddy's got a long reach, so you never know.'

As inconclusive an answer as any. Maybe they would learn more when Wee Freddy's men were interrogated. 'What about Arletta?' he said. 'Did she know you were undercover?'

'Not at first. But when I overheard Freddy talking about taking over the business, and what that meant to her safety, I sent her a message.' She shook her head. 'There was a time when I really thought she was going to pull it off, you know, make the family legit. But others didn't want to go along with that plan, which they believed could see them . . .' she grimaced, gave a rue smile, '. . . being eliminated.'

'By Arletta?'

'Yeah.'

'So much for making it legit.'

'Arletta tried to assure everyone that the transition would be done methodically, over a period of time. But . . .' She shrugged. 'What can I say? Some of these guys are lunatics, and they didn't believe her.'

'So she disappeared before Freddy could take over by force.'

'She always was a smart one, that Arletta.'

'And TK? Did you know about him?'

'What about him?'

'That he was helping Arletta?'

Taco's face deadpanned at that. 'Not until it was too late.' Her gaze shifted over his shoulder for a moment, as if she were looking deep into her memory. Then she came back, with, 'That was the turning point, TK being killed. That's when I knew Freddy was on the move, that the business was changing, that it was only a matter of time. They didn't like women. Didn't trust them. So I had no choice, really.'

'So you decided to make a break for it?'

'Time to go. But I couldn't leave you to die.'

Gilchrist said nothing, just held her blue gaze for what felt like minutes. If not for this woman's bravery, her decision to risk her own life to save his, he would not be sitting where he was at that moment. All of a sudden, flashes of memory returned to him – voices shouting, fists pummelling, a man's face, bloated and sweating from the effort of kicking the fuck out of him, eyes wide and wild from the thrill of it. Then a body on the floor, stomach rotund like that of a pregnant woman's, and the nickname came to him – Slim Jim – one of Bully Reid's henchmen, recently released from Barlinnie, no doubt with direct instructions to take out that skinny wee runt of a detective from Fife Constabulary. The echo of Bully's demented reasoning resounded in his mind—

'Are you okay, sir?'

Gilchrist looked down at the hand on his arm, her fingers white and tight. Then he looked into her blue eyes again. 'Sorry,' he said. 'I just . . . I was just having a moment.'

'Want me to get someone for you, sir?'

'No. It's okay.' A pause, then, 'You killed him though, didn't you? Slim Jim.'

She nodded. 'He didn't need to do what he did.' She tightened her lips for a moment, and he could read the anguish in her face. 'It was only him and me in the basement. Freddy and the others were in some meeting upstairs, worried about the backlash from killing Jake Cassidy. I watched him beat you up for as long as I could take it, thinking that Dainty would send in an armed unit any moment. He contacted me, but I knew they wouldn't let you leave the place alive. I told him that. Which was when we hatched the plan to get you out.' She ran a hand under her nose, and shook her head. 'But I didn't think you could take much more. So I told Slim Jim we needed a break. When he turned his back on me, I shot him in the head.'

Gilchrist felt his breath leave him, not so much at her callous way of talking, but at the closeness of his own death. 'You didn't have much time, did you?'

She shook her head. 'No. As soon as he was dead, I gave you a morphine injection. And before you ask, I'm a fully trained medic. I wasn't sure if you were capable of standing, let alone walking. But you surprised me.'

'I think I surprised myself.'

She smiled at that, and the stress seemed to slide from her features. She reached for his hand, gave it a squeeze. 'What we achieved today,' she said, 'not just you and me, but all of us, will make a difference. We've taken out one of the biggest crime bosses in Glasgow for years. And a real nasty one at that. It pleases me on a number of levels. One, that you got out alive. And two, so did I.' She shook her head. 'I knew the net was closing, and I told Dainty we were going to have to bring the operation to an end. You being kidnapped put a timeline on it.' She paused for a moment, then said, 'So in one way, you saved my life.'

He held her sky-blue eyes for a long moment, puzzling over the tears that welled in them. He wanted to thank her again for saving *his* life, but knew she would say that she was only doing her job. Instead, he offered a silent smile and a nod, pleased to receive a smile in return, then he turned and slid from the car.

CHAPTER 44

Mhairi drove into the car park of Hadwin Funeral Services, pulled to a halt in front of the main door, and switched off the engine.

'Doesn't look like much of a place,' DI Melton said.

'Maybe that's the idea. Low profile. Low public interest. Just get on with the job of getting rid of bodies.'

Melton offered Mhairi a lop-sided grin, as she reached for the door handle.

'We should wait for the others,' Mhairi said. 'They're only a few minutes behind us.'

'I'm going to check the back. See who's here. That'll give them time to catch up.' And with that, Melton strode down the side of the building.

It didn't take her long to confirm that Grant Hadwin was in the office. His car – some make and model way above her paygrade – sat parked in its marked space, alloy wheels road-dust free. Tiny beads of water from recent rainfall dotted paintwork that sparkled showroom new. Two cars of lesser prestige – Mazda and Toyota – looked diminutive parked beside it.

Melton had her mobile phone to her ear, when she returned to the front. 'Where are you?' she asked, then slipped her phone into her pocket, and said to Mhairi, 'They're two minutes out. Let's go.'

Sam Fishel looked up in surprise when Melton walked in and threw a warrant onto the reception desk. 'That's a search warrant for this place,' she said. 'Where's Hadwin?'

Fishel reached for her phone, then changed her mind when Mhairi marched along the hallway. She jumped to her feet and chased after her. 'You can't just barge in here like this,' she complained.

Mhairi stopped mid-stride at Hadwin's office door, then turned to face her. 'Yes we can. And you're under arrest.' She nodded to Melton, who grabbed Fishel's left arm, clicked handcuffs onto her wrist, and in an authoritative voice started to read out her rights.

Mhairi turned, gripped the door handle, and burst into Hadwin's office.

It took her a nanosecond of confusion to comprehend the scene – Grant Hadwin, eyes wild, fingers fumbling with a key, hands ripping open a drawer – and another nanosecond of realisation to take action.

She threw herself across his desk, at the same time as she shouted, 'Don't,' as his right arm raised up, and the short barrel of a black gun swung her way. She bundled into him to the sound of gunfire – more pop than bang – and together they crashed into the back wall with a force that shook diplomas off walls and pulled a grunt from Hadwin's twisted mouth. On top of him, Mhairi had the physical advantage, although she knew she was no match, and something was burning her left arm, which seemed to have lost connection with her brain.

'You're under arrest,' she roared into his ear.

But Hadwin was not for giving up. He'd recovered from his shock of moments earlier, and through the movement of his eyes, Mhairi read his thoughts. She cursed as she struggled to shift her position, snap cuffs on him – any one of his hands would do for starters – but found herself being heaved off his body to the hiss through gritted teeth of, 'Piss off, you bitch.'

'Fuck you,' she said, and brought her elbow down on his face.

At close range a hit with an elbow can be more effective than a punch, an impact force strong enough to fracture bones or crack ribs. Mhairi's effort burst Hadwin's lips and loosened a few thousand pounds' worth of teeth.

Hadwin grunted, then spat out blood.

Another thud with her elbow didn't have the same effect as the first, and she felt as if she was losing the strength to do anything but hold on. She elbowed him again, but that time to no effect. She fumbled for her handcuffs with a burgeoning panic that warned her she was losing strength as well as losing the fight. And in the cramped space behind his wooden desk, she could only look on as Hadwin found leverage to shoulder her aside, and free up his arm. A cruel smile pained his bloodied face, and the barrel of a gun appeared from his side, and pressed against her head.

'Say bye-bye, bitch.'

Mhairi gasped, 'No, *don't*,' as the gun went off, the same instant a boot from Melton battered Hadwin's arm upwards. The bullet hit the ceiling with a quiet thud as the gun flew into the air and clattered against the wall. Melton stepped in again, this time aiming her boot at his face. But in the restricted space, all she achieved was another grunt from Hadwin, who had freed himself from Mhairi and was struggling to pull himself upright.

On his feet, Hadwin was much taller than Melton expected. More muscled, too. Blood dripped off his chin, and a red-toothed smile warned her that she had to act fast. Time seemed to grind to a halt as she reached for her pepper spray, freed the canister from its holder, then swung her arm towards Hadwin's face in a practised movement that took less than a second in total. She squeezed the button as Hadwin's clenched fist hit her arm with a force that sent it spinning wide, and the canister free from her grip.

Then Hadwin had her back pressed hard against the wall, hands around her throat, fingers tightening and squeezing, thumbs crushing her windpipe. Bloodied spittle splattered her face as he gasped, 'You fucking pair of bitches.' Which was all he could say before his face contorted in pain at the sound of another dull pop, and a cursed scream hissed from his mouth as he released his grip and turned away from her.

Melton pulled in air for all she was worth. For a frightening moment, her world tilted, the room darkened, then recovered as she took in the scene in front of her – Hadwin moaning, holding his leg, hobbling towards Mhairi who was lying still on the floor, face deathly white, Hadwin's gun in her right hand, which slipped from her grip as unconsciousness threatened to take hold of her. Melton stumbled forward as Hadwin bent down, reached for his gun, fingers fumbling, taking hold of it, then turning around—

With every ounce of her strength, Melton swung her arm at his head, which jerked to the side as the heavy paperweight she'd picked up from his desk crushed his ear, fractured his skull, and sent him to the floor where he landed with a word-less thud.

On automatic now, she kneeled beside him, clicked the cuffs on one wrist, jerked an arm behind his back with a force that should have had him screaming, did the same with the other arm, and locked both wrists together. She then reached for Mhairi, and choked back a sob at the sight of her jacket and blouse sodden with blood that oozed from a bullet wound in her upper biceps. From the amount of blood, she suspected that the bullet had gone through the brachial artery, and she had seen enough dead bodies in her career to know that without help, Mhairi could bleed out in two minutes or so. From the colour of Mhairi's face, she might already be too late.

She needed to stop the flow with a tourniquet, and fast. But what to use? She turned to Hadwin who was coming to, struggling to sit upright. She punched him in the face, flattened him again, then unbuckled his belt and ripped it from his trousers.

Back to Mhairi, where she wrapped Hadwin's belt around her arm above the wound, pulled both ends as tight as she could. Then thumb over the joint, belt wrapped around it once, twice, then into the buckle, pull tight, and that was as good as she could do. She pressed her hand to Mhairi's wound, and gasped a sigh of relief that the bleeding appeared to have stopped, at least for the time being.

She pulled herself to her feet, removed her mobile from her pocket to call for an ambulance. But Hadwin had managed to push himself upright again, and was shuffling on his backside in an effort to stand.

'Not so fast,' Melton said, and with one step forward gave him a hefty kick in the face with the toe of her boot, which sent him on his back again, unconscious.

'Ah seen that,' a woman's voice shouted. 'That's police brutality.'

290

Melton turned to face Sam Fishel, who stood in the doorway, hands cuffed behind her back. Melton walked up to her, and said, 'What's that?'

'That's police brutality, so it is.'

Melton took hold of Fishel's lapels with both hands and glared into her eyes, while the thought that Mhairi was lying on the floor seriously injured, perhaps fatally, flooded her mind; that she, too, had come close to being throttled to death; that this self-righteous bitch in front of her had no right to be morally smug. Without a word, she launched herself at Fishel with a headbutt that flattened her nose, and dropped her to the floor, unconscious.

'*That* . . .' she said, 'is police brutality.'

Then she stepped over her to make the call.

CHAPTER 45

At the sight of Chief Superintendent Smiley, Melton swallowed a lump in her throat as she walked up to her. It wasn't normal for chief superintendents to make themselves present at the scene of an arrest, and Melton suspected that her presence now spelled trouble for her – big time. Fishel had been carted off in the back of a marked police car, slurring like a drunk, and threatening to sue the police for assault against an innocent citizen. Melton now worried that the chief super was here to give her a talking to, or worse, suspend her.

'Ma'am?' she said to her.

'DI Melton.' Smiler's gaze danced all over her, noting the jacket and blouse covered in blood from dealing with Mhairi, and the bruise on her forehead from headbutting Fishel. 'DCI Small asked me to pay this place a visit.' She looked around her, as if seeing the funeral home for what it was for the first time. Then back to Melton, and another quick scan of her face. 'You look as if you've been through the wars.'

'There was a bit of resistance while making the arrest, ma'am.'

'Yes. I heard.'

Silent, Melton waited for the onslaught. She didn't know anything about CS Smiley, but knew that she wouldn't have reached that position without having had a spotless career. Melton worried that headbutting a handcuffed perp could be sufficient to end her career.

Smiler's mouth shifted to show a set of white teeth, but it couldn't be mistaken for a smile. 'Run it past me,' she said, 'how you made the arrests.'

'Yes, ma'am.' Melton tried to force some command into her tone. 'DC McBride and I arrived ahead of the others. On checking with them, I confirmed they were more than five minutes away, ma'am.' Not strictly true, but close enough.

'Why didn't you wait for them?'

'We believed time was of the essence—'

'Did you now?' Smiler snapped. 'Why did you believe that?'

'Because of the police raid on the Dilanos residence in Glasgow, ma'am. I received a call from Dainty ... I mean, DCI Small, ma'am ... stressing the urgency to make the arrests.' She hadn't wanted to mention Dainty's name, but she knew she was in so deep she needed all the support she could muster. 'We feared it was only a matter of time before word reached Hadwin and—'

'Feared?'

'Yes, ma'am. One phone call from one of the gang members in Glasgow was all it would take.' A tremor had begun to take over her legs, and she worried that it would work its way to her lips.

'Then what?'

Melton's mouth felt dry, and a lump in her throat was doing what it could to make itself known. She pursed her lips for a moment, then said, 'We entered the property, ma'am, and presented the receptionist, Samantha Fishel, with the search and arrest warrant.' This was the tricky bit, the part of her story that Mhairi could not corroborate. And with that thought, and the memory of Mhairi being gurneyed unconscious into the helicopter, she felt tears well in her eyes. Shit, and damn it.

'Do you need a moment, DI Melton?'

Christ, the formality of it all was getting to her. 'No, ma'am. I'm fine.' She sniffed, forced herself to stay focused. 'As I was saying, ma'am, once the warrant was presented, DC McBride left me to arrest Ms Fishel, while she went to arrest Mr Hadwin.' She paused for a moment. This was where it all went off-track. 'While attempting to arrest Ms Fishel, ma'am, I heard a gunshot. That's when everything kicked off.'

'Kicked off? In what way?'

Melton held Smiler's gaze, a hard look that showed no signs of friendship; a poker face that could put a statue to shame; and knew she was on her own. Time to retaliate, she thought. 'What do you mean, ma'am?'

'I thought the question was clear, DI Melton. How did two arrestees come to have bloodied faces, and one of my officers helicoptered to A & E, now fighting for her life? Is that clear enough for you?' Smiler stepped in closer, as if to check there was no alcohol on her breath. 'And be careful how you answer this, DI Melton. You understand?'

'Yes, ma'am.' She took a deep breath, then let it out slowly. She would have to tell the story closer to the bone than originally intended. 'At the sound of gunfire, I left Ms Fishel and went to assist DC McBride. On entering the office, I saw DC McBride on the floor, and Mr Hadwin with a gun pressed to the side of her head.'

'What?'

'Yes, ma'am. Mr Hadwin looked as if he was about to pull the trigger.' For the first time, Smiler's face gave a twitch of uncertainty, as if her assumptions about what happened were about to be thrown to the wind. Melton pressed her advantage. 'I ordered him to drop the gun, and when I noticed some hesitation in his manner, I stepped forward and managed to kick the gun from his hand. At which point he attacked me. I was quickly overpowered. Mr Hadwin had his hands around my throat, with clear intent to kill me. I almost blacked out, but DC McBride somehow found his gun and shot him, before passing out.'

Silent, Smiler nodded, and her gaze shifted over Melton's shoulder before returning. 'So that gunshot you said you heard. That must've been the shot that hit DC McBride.'

'Yes, ma'am.'

'So when you entered the office to find Hadwin with his gun to DC McBride's head, she'd already been shot.' Not a question. 'Did you see her gunshot wound? Did you notice any blood?'

'Not at that point in time, ma'am, no.'

'Mmhh.' Smiler grimaced for a short moment. 'Seeing your partner bleeding from a wound, then about to be shot in the head, would strengthen the need for you to take quick, decisive, and dare I say, *aggressive* action.' She nodded. 'Are you sure you didn't see any blood?'

Melton stared at Smiler, who held her gaze with an expectant look, eyes wide, head giving the tiniest of nods in anticipation. 'It all happened so fast, ma'am.'

'Yes?'

'But on reflection I do believe I did in fact notice DC McBride's gunshot wound bleeding . . . heavily.'

'Much better. Remember that when you provide your written statement. And the other person? Sam Fishel, you said? How did she manage to have her nose broken?'

'She came at me, ma'am, and in an effort to defend myself, I hit her on the face.'

'I thought she was handcuffed.'

Melton froze, caught head-on in a lie. 'I . . . eh . . . I—'

'Perhaps she resisted arrest and you had to forcefully restrain her . . . *before* you saved the life of DC McBride?'

Melton felt her Adam's apple bob like a cork in water. 'Perhaps, ma'am, yes.'

'Good.' She smiled for the first time, a genuine smile that reached her eyes and took years off her. Then she took hold of Melton's shoulder and gave it a motherly squeeze. 'You handled the situation exceptionally well, DI Melton. You put your own life in danger to save the life of one of our own, and all in the line of fire. That takes real courage.' She nodded, as if pleased with what she'd just said.

'Thank you, ma'am.' Melton paused for a couple of beats, then said, 'Do you have any word on how Mhairi is? I mean, DC McBride, ma'am?'

'She's stable. But not out of danger yet. That's the last I heard. I'll keep you informed as soon as I hear something.'

'Thank you, ma'am.' Melton wasn't sure if she should follow up with a question on Gilchrist's situation. She'd heard he'd been found alive, but badly beaten, and was stable in Glasgow Royal Infirmary. Instead, she kept it short. 'Is there anything else you need me to do, ma'am?'

'Get your written statement completed by close of play today.'

'Yes, ma'am.'

And with that, Smiler turned on her heels, and strode off, leaving Melton to wonder what in the hell just happened?

CHAPTER 46

Early evening, Friday
Glasgow Royal Infirmary

Gilchrist was surprised to see Maureen, and was taken aback when she handed him a pack of four miniature whiskies, and leaned down to give him a peck on the cheek.

'What's this for?' he said.

'How about – lovely to see you, Mo, and thanks so much for the present?'

'Sorry,' he said. 'I didn't expect anyone to visit. I'm only in for observation.'

'They're going to keep you overnight. That's what I heard.'

'No they're not.'

'I tried to tell them you wouldn't stay in bed, but they're adamant you can't drive. Not on the painkillers they've got you on anyway.' She frowned as her eyes took in the damage. 'You look pretty bad, although I'm assured it's mostly superficial. How do you feel?'

· 'If I felt half as bad as I look, I'd be happier.' He forced a smile to his lips, but his jaw was swollen, and he didn't think he pulled it off. He tried to hold her gaze, but his right eye was half shut, and he still couldn't find a comfortable position, even lying on his back. 'The good news is that nothing's broken,' he said.

Maureen gaped at him. 'Nothing's broken? Your collarbone's fractured, and your hip was dislocated.'

'That's what I said. Fractured, not broken. Dislocated, not broken.'

Maureen shook her head. 'Anyway, I've had a chat with Ty, and knowing how pig-headed you are, and that you'd refuse to be kept in bed, we've arranged to drive you home to St Andrews.'

'You have, have you?'

'It's either that, or you spend the night in this ward.' She shook her head. 'Which wouldn't be a bad idea.' She rummaged in her bag, pulled out a make-up mirror, and opened it. 'Here,' she said, holding it out for him. 'Have a look.'

He did.

'Still think you should go home?'

He almost agreed with her. Swollen eyes, bruised and cut cheeks, although he thought his hair being shaved in patches, where cuts had been sutured, made the damage look worse than it was. It had taken a total of twenty-two stitches – well, staples nowadays – in three locations to close all the wounds.

He adjusted the mirror, and eyed a bloodied V-shape above his left ear where a flap of skin had come loose from the beatings. A turn of his head and an adjustment of the mirror let him view a stapled bare-patched lump just behind the crown of his head, the first blow that had knocked him unconscious. X-rays confirmed a small fracture to the skull, but incredibly no bleeding of the brain, or concussion. *You're a lucky man*, the consultant had said to him. *Bones as hard as steel.* He almost smiled at the memory, as he handed the mirror back to Maureen.

'It's worse than it looks,' he said.

She closed her compact case and returned it to her bag. 'You think so?' she sneered. 'Wait until the painkillers wear off. I'm in two minds whether or not to take you home.' She clipped her bag shut, and sat with it pressed to her knees, lips pursed tight. For a disturbing moment, she reminded him of his late wife, Gail, Maureen's mother, settling into a dark mood for the evening.

But what could he tell her? He had to be back in St Andrews for the promise he'd made to Irene, and her daughter, Joanne. Just the three of them. No one else. And Sunday night was the deadline Irene had set for them. Even if he wanted to stay overnight, he wasn't sure he'd be in any fit state to drive to St Andrews in the morning. So maybe it wasn't such a bad idea for Mo to drive him home that night.

'How about I'll keep taking the pills until the stitches are removed? Does that work for you?'

'It's not me they have to work for, Dad. It's you.'

'Well in that case, I think we're good to go.' He flickered a smile at her. 'Can you help me up?'

Mo pressed her lips together for a long second, then shook her head. 'You know, Dad, at times you can be infuriating.'

'So that's a yes?'

'That's a yes. But I have to talk to Ty first. He's going to drive me back to Glasgow from St Andrews. I think he might be able to get some time off from what he's working on.'

For a moment, Gilchrist thought about Mo and Ty working together in Strathclyde Police, then said, 'You know, I haven't heard anything more from Dainty or the others.'

'That's because they're up to their ears in it. They've arrested eighteen people in total, and already they're pointing the finger at each other, so Dainty *et al.* are going to be up most of the night with back-to-back interviews.'

He almost smiled at that, the possibility of Elgin's murder and the disappearance of Hazazi, Saliba, and maybe even Ryan Hadwin, being resolved by some of Freddy's men turning Queen's evidence to save their own skin. And more recently, too, Jake Cassidy's and TK's murders. But something in the way Mo struggled to return his look, told him that she was holding something back, not telling him the full story. 'All of Freddy's men?' he said.

'As far as I know, yes.'

'And Hadwin's funeral business? Anything happen with that?'

'Yes.' She flicked him a smile. 'They got him, too.'

Gilchrist felt a chill slide through him. 'Mo,' he said, and reached for her hand. But she seemed reluctant to take it. 'What're you not telling me?'

She looked away for a couple of beats, and when she turned back, face pale, eyes moist, he feared she was about to tell him the worst. Her lips tried a quick smile, but it died before it surfaced. 'No one was killed,' she said.

'But . . .?'

'Hadwin had a firearm. A SIG Sauer. Semi-automatic. Which he used.'

'And . . .?' He gripped her arm, gave it a shake. 'Jesus Christ, Mo, just tell me.'

'I'm sorry, Dad, I'm sorry. I don't know the full story. I only know that Mhairi was shot arresting Hadwin. She lost a lot of blood and was airlifted to Forth Valley. That's all I know. I'm sorry.'

'Forth Valley?' he said. 'That's for trauma victims.'

'I know, Dad. She's in good hands.'

'What's the latest?'

'I don't know. I think she's still in surgery. But I could find out for you.'

With a spurt of blood, Gilchrist tore the canula from his arm, then pulled the sheets to the side.

'What're you doing?' Maureen gasped.

'Going to pay Mhairi a visit.'

'There's nothing you can do for her.'

'Yes, there is.' His feet slapped to the floor, and his world tilted for an unsettling moment, then righted itself again when Maureen gripped his arm.

'You're not fit to go anywhere,' she said.

He almost agreed with her as he pushed to his feet. With his right eye almost closed, his depth of perception was more or less non-existent, and he fumbled for his mobile.

Maureen picked it up for him. 'I'll take it,' she said. 'And sit down on the bed while I sort out your clothes and have a talk to the ward sister.'

For the first time since she arrived, Gilchrist did as instructed, and sat in silence while she removed a bag from the bedside cabinet and placed it on the bed beside him.

'Can you manage to dress yourself, or do you need a hand?'

'I'll manage.'

She reached up, took hold of the curtain, and slid it along the overhead rail, all the way around until he was in a space of his own. 'I'll be back,' she said, 'once I've had a talk to the sister.' Then she slipped through the closed curtain, leaving Gilchrist to wonder if he was doing the right thing, or not.

CHAPTER 47

Forth Valley Royal Hospital, Larbert

It was pitch black by the time Maureen parked her car. Thick clouds blocked the night sky, and an easterly wind seemed to be gaining strength. It blustered around her, raked ice-cold fingers through her hair, buffeted her in freezing gusts while she unpeeled Gilchrist from the passenger seat.

Outside, he pulled himself upright, holding onto her with one hand, steadying himself with his other on top of the door. Whatever painkillers he'd been given were wearing off, and a headache that seemed to beat in time with his breath, had him squinting his eyes from the pulsing pain. As he turned to the side, he grunted from a sharp pain that felt like a spear piercing his ribs.

'Can you stand?' she said.

'I thought that's what I was doing.'

She tutted, then said, 'I'd offer to go for a wheelchair, but I know what you'd say.'

'Correct.' He put an arm over her shoulder, and didn't object when she slid an arm around his waist.

'You're still too thin, Dad. You need to put on some weight.'

'So you keep telling me. Come on. Let's go.'

She hesitated for a moment, looked around her, then said, 'It's too cold.' She retrieved her arm, and he almost lost his balance. 'Here. Let me sort you,' she said, and made to adjust his jacket collar, tug it tighter around his neck.

But he brushed her off. 'It'll be warmer inside,' he said, as he eyed the circular facade and the covered walkway that led to the entrance, and hinted at some shelter from the blustering wind.

Together they shuffled across the car park, and at one point had to work their way between cars parked too close. 'Can you manage?' Mo said.

'Of course.' But the look on her face warned him she was reaching the limits of her patience.

'Stay put,' she said, 'and don't answer back for once in your life. I'll be back in a jiffy.' She removed her beanie hat, and placed it with care over his head, careful not to touch his stitches. 'That should keep you warm.' And with that, she turned and jogged towards the entrance.

He watched her go, marvelling at how limber she appeared, her loping stride eating up the yards with effortless ease. He used to be able to do that, he thought, jog the length of the West Sands and back, his breathing steady, his heartrate controlled, every step clearing his mind, strengthening his resolve for what lay ahead that day. That's what jogging had been grand for, he realised, as if seeing it for the first time – not just for physical fitness, but for refreshing his mental strength, as if it wiped out whatever horrors he'd seen in the previous day to set him up with a clear mind to face the horrors of the upcoming day. Now, it seemed, he'd not only lost the desire to run and keep himself fit, but the physical ability, too. As a friend of his used to say – *this getting old is for the birds*. Of course, it didn't help that he felt as if he'd been kicked from one end of the pitch to the other, and back.

Maureen didn't take long. Which was just as well, as he was beginning to struggle to keep himself upright. She positioned the wheelchair just so, and he shuffled around then fell into it with a satisfying grunt.

'Better?' she said, wheeling the chair around.

'Much,' he said, and uttered nothing more while she whisked him across the car park, then through the sliding doors into the spacious warmth of the entrance lobby. The lift opened timely for them, as if by remote control, and they waited in silence while it emptied. Then she wheeled him inside – just the two of them.

The doors closed to the sound of the recorded voice.

'Do you know which floor?' he asked.

'Of course.'

When they exited, he thought silence his best option as she pushed him along wide corridors and around corners with an uncanny familiarity that had him convinced she'd been there before. When she drew to a halt outside a windowed office, in which two nurses were busy at their desks – one marking up a chart of sorts, the other on the phone and pointing at something on her computer monitor – he said, 'Have you been here before?'

'It's where I met Ty.'

He mouthed an Aahh, but said nothing more while she interrupted one of the nurses, then despite his excellent hearing had a quiet chat with her out of his earshot.

Back behind the wheelchair again, she said, 'She's been moved. She's in a different ward.'

It didn't take long for her to locate Mhairi, alone in a small side room with just one bed. She was asleep, and hooked up to a mobile drip tube and some electronic monitor that showed her vital signs as steady and healthy.

'Okay,' Maureen whispered. 'Here we are. Now what?'

Now what? indeed. He hadn't given any thought to what he was going to say, had just felt an urgent need to see her, be by her bedside, let her know he was there for her, even hold her by the hand if that would help in any way. Now, as he sat by her bedside listening to her steady breathing, glancing at the red and yellow numbers on the monitor, he felt reluctant to wake her up. He looked up at Maureen, and said, 'We wait.'

Maureen nodded, as if she'd expected to hear that answer, then said, 'Coffee?'

'Sure.'

She squeezed his shoulder. 'I won't be long.'

He tapped her hand in return, then reclined in the wheelchair once he heard the door click. After a few minutes, he sensed Mhairi stirring – a flutter of her eyelids, a twitch of her finger. He leaned forward, rested an arm on the bed. Had he imagined it? Or maybe she was just dreaming. Then her eyes opened, and as if she'd known he was there she turned her head and looked at him. She said nothing, just frowned as she took in the damage to his face.

He reached for her hand, and jerked a smile. 'You should see the other guy,' which pulled a grin to her lips. He squeezed her fingers. 'How d'you feel?'

She half-nodded, and mumbled. 'Tired.'

He glanced at the IV drip. 'They've got you on painkillers. You'll be doped up for a while.' He leaned closer, conscious of her frowning at his swollen eye, his bruised cheek, his torn lips. At least with Maureen's beanie hat on, she couldn't see the stitches on his head. 'You were lucky,' he said. 'I was told that Annie acted quickly.'

Mhairi frowned at that, as if struggling to recall who Annie was.

'DI Melton,' he said. 'Annie. She wrapped a tourniquet around your arm using Grant Hadwin's leather belt. Pulled it from his trousers.' He smiled, hoping she could see some irony in that.

But she winced, as if in pain, then whispered something he failed to catch.

'Are you okay?' he said.

'Annie,' she said, her voice stronger. 'She wouldn't wait.'

'What d'you mean?'

'When we got to Hadwin's, she wouldn't wait for backup. She just . . . I don't know . . . she just seemed in a rush, somehow. Like she couldn't wait.'

'Did she say why?'

'No. She just got out the car and barged in. I had no option but to follow.'

Gilchrist gave that some thought. By not waiting for backup, had Melton put her and Mhairi's lives in danger? Had she misjudged Hadwin's resistance? After all, he'd had a gun, and used it. But Mhairi was right. They should have waited for backup to arrive.

Mhairi interrupted his thoughts with, 'And she said . . . she said something strange.'

'What d'you mean?' Which seemed to be all he could say.

'After the arrest, she ordered food, I think.' Mhairi frowned at the recollection. 'Or did I imagine that?'

Gilchrist chuckled to make light of the moment. 'Probably imagined it.'

'No, no, it wasn't a dream. I had . . . I had moments of clarity . . . drifting in and out . . . but I remember . . . I remember food. She ordered food. On the phone.' She looked at him then, and puzzled wrinkles creased the corners of her eyes. 'Strange . . . don't you think?'

Gilchrist nodded. Whatever they were drip-feeding Mhairi was affecting her mind. He glanced at the IV drip again. Valium maybe. Or something stronger. Morphine?

She tightened her fingers. 'I remember thinking . . . thinking it was odd.'

'Well . . . if she ordered food, I'd agree with you that it was odd.' He held her gaze for a long moment, then said, 'Are you sure?'

'She ordered Mexican food. Which is why I remember it. I like Mexican. Quesadillas. Guacamole.' She smiled. 'And tacos. With cheese. And jalapeño peppers. That's one of my favourites.' She frowned again. 'But why order only one?'

'What d'you mean?' Christ, could he think of nothing else to ask?

'Why would Annie order only one?'

'Well, you were out of it, weren't you?'

'No. Not that.' Another frown at the memory. 'Taco, she said. I remember that clearly now. Taco. Just the one. That's what she said. Taco.'

Ice flushed through Gilchrist's system as his mind struggled to make sense of what his logic was telling him. Dainty knew about Taco. But why would Melton phone Dainty and mention Taco? It made no sense. Then slowly, the fog lifted.

Only one other person knew who Taco was.

CHAPTER 48

'Best I could get,' Maureen said, and handed Gilchrist a cardboard cup. 'Took me ages to find a machine. One that worked, anyway. And why aren't you in that wheelchair?'

'Feeling better.' And he did indeed, although still a tad wobbly.

Then she glanced at Mhairi, who had closed her eyes again, and seemed dead to the world. 'How's she doing?'

He sipped his coffee – lukewarm, weak – then nodded. 'She's doing well. Better than expected.'

'Did you speak to anyone?'

'No.' He glanced at Mhairi, then said, 'Can you keep an eye on her?'

'She's not going anywhere, Dad.'

'You know what I mean.' He placed his coffee mug on the side table. 'I'll be back in a jiffy.' And before Maureen could object, he slipped from the room.

He found a quiet spot at the end of a corridor, removed his mobile from his pocket, and turned his back to the wall. He held onto his mobile for several seconds, all of a sudden unsure if it would be better to have this confrontation face to face, rather than over the phone.

Then, decision made, he dialled the number.

It rang out.

He dialled it again, cursing under his breath at the way the game had to be played.

This time it was answered with silence.

Gilchrist held onto his mobile for several seconds, then said, 'Arletta?'

'This is the last time we'll speak on this number. You got that?'

'Who else has this number?'

'No one.'

'You sure?'

'Positive.'

For a short moment, doubts reared up in his mind, then evaporated. She was playing her cards close to her chest, not letting on, never telling the truth – first time round, anyway – which was how she'd survived for so long. Nothing for it but to just come out with it.

'DI Annie Melton has this number,' he said.

The line fell silent for several seconds, then died with a hard click.

Which told him all he needed to know.

One more call to make.

Dainty answered on the second ring with a disgruntled, 'Where the hell are you, Andy? I heard you checked yourself out of the Royal. Are you all right?'

'I'm fine,' he said. 'Maureen's driving me up the road.' For some reason, he didn't want to tell Dainty that he was in Forth Valley, and decided just to go for it. 'How's Taco doing?' He could tell from the pregnant pause that Dainty knew he was about to be tackled on something he didn't want to face – either head on, or over the phone.

'She's being taken care of,' Dainty said. 'How are *you* doing, is more to the point.'

Typical Dainty, Gilchrist thought. Throw you off track by changing the subject. Two could play at that game. 'Run it past me again, how many people knew about Taco?'

'Fucksake, Andy. No one. Just you. I already told you that.' A pause, then, 'Why? What do you know?'

But Gilchrist wasn't up for bringing Dainty up to speed. Not just yet anyway. 'The reason you pulled me into your investigation,' he said, 'wasn't just for a second opinion on how Mike Elgin died, was it? You wanted me to find Arletta for you.'

'Yeah. I told you that, too.'

'Actually, it wasn't you who told me. It was DI Melton.'

'Same difference, Andy. I told Annie to tell you what I wanted. I mean . . . Jesus . . . what the fuck're you on about?'

He ignored the question, and pressed on. 'But DI Melton didn't know about Taco, did she? Or that she was deep cover.'

'I've already fucking told you that.' A pause, then, 'Look, Andy, you're beginning to piss me off—'

'She also didn't know where Arletta was,' Gilchrist interrupted. 'Did she?'

Silence filled the line for so long that Gilchrist thought he'd lost the connection. Then Dainty came back with, 'Stop fucking me around, Andy. What've you found?'

'Can I trust you?'

'Of course you can fucking trust me,' Dainty roared. 'Jesus Christ, Andy, what the fuck's going on?'

It struck Gilchrist all of a sudden that maybe he had it all wrong. Maybe Mhairi had imagined hearing Melton mention Taco by name. She'd just been shot in the arm, was losing lots of blood, and suffering from shock. Maybe Melton had been ordering food. Or talking to someone about food. But even as those thoughts flashed into his mind in a millisecond, his recent call to Arletta nailed it for him. Mhairi hadn't misheard. She'd got it right.

'How long have you known DI Melton?' he asked.

'Come on, Andy.'

'How long?'

'Years.'

'How many?'

'Christ, Andy, I don't know. Fifteen. More. Why?'

'Do you trust her?'

'Why? Are you going to tell me that I shouldn't?'

Gilchrist let silence give Dainty the answer.

'Ah fucking shit,' Dainty hissed. 'Don't tell me.'

Gilchrist took a deep breath. What he was about to tell Dainty was not based on facts, but on the conclusion of deductive reasoning – so he believed. Or perhaps more correctly, so he *hoped*. It flashed into his mind again with a force that had him gritting his teeth, that he had it wrong, that he was about to accuse one of Strathclyde's finest of dishonesty, maybe even outright criminality. Which had him easing into it with Dainty, rather than blasting him with both barrels.

'I could be wrong,' he said, 'but I believe Annie Melton's been in touch with Arletta all along.'

'What makes you think that?'

Christ. Here it comes. He squeezed his eyes tight for a brief moment, then said, 'She knew about Taco.'

'Impossible, Andy. No one knew about her. I told you that.'

'She mentioned Taco by name in a phone call to Arletta.' There. He'd said it. The quantum leap in logic that was

311

impossible to justify, let alone prove. But hadn't Arletta told him as much by ending the call? Who else could Melton have been phoning? Anyone on the planet, came the disappointing answer.

Dainty interrupted his thoughts with, 'When did Annie mention Taco by name?'

'After she arrested Hadwin.'

'Did you hear her say that?'

'No.'

'So who told you?'

A pause, then, 'DC Mhairi McBride.'

'I thought she'd just been shot.'

'She had.'

'Shot. In the fucking artery. Blood spouting everywhere. Only minutes before she lost the fucking lot. Saved by Annie tying a tourniquet. And you're trying to tell me she had the mental wherewithal to stay awake and listen to Annie on the phone?' he said, voice rising in anger or frustration, maybe both. 'Is that what you're trying to tell me?'

'Yes.'

'Unless she's fucking superwoman, she would've passed out from loss of blood.'

'That's what DI Melton thought, too.'

Dainty hesitated for a moment, then said with firm finality, 'I don't buy it, Andy. Sorry, but you've got this one wrong.'

'I spoke to Arletta.' Not strictly true, but close enough.

That stopped Dainty.

'Annie'll have a burner,' Gilchrist said. 'Look for that first.'

'You'd better be fucking right about this, Andy, or so help me.'

Then he killed the connection.

CHAPTER 49

Sunday morning
St Andrews

Gilchrist pulled himself from bed, unable to shift a heavy sense of depression that weighed him down like an anchor, as if it had depleted the muscles in his limbs, sucked the life out of them. A look in the mirror didn't help, although the swelling around his left eye had diminished enough that he could now see out of it. And his cuts and bruises no longer looked as fierce. A piping hot shower usually worked its magic, but that morning he could only handwash himself, taking care to keep his cuts and stitches dry, while an aching pain that seemed to hover around his ribs only to stab him with a white-hot poker at the slightest movement, added to his deflated mood. Even a shave did little to lift him.

Downstairs, he entered the living room. The curtains were open, and in the shadow of the dawn light he could make out the still form of Irene asleep in bed. He walked over to her, pulled up one of the chairs at the side of her bed, and sat.

What could he do? What could he say?

He leaned forward, pressed his lips to her forehead, then took hold of her hand.

'Good morning,' she whispered, and opened her eyes.

'I'm sorry, I didn't mean to wake you.'

'I was only dozing.' She squeezed his hand, then settled into a frowning look. 'I can't get used to you wearing a beanie hat. Don't you want to take it off?'

'Best that I keep it on. Believe me.'

She lifted a hand to his face, and ran her fingers around his eye. 'Does it hurt?'

'Only when I laugh,' he said, and tried a grin.

She smiled at his silly joke. 'You smell nice, though. Is that the aftershave I bought you for Christmas?'

'Of course.'

'Lean closer.' She breathed him in as he did so. 'It reminds me of springtime. Fresh and light. Lovely.' She tightened her grip on his fingers. 'Will you wear that tonight?' she said, and from the look on his face, added, 'For me.'

His lips flickered a smile. 'Of course.'

'When's Joanne coming over?'

'She didn't say. Sometime in the morning, I think. Definitely before midday. Maybe eleven-ish. Or before. I'm not sure.' He felt as if he was havering, but didn't know what else to say.

Irene smiled, and nodded. 'It'll be all right, Andy. C'mere. Give me a hug.'

He leaned down, pressed his face to her cheek. It felt warm and clammy.

She patted his back, kissed the side of his face. 'It's time,' she whispered. 'I've told you that. And Joanne knows that, too.'

He pushed himself upright, tried to give a smile of acknowledgement, but failed.

'I'm not afraid,' she said. 'I'm ready. I just need you and Joanne to be with me.'

'Of course.' Christ, could he not think of anything else to say? He swallowed a lump in his throat, tried to fight back the nip of tears, then said, 'Let me put the kettle on, shall I?'

She nodded, and eased her hand free.

In the kitchen, he tried to make sense of his cascading emotions. One second he felt comforted by Irene's confidence, her assurance that she was ready, was not afraid, the time was right, that she'd made peace with herself. The next second, the thought of her not being around tomorrow and every day after, swamped him in a debilitating wave that threatened to have him doubting everything she'd said and reduce him to a sobbing wreck. He gritted his teeth, turned on the radio – some random channel that offered background music that could be coming from a different planet, where death didn't linger in the shadows, and life was there to be lived and enjoyed. He glanced over at Irene, saw she was asleep – her eyes were closed at least – then turned away and gave his eyes a quick wipe.

The morning hours passed slowly. Every second of every minute took twice as long as normal, it seemed. He checked his mobile for the umpteenth time – he couldn't say how often he'd done that every hour – but found no messages. Yesterday could have been the same, but he'd spent most of the day in his office, reading reports, batting calls from all and sundry – yet nothing from Dainty – while being doped up with prescription painkillers. By mid-afternoon, Smiler had told him in no uncertain terms to go home and not to return to the office without a doctor's sign-off. Failing that, she would suspend him.

He'd reluctantly gone home, but since then had heard nothing.

It was as if everyone knew he should be left alone today, that this was a day not to be interrupted. But how could they? No one knew? He and Joanne had made a pact to keep Irene's decision to end her life between them. Just the two of them. Not Jack, and certainly not Maureen who would no doubt argue against Irene's wishes in her own strong-minded way, and challenge the legality of what they were about to do.

But Gilchrist knew that in England and Wales, assisted dying was illegal under the Suicide Act 1961, whereas in Scotland there was no specific crime of assisting a suicide. Even so, helping someone to end their life could be argued a crime, and could in turn lead to prosecution for murder, culpable homicide, or even reckless endangerment, which was why he and Joanne had taken the earlier precaution of having Irene's GP – Doctor McIntyre – examine her at home, and reach the conclusion – with persuasive assistance by Irene – that it was simply a matter of time before her body could no longer support her, and that her death was not only unavoidable, but imminent.

Suitably satisfied, McIntyre issued a VOED – Verification of Expected Death form – which meant that on Irene's passing, one of the qualified district nurses who visited her at home regularly, could verify that death had occurred, negating the need of a GP's visit, a post-mortem examination, or a police investigation into the circumstances surrounding her death. Following that, Form 11 – Medical Certificate of Cause of Death – could then be signed off by Doctor McIntyre as a matter of course.

When Joanne turned up just after eleven, carrying a bunch of colourful flowers which she tearfully presented to her mother, Gilchrist excused himself – to permit mother and daughter some private time together. He threw on his jacket with an over-the-shoulder comment that he was going out to buy a newspaper and would be back in an hour or so.

Outside, a chilling wind hit him with its icy bite, making him regret not coming out with a scarf or gloves. But he tugged up his collar, adjusted his beanie hat, tugged it down over his ears, and set off for a brisk walk through town.

His original intention had been to walk the West Sands, face the sea, breathe it in and pray to a God he didn't believe in and ask for forgiveness for what he was about to do. He'd witnessed death before, many times. He'd even been there at the moment of some victim's passing, noting only that it was indeed a sad and final event. What he had never experienced, and what he swore he would never let himself be talked into again, was to sit with someone while they wilfully took whatever medication they knew would end their life.

He arrived at Bruce Embankment where the wind was at its strongest, the sea at its most expansive, when his mobile rang. He removed it from his pocket – ID Dainty.

'What's up?' he said, without introduction.

'Fucksake, Andy. You were right.'

Gilchrist stopped. He stared across the bay to Tentsmuir Beach, nothing more than a light line against a verdant backdrop under a dull morning sky. 'Annie confessed?' he said.

'Not a chance.' Dainty let out a heavy sigh, then said, 'No, I've just spent the last ten minutes on a conference call with Tom Ravenscroft, and big Archie.'

'Archie McVicar?'

'The one and only.'

Gilchrist frowned. Ravenscroft was the chief constable for Strathclyde Police. But why was Fife Constabulary's Chief

317

Constable McVicar involved? 'I'm listening,' was all he could think to say.

'Told me to drop all investigation into DI Melton. Not Annie. But *DI* fucking Melton, just to make sure I understood that what they were telling me was official. And serious.'

'How serious?'

'That's what they wouldn't tell me. Warned me away from Annie, who was under instruction to notify them immediately if I disobeyed their instruction.'

'For crying out loud, Dainty. I don't know what to tell you.'

'Well, Annie and I go back a ways. That's what neither of those bastards understood. So what I'm about to tell you, you know nothing about, and God forbid if you ever let it slip. But if you do, you didn't hear it from me, and I'll deny all knowledge. Okay?'

Gilchrist pressed his mobile hard to his ear. 'Okay.'

'She's Arletta's controller.'

'She's *what?*'

'Ever since Tony Dilanos was killed and Arletta took over the business, Annie's been able to contact her all the while.' Dainty hissed a curse, then said, 'Keeps her on a tight leash, is what she said. Can't so much as have a fucking shite without Annie's say so.' He coughed out another curse, and said, 'She kept that fucking quiet.'

'She'd have to. It'd be too dangerous otherwise.'

But Dainty carried on, as if Gilchrist hadn't spoken. 'With Wee Freddy now heading to the Bar-L for the rest of his natural, the road's finally clear for Arletta to turn the family business legit. Of course . . .' He let out a long sigh, then said, 'There has to be a bit of dodgy stuff before she turns it around. Hence Annie. To make sure she abides by the law. Within reason, that is.'

Gilchrist wasn't sure what to make of it all, but he thought he saw one outcome that made sense. 'So with Annie and others making sure Arletta toes the line,' he said, 'one of the longest lasting criminal families in Scotland becomes extinct. Is that it?'

'Precisely.'

'You think it'll work?'

'Who knows? What I can tell you is, I'm not buying it. If Arletta or any of her mob step over the line, they'll be arrested and charged under the full force of the law. And that goes for Annie, too. So she'd better watch her fucking step.'

So much for friendships. You really did mess with Dainty at your peril. A thought came to Gilchrist. 'With the Shepherd family no longer a criminal force,' he said, 'won't that open the door for the Cassidy clan to take over?'

'Apparently there's a similar operation still under wraps that's gonnie clean up the east coast and beyond, which'll wipe every Cassidy off the map. Of course, minions like us don't get to have a say in any of it, the bastards.' The line clattered all of a sudden, as if his mobile had been dropped, then Dainty came back with, 'Gotta go, Andy. Not a word.'

The connection died.

Gilchrist stared off across the bay, trying to make sense of what he'd just heard. Key members of the police force were infiltrating the Shepherd family – the Cassidy family, too – with the intent of dismantling Scotland's foremost criminal gangs. Would it work? As Dainty said, who knew? A bold plan that was surely doomed to fail in the long run. Criminality was almost inbred throughout the UK now, and there would always be someone ready to jump at the opportunity and take over.

With a heavy heart, Gilchrist slipped his mobile into his pocket and turned for home.

CHAPTER 50

From the second-floor living room, Gilchrist looked down on the scene below, South Street alive with people going out for, or coming back from, a Sunday night's entertainment; a bite to eat, a beer or glass of wine or more, or just a pleasant walk through town, shop fronts and windows festooned with fairy lights that glowed steadily like stars, or twinkled off and on like flitting fireflies, carrying with them the promise of a wintry Christmas. It all seemed surreal somehow, the world going about its business like everything was normal, while here, in this room, Irene was on the verge of breathing her last.

He pressed his palm against the pane, felt its coldness creep up his arm, and in doing so caught his reflection in the glass – thin face, bruised and cut, half-closed left eye, stitched hairline hidden by a beanie hat he knew didn't suit him. From behind, Joanne's quiet sobbing broke the ambient silence. He closed his eyes for a moment, took a long breath, then stepped away from the window.

Joanne sat at her mother's bedside, holding her hand, rubbing her fingers, never lifting her eyes from her face, as if worried that by doing so she might feel she'd somehow missed the exact moment of her passing.

Gilchrist felt differently. He'd held Irene's hand until the pills and the alcohol took their toll, and she closed her eyes for the last time. Then he'd lifted her limp hand to his lips, and in his mind whispered to her once more that he loved her – more than he'd ever loved anyone – that he would miss her, that he would never forget her, that he would look after Joanne for her, and together they would scatter her ashes over the West Sands, just as she'd wanted. He'd tried to remember what her last words to him had been, but she'd mumbled incoherently – to him or Joanne, he couldn't say – and the moment slipped by.

Now, it was a waiting game – only minutes, maybe even seconds.

He took his seat opposite Joanne again, and reached for Irene's hand. It felt cool, limp, her fingers slack, free of tension. He brushed his fingertips over the side of her face, down the soft skin of her neck, and felt the weakest of pulses.

Joanne looked at him, eyes pleading, heavy with grief. 'Has she . . .?'

He shook his head. 'Not long now.'

She choked a sob, pressed her mother's hand to her lips, squeezed her eyes shut.

Gilchrist eased his chair back, and stood. He'd done all that had been asked of him. All he could do now was give Joanne some privacy to share her mother's final moments. He gave her shoulder a gentle squeeze in the passing, and made his way into the kitchen.

On automatic, he filled the kettle and plugged it in. From there, he had sight of the living room, and of Joanne by her mother's bedside. He had just added milk to two mugs, when he noticed Joanne leaning towards her mother and resting her head by her cheek. He could tell by the way her shoulders moved that the moment he'd been dreading for months had arrived. Irene had passed away. She was no longer hooked up to goodness knows what, or confined to bed for the duration, or to shuffle around the room only as far as her strength would allow, but was free at last to leave this world of pain and worry behind her.

Something swept over him then, a strange coldness that pulled tears to his eyes, and left him standing there, immobilised, as if his nervous system had lost all connection with his brain. From the bedside, he could hear Joanne's muffled whispering, as she fussed and faffed with the sheets by her mother's neck, fluffed up the pillows just so, leaned down and pressed her face against her cheek. Then she turned to face him, and without a word he found himself walking towards her, to hold her as she stumbled into his arms.

Together they shed tears in silence, each comforted in some way by the other's pain, as if to share the aching was less than half the burden. They stood like that for a long moment until he felt her grip loosen, and they parted slowly.

She looked up at him, and sniffed, then ran a hand under her nose. He swiped a tear from her cheek with his finger, then pushed a loose strand of hair behind her ear, all of a sudden conscious of how he used to do that with Irene. There seemed no need to speak as they parted, and together they returned to stand side by side where Irene lay. He thought she looked at peace, and it pleased him that in the end she hadn't suffered, that she had taken control of her life, and chosen the manner in which she'd wanted to die.

And was that too much for anyone to ask?

Over the years, he'd witnessed many deaths, but as he stood in silence and looked at Irene, he came to understand, as if for the first time, the utter finality of death, how tenuous life was, how people went about their daily business as if unaware that only a hairsbreadth separated them between the living and oblivion. Now, Irene had crossed over that narrowest of gaps, and no one could do any more for her.

Irene was gone. He leaned down, kissed her forehead and whispered words of love. Then he pulled himself upright, gave Joanne a grim smile, another squeeze of her shoulder, and removed his mobile from his pocket. He powered it up – they'd both shut their mobiles down for the afternoon – and phoned Jessie. He and Joanne had spoken of this moment, what they would do when Irene finally passed. They'd stayed with her through the final stages of her life, topped up her glass with another hefty measure of brandy – Irene's go-to drink when she'd wanted to drown out the darkness of an earthly world – helped her swallow the last of the Valium pills before the drugs and alcohol had a chance to work on her central nervous system, and slow her heart and lungs until her body shut down, held her hands while her life slipped away.

Now, they had to clear all evidence of their assistance.

Gilchrist already had the VOED form signed off by a doctor, which would negate the need of a post-mortem. However, suicide by overdose was different from dying by natural causes as expected, and questions might be raised as to what had happened, and where exactly had Gilchrist and Joanne been at the moment of Irene's passing. Spending a quiet hour with Jessie would be the answer, because he and Joanne had sensibly agreed to Irene's final wishes to leave her to end her life alone, and thus avoid any legal dubiety of their being complicit in her suicide.

Joanne had closed all the curtains – to allow Irene the privacy of her suicide – while back at the bedside, Gilchrist slipped on a pair of latex gloves. Next, he wiped the bottle of Courvoisier VSOP and the crystal glass clear of fingerprints, leaving the rim untouched where Irene's lipstick had stained it – she'd insisted that if she was going to end her life, she could at least make the effort to look her best. Then he adjusted her hand, pressed the bottle onto her fingers, shifting it around to make it look as if she'd helped herself to several drinks. Next, he did the same with the glass, feeling oddly criminal as he did so. And finally, the bottle of Valium pills, which Irene had been prescribed months earlier when sleep really had eluded her. One last look over the room, then he held out his arm for Joanne to follow him.

Downstairs, in the hallway, they slipped on their respective coats – scarf and gloves and leather jacket for Gilchrist; fawn cashmere woollen coat and matching scarf, gloves and hat for Joanne. Now that the focused excitement of removing all trace of their involvement was over, grief struck Joanne again. She sobbed, shook her head in disbelieving despair.

Gilchrist pulled her to him. 'It'll be okay,' he said. 'As far as Jessie and everybody else is concerned, we left your mum in bed alone and alive, at her own request.'

Joanne sniffed, nodded, choked back a sob. 'I still can't believe it.'

What could he say? That he didn't believe it either. But he said nothing, just opened the door and followed Joanne outside. He secured the lock, then put an arm around Joanne's shoulder, and together they strode into the cold November night.

ACKNOWLEDGEMENTS

Writing is indeed a lonely affair, but this book would not have been published without the considerable help, advice and support from the following: Beta readers, Tom, Jane, Ian and Sheila; Sean Russell, Crematorium Manager; Lisa Somerville, Assistant Crematorium Manager, for explaining to me the behind-the-scenes workings of a crematorium; Alan Gall, retired Chief Superintendent, Strathclyde Police, for police procedure; Howard Watson, for professional copyediting to the nth degree; Jen Shannon, editor; Rebecca Sheppard, editorial manager; Meg Shepherd, cover designer; John Fairweather, production controller; Ellen Turner, publicist; Jessica Callaghan, audio editor – all for working hard behind the scenes at Little, Brown to give this novel the best possible start; Krystyna Green, former publishing director at Constable, for twisting my arm and convincing me to write one more Gilchrist. And finally, Anna, for putting up with me, believing in me and loving me all the way.

RAISING READERS
Books Build Bright Futures

Dear Reader,

We'd love your attention for one more page to tell you about the crisis in children's reading, and what we can all do.

Studies have shown that reading for fun is the **single biggest predictor of a child's future life chances** – more than family circumstance, parents' educational background or income. It improves academic results, mental health, wealth, communication skills, ambition and happiness.[1]

The number of children reading for fun is in rapid decline. Young people have a lot of competition for their time. In 2024, 1 in 10 children and young people in the UK aged 5 to 18 did not own a single book at home.[2]

Hachette works extensively with schools, libraries and literacy charities, but here are some ways we can all raise more readers:

- Reading to children for just 10 minutes a day makes a difference
- Don't give up if children aren't regular readers – there will be books for them!
- Visit bookshops and libraries to get recommendations
- Encourage them to listen to audiobooks
- Support school libraries
- Give books as gifts

There's a lot more information about how to encourage children to read on our website: **www.RaisingReaders.co.uk**

Thank you for reading.

hachette
UK

[1] OECD, '21st-Century Readers: Developing Literacy Skills in a Digital World', 2021, https://www.oecd.org/en/publications/21st-century-readers_a83d84cb-en.html

[2] National Literacy Trust, 'Book Ownership in 2024', November 2024, https://literacytrust.org.uk/research-services/research-reports/book-ownership-in-2024